"They're having a ceremony tonight . . ."

Phillip Owens and his wife, Paige, should have heeded the Haitian innkeeper's warning not to delve into forbidden things . . .

In the middle of the graveyard, thirty forms swayed in rhythm to the drums. The priestess, an evil old crone, held a knife over her head. A young girl lay stretched naked across the top of a flat tomb.

The blade flashed down. The priestess reached into the chest cavity and removed a beating, quivering heart. She began to eat . . .

VOODOO FURY

VOODOO FURY

Gregg Loomis

DIAMOND BOOKS, NEW YORK

VOODOO FURY

A Diamond Book / published by arrangement with the author

PRINTING HISTORY
Diamond edition / January 1991

ISBN: 1-55773-447-X

Diamond Books are published by The Berkley Publishing Group, 200
Madison Avenue, New York, New York 10016. The name
''DIAMOND'' and its logo are trademarks belonging to
Charter Communications, Inc.

PRINTED IN THE UNITED STATES OF AMERICA

10 9 8 7 6 5 4 3 2 1

To the women in my life:
Suzanne,
who endured my writing this,
and Mary Jack,
who found it a home

Chapter 1

Ш

CAP-HAÏTIEN, HAITI, 1986

Phillip Owens awoke with a start, unsure if the sound he had heard belonged in the dim dream world that was slipping from his mind. Next to him, Paige was breathing with the rhythm of deep sleep. He sat up, careful not to disturb her. God, how could anyone slumber so peacefully after what had happened only hours ago? He stared out of the window where a late moon was paving a road of silver across the harbor below. Maybe what had happened was a dream, maybe . . .

There it was again, no mistaking it: something was moving in the far corner of the hotel room, making a sound like the rustling of fallen leaves. Although moonlight illuminated most of the room, it also created shadows that clung to the corners as though the space there refused to be stripped naked of gloom.

Slowly, he got out of bed with the uncertainty of one in unfamiliar surroundings. He was careful to give wide berth to the suspect corner as he groped for the switch to the lamp. With his tug, bright light painted even the menacing corner with a cheery yellow. Somehow, he'd known there would be nothing there. Paige mumbled something and turned over as he slipped back into bed.

1

Sleep, at least for the moment, was going to be impossible, he realized. He was awake now with the memory that kept playing across his mind like a TV he couldn't turn off. Was it only this afternoon that all this had started? It seemed years ago since he had stood on the balcony, staring at the rain forest across the harbor, staring and thinking that Haiti looked as dark and foreboding as the news—what there was of it—had made the country seem. He had stroked his neat beard, watching the afternoon's herd of thunderstorms make its way out to sea. Steam came up from the jungle like smoke from a thousand campfires. Haiti. Land of mystery and paradox, he had then thought. And terror, he now knew.

He had come here to research a series of articles and had found terror—terror he had, until now, believed existed only in fiction. At first he had found a country beautiful with orchids cascading down hills dotted with crude mud huts. There was no need for locks on the doors, yet there was shooting in the streets. Most of the country consisted of eroded hills, but here on the north coast, everything grew in profusion. Contrasts, contrasts . . . and the most frightening experience of his life. Not that you would know it from Paige's peaceful sleep.

Paige. She had insisted on coming along, vacationing from her law practice while he searched out hard facts, facts that had been few since the departure of the Duvalier government. Not that anyone was hiding the truth, but rather no one seemed to know what was happening. Before coming to Cap-Haïtien, the country's second largest city, he had spent four days in the anarchy of Port-au-Prince where he had prowled government offices in search of someone, anyone, to interview. Most of the former occupants had taken leave of their posts shortly after the President for Life had boarded a U.S. jet for permanent residence in France. Those who remained had nothing to administer and no means to do so. Chaos had been the only consistency in the capital, chaos as complete as he had witnessed in Saigon or Tehran, if less violent. From what he had seen in Port-au-Prince only weeks after the government dissolved, no one was in charge.

However he phrased the onset of turmoil, he was convinced that it would either be years before order was re-established democratically or months before another dictator stepped onto the national stage. He sighed. At least here on the north coast, life went on at its normal frantic pace and there was no gunfire at night.

There it was again: that scraping, crawling sound that made him break out in a cold sweat despite the room's air conditioning. He listened, turning his head to determine the source of the noise. This time it was in the bathroom. Something was crawling across the floor! Again, he got out of the bed and, bare feet slapping against ceramic tiles, made his way across the room. Fear clutched at each step, making his arm heavy as he reached for the light switch that flooded the bathroom with a brilliance enhanced by white porcelain. The commode and bidet mocked him with mundanity. No creature was slithering across the floor. The only life was a cockroach scurrying for cover. Wearily, he returned to bed. Visible or not, he knew it was in the room. This afternoon he would have scoffed at the idea. But this afternoon was a long time past.

Was it really only this afternoon that he had turned to watch Paige stretch after her nap, a long sensuous movement of her slender body that emphasized breasts still firm despite her forty years and motherhood? She had run slender fingers through long dark hair just beginning to show silver streaks that she refused to color. And why should she? Her face was as young as that of a twenty year old.

"Well," he had said, grinning, "Sleeping Beauty awakes!

I was beginning to think you'd snooze away the rest of the afternoon.''

Her large coffee eyes had twinkled merrily. ''And miss one last shopping expedition? No way.'' She slid her arms around his waist. ''This may be just another story to you, but it's my vacation, remember?''

He recalled their argument, one of the few they'd had in ten years of marriage. He had insisted this country was not the place for her. She had insisted that *she* be allowed to face whatever might confront him. As usual, he had been the one to grudgingly concede. Besides, the greatest perils they had experienced so far were the pothole-studded strip of paving that served as the only highway from the airport and the wheezing antique of a taxi that barely made it to the hotel.

He feigned disapproval. ''I haven't even written anything yet, much less sold it. Now you want to spend every nickel I might get paid.''

''Gourde,'' she corrected, referring to the national currency, the wrinkled paper that, if readable at all, announced its own worth as being twenty U.S. cents. Her eyes had the mischievous sparkle they assumed when she kidded him. ''Apparently you haven't haggled with the locals. You could almost buy the whole town for what one of your articles brings.''

There was some truth in her exaggeration. Although low, prices in Haiti had fallen even lower since tourists perceived the country to be unsafe. Consequently, the shops that dealt in the frenetic and colorful art that mirrored the Haitian lifestyle were selling their wares for half their usual price, as were the shops that carried the carved mahogany salad bowls and the hand-woven cottons.

''And just what were you planning to buy?'' Phillip was

intentionally prolonging the banter. "There isn't exactly a Saks here, you know."

Paige stretched again, pushing against him. He caught the suggestion of her perfume mixed with the feminine, musky odor of her body as she flashed a smile. "I'd like to get a couple of those paintings we saw near the market. At least two of them are Braziles. Do you have any idea what his work brings in the States?"

He was consistently awed by the knowledge of comparative prices his wife seemed to carry around in her head. A brand-name watch, diamonds by the karat, the quality of Haitian paintings, it didn't matter. Had she been *born* with the information? Phillip shook off the question. "What does it matter what his pictures go for? You don't have any intention of selling them once you get them into the house. Admit it," he kidded.

She gave him a reproachful look. "You never know when we might need the money. Besides, these are extra large. They'll look great on the sun porch."

"Good grief, woman!" he said, pretending astonishment. "How do you expect me to get those things on the plane?"

"I'm sure you'll find a way. Maybe you should have held out for a bigger model."

He pouted in mock wounded pride. "I thought I did a hell of a job convincing the magazine that renting a private plane was the only way to get around this country."

"And let them pay to keep your license current by doing so. Let me slip on a dress and we'll be ready to go."

Paige had noted Haitian women never appeared in pants or shorts. With her usual sensitivity, she had exchanged her cutoffs for a skirt every time they had left hotel property.

Phillip and Paige walked hand in hand through the open space that served as a lobby. Outside, Phillip could see

Louis, their self-appointed guide, waiting with the easy patience common to Haiti's people. With his broken English, Louis had attached himself to the couple on their first trip into town.

"Guide, Missa, Madam?" he had asked, brilliant white teeth accentuating the blackness of his face.

"Aleoue, pou!" Phillip had replied with one of the few Creole phrases his tone-deaf ears had been able to pick up.

"No." Paige had put a restraining hand on his arm, understanding the inflection if not her husband's words. "He can translate for us. Besides, he looks like he could use the work."

Both observations were true. Thin to the point of emaciation, Louis had been wearing clean, if shabby, trousers. Only the rope around his waist kept them from falling. Toes stuck out of worn sneakers that had never quite fit. Incongruously, his guayabera, the loose-fitting cotton shirt ubiquitous in the Caribbean, appeared new.

Phillip had shrugged his broad shoulders. "Okay," he told Louis, "you be our guide, but five bucks—dollars—is it, understand?"

More bright teeth showed as Louis nodded violently, "Sho' thing. Make good guide, get cheap price ever'-where."

And he had. When a shopkeeper fell into a sullen silence at Paige's top offer on a carved figure, Louis had become animated, jabbering away in the tongue that was a mixture of French, Spanish and West African. The merchant had replied in kind, his arms gesticulating wildly. Finally, the antagonists had paused, breathless.

Louis had given his now familiar broad grin. "Give the man four dollars, U.S."

"But that's less . . ." Paige had gasped.

"Pay him 'fore he change he mind," Louis had insisted gently.

So it had gone. Louis had proved to be a shrewd bargainer and seemed knowledgeable about points of interest the town had to offer. Better, from Phillip's point of view, their guide had kept at bay the swarm of nearly naked children who surrounded the Americans with outstretched hands and supplicating eyes.

Now the Haitian smiled in recognition as Phillip and Paige, as one, put on sunglasses against the late afternoon glare.

"How do you suppose he knew we would be going out?" she asked.

"He didn't," Phillip replied. "He was just waiting in case we did. What else does he have to do?"

"Poor thing," she said softly, pulling her purse strap over a shoulder. "If we hadn't decided to make one more trip, he'd have waited out in the heat and rain all afternoon!"

Once Paige told Louis that she wanted to see some of the local art, he nodded and set off down the steep slope toward the town where the sinking sun already was casting shadows off the low buildings on the narrow streets. Phillip slipped his hand around Paige's to help her keep up with their guide.

WHUMP!

A flat, toneless sound like a hand on a flat surface—a sound more felt than heard—reverberated across the valley. Startled, Phillip looked around for the source. From her puzzled expression, he guessed Paige had heard it also. Suddenly, he experienced a chill as cold and as certain as a gust of winter air. He shivered although they were still standing in full sunlight. He reached to the front of his khaki safari shirt, making sure it was buttoned.

Paige stopped, looking at him quizzically. "What's the matter? You don't look like you feel well."

The warmth flooded back into his body as suddenly and inexplicably as it had left. "Don't know. A rabbit ran over my grave, I guess."

She reached up to run a hand across his back. "If you're ill now, wait till you see how much I spend on Haitian paintings," she teased, but her expression was serious, searching his tanned face.

Louis was already at the bottom of the hill, standing astride one of the many rain-filled potholes. "This way," he indicated. "Store close soon."

At six feet two inches, Phillip's stride was nearly twice that of his wife's, yet he had to make an effort to keep up with her and the guide. The fear of missing a final chance to shop was, he was certain, lending her speed. The three were walking hastily down a narrow alley lined with stuccoed, multicolored houses. Windows were already shuttered against the approaching dusk.

"Shit!" Phillip swore.

Louis stopped in mid-stride while Paige giggled and said, "You look a little silly with your foot stuck in a mud hole."

"I couldn't see the damn thing. The street's too dark," he growled, stepping gingerly onto the ragged paving. He glumly watched brown water ooze out of his sneaker as he put his weight on the offending foot. "God knows what sort of jungle rot I'll catch." He shot what he intended to be a glare at Louis, whose normal smile had widened noticeably.

Paige was trying to suppress her laughter with only moderate success. "Just as long as you don't have to have your foot amputated before we get home, you'll survive."

Louis pointed. "The store right here."

Two houses down, wooden double doors stood open onto a single room. Dim light from inside revealed walls covered with busy, primitive art. The pale yellow glow of an electric bulb gave a sinister appearance to the canvasses. The pictures seemed to move.

"Why don't you go over a couple of blocks?" Paige suggested to her husband. "I saw the sun still shining on the church there. You can sit and dry out your sock while Louis and I do the haggling. Besides, I know how you hate to shop."

Louis gave an uneasy glance in the direction she indicated. "Sun be behind de hill."

"No, it's not," Paige gently corrected. "We don't need him here, anyway."

Phillip perceived a reluctance on the guide's part. But at what? To hell with both of them standing there laughing at his misfortune. Anyway, Paige would be perfectly safe. Despite the national poverty, there was no street crime Phillip had ever observed. "Good idea. I'll be in the churchyard when you finish."

WHUMP!

That sound again. No closer, no more distant than before. It seemed to come from nowhere and everywhere.

Phillip, who had already started up a side street, turned. "Louis, what was that?"

The dark face was unchanged as though he had heard neither the sound nor Phillip.

Paige repeated the question, "That sound, what is it?"

"Drum," Louis responded, his mouth immediately clenching as though to prevent more information from slipping out.

Phillip and Paige looked around the empty street. Phillip was the first to verbalize what they both thought. "I don't see any drum."

"And I never heard one like that," she added.

"In the jungle." Louis jerked his head toward the mountains whose top could be seen above the low buildings.

"But how could we hear it from so far away" Phillip protested.

"Drum in jungle." It was obvious Louis could not or would not elucidate. "Store be closed soon."

Paige gave Phillip her "Oh, well" look and said, "We'll ask back at the hotel. Now go dry off while I shop."

Phillip watched his wife and the Haitian step inside the building before he turned the corner. His shoe squishing like a wet towel with each step, he looked down the two blocks ahead. The church, the largest building in Cap-Haïtien, reflected the fading sunlight from is stark white sides. Instead of a steeple, the structure was topped by a metal cupola, its burnished surface glowing invitingly. Beyond, the rain forest washed up the mountainsides, a sea of green interrupted by a single island where banana trees grew at impossible angles.

As Phillip crossed the street to the church's plaza, he felt the warmth of the sun and imagined his wet sock steaming in the heat of the dying day. He sat on a stone bench, letting his eyes adjust to a brilliance even his sunglasses could not dim while he took off his sneaker and lay the still soaking sock beside him. His eyes fastened on the massive wooden doors of the church. They were shut, exposing primitive carvings of what he supposed were biblical episodes. For no reason, he remembered what an Englishman in Port-au-Prince had told him; the Creole word *pa* meant both fear and Catholic priest. Phillip guessed that said something for the view the Haitians had of the religion that over ninety percent of them ostensibly embraced.

He squinted at the carvings, got up, and limped over on one shoe to run his fingers across the mahogany. One scene depicted what he surmised was the Garden of Eden. A huge snake hung from a tree, apparently watching two human figures. One male, one female. Adam and Eve. But the two people seemed to be beckoning, supplicating the reptile. Hardly Genesis as Phillip remembered it. Another panel consisted of pairs of animals trudging toward a boat, a ship similar to the small fishing vessels he had seen in the harbor. Noah's Ark? The beasts were not merely crudely done, they were grotesque, misshappen. Except one—the same serpent. Larger than all the other creatures, it writhed around the mast.

Phillip jumped back and blinked. The thing, the snake had . . . moved? No, the shadows were playing tricks just like the paintings, of course. Nonetheless, he backed away from the entrance, convincing himself he had not seen what his eyes had tried to tell him.

Absurd, he thought, sitting back down on the bench. Some rogue cell of his brain would not be hushed: that thing curled around the carved rigging had slithered! Nonsense, logic answered indignantly. Carved snakes are as inanimate as the wood of which they are a part.

Now, in the hotel room, alone with the night except for his sleeping wife he wasn't so sure. The unwanted memory continued . . .

He had glanced around to see if anyone had noticed the tall, bearded American jumping backward from the church doors and shivering in the tropical heat. He must look demented. The plaza was empty, he observed. Odd. This afternoon was the first time in Haiti, outside a hotel, when he had seen no natives. Everywhere before, they had surrounded him, moving at that half-walk, half-trot that was as indigenous to the country as the banana trees on the mountainside above him. The contrast between the normally seething population and this empty space was eerie.

Phillip shook himself. This was ridiculous. He looked

around again, this time to find something to occupy a mind that didn't seem to have enough to do without seeing carved wood move and something sinister in an empty plaza. For the first time, he noticed a wall at the far end of the square, almost hidden behind the church. He put his still-damp sock back on, laced his wet sneaker, and crossed the plaza, curious as to what might be on the other side of that wall. Standing on tiptoe, his height allowed him to peer down into a graveyard of about an acre. Each tomb was a separate structure, a white-washed stucco box about seven feet by four feet. Some of the tombs were in a state of advanced disrepair, others looked new. Many displayed photographs, presumably of the deceased. Phillip was reminded of New Orleans where the water table also necessitated above-ground burials. Then he observed something odd: each tomb was adorned with a white flower. The decorations had to be recent or the afternoon rains would have washed them away. Perhaps this was one of the saints' days so common on the Catholic calendar.

His eyes followed the wall to a gate at the opposite end. He was walking toward it when Paige called to him. She was standing across the street with Louis, a canvas under each arm. Phillip joined them, pointing. "Louis, is this some special day? All the graves have flowers on them."

Paige looked where her husband indicated while the Haitian shifted his weight from one foot to the other.

Phillip tried again. "A saint's day, perhaps?" Why did he feel as if he wasn't going to get an answer?

Louis was looking at the wall as though he had never seen it. "A Catholic church," he intoned. "Build here by the French in 1803."

"I know it's a Catholic church, but the little tombs. . ."

"Catholic church, build here by the French . . ." Louis

was beginning to sound like a record skipping on the wrong speed.

Phillip made no effort to keep the irritation from his voice. "Look, I know it's a Catholic—"

Paige touched his arm. "Phillip, hush! Obviously the man doesn't know the answer to your question and you're embarrassing him with that reporter-seeking-a-story way of yours. Come on back to the hotel and we'll ask around. There you can get your facts over a Barbancourt and tonic."

On the way back up the hill, the thump that Phillip mentally referred to as "The Noise" sounded twice more. Despite his efforts to locate the source, it seemed to come from the sky, the ground beneath his feet, and the mountains. Or from no place at all. He rationalized the apparent paradox by the hills' ability to echo and distort sound.

As soon as he set down Paige's acquisitions in their room, he reached for her, but she danced away, giggling. "Not now! If you're so eager to find out the reason for those flowers on the graves, go downstairs and ask! Besides"— she wrinkled her slender nose, accenting its upturned tip— "you need a shower."

Reluctantly, Phillip abandoned what he'd had in mind and took a shower. After stepping from the stall into the foggy steam of the bathroom, he used his towel to wipe the moisture from the mirror. He had believed that growing a beard would obviate the necessity of daily shaving. Not so. In order to keep neat the fringe of chestnut hair that outlined his square jaw, he had to trim it away from his throat. Paige had made it quite clear that looking like Wolfman Jack was simply not okay. As he carefully shaved under his chin, he took an appraising look at the oval face that stared back at him. No new wrinkles, although the crows feet around his green eyes might have become a shade more pronounced. Having the tan he immediately acquired in the tropics added to his forty-two years. Consequently, he usually wore a hat despite the full head of hair that was just now beginning to exhibit silver. Too bad about the hat. The damn thing had blown off his head and into the harbor within minutes of his arrival in Cap-Haïtien and he had been unable to find a suitable replacement.

He stepped back, wiping the lather from his neck. He was pleased to note the tautness of his stomach muscles even after the rich cuisine of Port-au-Prince and this place. The country may be poverty stricken, but the Haitians could cook an old tennis shoe and produce a delicious meal. Well, the daily workouts in the gym back home should take care of any excess poundage that had attached itself. Satisfied middle-age spread was not imminent, he picked up the hair dryer Paige had left out and switched it on.

While one is blow-drying one's hair, there is little to do but admire oneself in the mirror, he rationalized as he continued to take stock. He had meant to have his nose fixed shortly after it had been broken in a college football game, but after all these years, he found its irregular ridge comforting, an old friend, although it made his face resemble that of an aging boxer. He grimaced. Teeth okay. He was certain they were getting whiter since he'd quit smoking a year ago. His hair dry and personal inventory complete, he stepped into the bedroom to see Paige leaning over the dresser, applying makeup.

"Okay," he grunted, circling her waist with an arm, "I'm squeaky clean and ready for romance."

"I thought you wanted to find out about those graves," she teased.

He gently pulled her to the bed. "Who cares? I can't imagine it mattering what the occasion is."

Now, tonight, he knew it mattered very much indeed.

Jesus! That crawling thing was under the bed! With the

irrational thought process of fear, Phillip wondered how long it had been since he had imagined something under the bed. This, though, was no imagination. He could hear all too clearly the sound of scales writhing across the tiles. Maybe if he refused to look—just like he had when he was a terrified boy, certain the wolfman was lurking right below the box springs—this, too, would go away, along with the cold fingers of fear that were running up his spine.

He had no one to blame but himself. Had he taken Jean's advice this evening, had he stayed at the hotel instead of being curious. . .

Involuntarily, the image of a meal in the tropical night appeared, a meal that would be the last really peaceful moments he would know for some time.

Chapter 2

By the time they had finished dinner on the hotel's open patio, "The Noise" could be heard at regular intervals. Phillip checked his watch. "About every two minutes," he observed.

Paige put down her coffee cup. "If you're so interested in that drum, or whatever it is, why don't you ask Jean to come over for a drink? He'll probably know about it." She nodded toward the hotel's tubby proprietor who was fussing with linen a few tables away.

"Good idea," Phillip agreed, waving to their host.

Jean approached, eager for conversation. Talking, Phillip had observed, was one thing the portly little Frenchman was always willing to do.

"Everything satisfactory?" he asked, rubbing his hands together.

Phillip pushed back from the table. "I'd like to get some information. I'm willing to pay for it with your choice of after-dinner drinks."

The hotelier smiled, showing little yellow teeth that reminded Phillip of a small animal with a round face. "Fair enough, M. Owens. Usually you reporters want your facts

16

for nothing, eh?'' He beckoned to one of the white-coated waiters and looked questioningly at Paige.

''Nothing for me, thank you,'' she declined.

''Two Calvados,'' Jean requested quietly. ''My special stock.''

Phillip winced at the thought of the fiery apple brandy of his host's native Normandy and the monumental hangovers it produced.

Jean watched the Haitian waiter slip away on silent feet while he pulled the black stub of a cigar from his shirt pocket. ''Well, what can I tell you that you are willing to pay so dearly for?'' His face blurred in a haze of blue smoke as he touched the flaming match to the tobacco and took the first puff.

Phillip managed to hide the distaste a reformed smoker has for the smell of his former vice. ''The drum, or whatever that thumping is . . .''

Jean's good nature vanished, his thick eyebrows coming together under a forehead suddenly wrinkled. ''The damn natives!'' he spat. ''Always something! First this idiot revolution that accomplishes nothing other than replacing a bad government with no government at all. The, how would you say, unrest? Yes, the unrest, that is the reason this hotel is almost empty—and for nothing!''

''But the drum,'' Phillip persisted.

Jean waved a dismissive hand, almost knocking the two glasses from the tray that had appeared, along with the waiter, behind him. ''Ah! These superstitious people are having one of their heathen ceremonies, no doubt. With no one in charge, no police to enforce the laws, these things are now done openly. The country starves while ignorant blacks slaughter pigs and chickens for African gods. The people get drunk on their monkey bag cane whiskey and act as savages. As if that isn't bad enough, we have to listen to that . . ." He paused to acknowledge the server's presence with a string of Creole.

Phillip seized the chance to interrupt. "You mean voodoo?" Every time he had brought up the subject of the sinister religion, he had encountered either cold stares or denials that such a thing existed. He wished he had brought his tape recorder from his room.

Jean took an appreciative sip from one balloon glass and handed the other to his guest. "Voodoo, verdun, whatever you call it, it's damn nonsense, a belief of wretched people to get their minds off their wretched lot."

"They're having a ceremony of some sort tonight?" Phillip was leaning across the table, his drink forgotten. "I noticed the cemetery's graves all had white flowers. Would that be where . . . ?"

Jean shook his head, his flaccid jowls trembling. "Don't even think about it, M. Owens. Those people who, er, conduct such things are probably drunk and certainly lawless."

Paige, leaning forward also, knew what was going through her husband's mind. "You're saying it would be unsafe?"

Jean studied her face a moment before answering slowly, "Mme. Owens, you must remember, enforcement of the laws has all but stopped here. The participants in whatever ceremony or rite may be going on will have been drinking as well as, er, intoxicated on their damned gods. They might not be happy to see an intruder, particularly a white one. Besides, why would you want to see natives butcher a chicken or pig?"

"Because my editor would love a firsthand account of a voodoo ritual. A real one. Not some show the locals concoct for tourists and foreign writers." Phillip's mind was already decided. In his memory, he saw the snake move on the wooden surface. Illusion or not, it had seemed real enough. A prank of the optic nerve?

"Do snakes play any prominent role in voodoo?" he asked, careful to make the suggestion sound offhand, an academic inquiry.

Paige gave him a look of curiosity.

Jean drained the rest of the amber liquid and looked sadly at the empty glass. Was he concealing a surprised expression?

"Too bad we cannot get Calvados in Haiti. I had to bring it in myself." His attention returned to his guests. "Snakes, dogs, what matter? It would be very foolish of you to do what you are thinking, M. Owens. Even more so to include your wife." He stood up with a surprising abruptness. "If you take my advice, you will enjoy the after-dinner music here. The band, though native, is quite good. Excuse me, but I must see to my help."

Phillip watched the hotel keeper, trailing smoke like a locomotive, waddle off into the shadows before he spoke, "Boy! He was sure clear on not wanting us to attend whatever is going on down there."

Paige reached across the table to take his hand. "Maybe he's just concerned about our well-being." A wisp of mischief danced across her face. "After all, if we get turned into toads or something, we couldn't pay our hotel bill."

Phillip acknowledged the remark with a tight grin. "It's too much of an opportunity. . . ."

"You're not really going to . . ." She knew he was.

"As soon as I can get the recorder from the room."

"Then I go."

"You heard what the man said. It could be dangerous." If there was a risk, he felt he had to protest even though her jaw had already assumed that firm set that said her mind was made up.

"No more hazard involved than getting shot at in Belize a few years ago," she remarked.

"We weren't exactly 'shot at,' " he corrected. "The rebels just fired a couple of rounds through the hotel window. I don't want our son to wind up an orphan."

Paige had heard it before. "Neither do I. Nor do I want to be a widow. We go or stay together."

Phillip shrugged his defeat as he stood and headed for the room. "Back in a minute."

"The Noise" was reverberating through the town when they reached the bottom of the hill. Now the sound had direction and, by unspoken consent, they groped along the darkened streets toward it. Their route was occasionally illuminated by flickering candlelight seeping around the edges of shuttered windows like water escaping from a cracked cup. Within a few blocks, they could hear the sound of other, lesser drums sounding a quickening cadence that seemed to match the increase in Phillip's heartbeat, an increase fueled by the apprehension that was a growing block of ice within him. A chant, the wailing of many voices, gave goosebumps to Phillip's flesh despite the warmth of the night, and he began to wonder if he would not have been wise to have heeded Jean's advice. If Paige had any such doubts, she didn't show it as she surged ahead around a corner.

Phillip followed and almost collided with his wife. They both stood, fixed by the sight of the church. Somehow Phillip had known the sounds would lead them here. The outline of the building was visible only as a more distinct feature against the velvet blur of mountains behind it, and the star-studded sky. From the graveyard, pale lights flickered, projecting giant forms that wavered across the side of the church like images on a movie screen.

"Come on!" Paige whispered, tugging at his hand,

oblivious to the nameless dread that was slowing his steps. "We can't see from here."

Phillip choked back the impulse to tell her of his experience in front of the doors that afternoon. The eerie light and keening, rhythmic voices silenced the rational part of his mind. Not the time to mention it, he decided. This was creepy enough. He took the lead, crossing to the plaza and then sliding along the wall to the gate he had noted earlier. It was open and the area was dark except for shifting patches of torchlight.

In the middle of the graveyard, around one of the flat-topped sepulchers, thirty or so forms swayed in rhythm to the drums and chants; human reeds in a breeze. The women wore white. The men were bare-chested, sweat on their torsos reflecting light like polished ebony. Phillip was certain others stood outside the flickering amber light. A buxom woman crawled on her belly, her hands clasped behind her. She lifted her head and shoulders, weaving to the beat. Phillip felt a cold chill spread down his back when he realized the woman was doing a fair imitation of a snake.

Another woman, this one emaciated by age and with white hair that glimmered orange from the sputtering torches, stood solidly beside the tomb, the center of the crazily flowing circle of . . . worshipers? Communicants? Her hands above her head, she clasped something that glinted, something long and metallic. A knife, Phillip decided. She cried out and the crowd responded in a strangely musical language that Phillip had heard in one of the West African republics two years ago. Again she half crooned, half shrieked. The group responded. Slowly at first, then with increasing speed, she, too, began to sway, the drum's beat speeding up with the chants of the old woman and her throng. There was another movement at the back of the group. Two men were pushing their way through those in front. The pair were carrying an object between them.

"Too big for a goat, must be a pig," Phillip whispered, although he could have spoken out loud with little chance of being heard by the dancers. "Sure you're up to this?" He reached inside his shirt pocket and turned the recorder on.

Paige choked on her answer. "That's no pig, it's . . ."

He followed her horrified stare and his mouth went dry, his throat unable to swallow. The two men and their burden were now clearly defined by the wavering torchlight. Between them was a woman, nude. A young girl, really, Phillip corrected himself with journalistic detachment as he noted the lithe figure and breasts just beginning to swell. Her eyes appeared to be closed in death. No, the small chest moved. She was breathing. Her bearers, one holding her arms, the other her feet, stretched her across the top of the tomb. Her eyes flew open and she began to twist frantically, aware of what was to happen.

"Phillip," Paige said in a voice that crackled with the panic beneath it, "either do something to stop this or—"

"Shhhh!" He was certain she was mistaken. Surely these people were not going to . . .

But they were.

At a wail almost lost in the drumbeat, the blade flashed down, a silver blur of death. Blood, black in the smoky light, erupted from a slash from the young girl's pubis to her chin. Paige gagged as the executioner reached into the still thrashing chest cavity and removed an object the size of a softball. As she held her prize aloft in gore-soaked hands, Phillip felt the bile rise in his throat. She held a beating, quivering heart. Phillip tried to force back the acrid, bitter taste in his mouth as the crowd's chant and the drums reached a peak of frenzy. The woman, priestess, whatever, slowly lowered her hands to her lips, and, with slow deliberation, she began to eat.

The horror that numbed Phillip's mind was so great he

was unaware he was retching, only slightly aware of a whine that rose to a scream just as the drums ceased. Paige was shrieking. Not a single, pitched sound, but a series of wails and sobs. Her hands were pressed to her eyes as though to erase what they had witnessed. He reached for her, seeking to give her comfort he did not feel.

Thunk!

The sound of metal striking stone near his head distracted him from Paige. He whirled around to see an object arch into the air, its surface shining malevolently in the flickering light. He shoved Paige out of the way before the machete also struck stone with another evil reverberation. The long blade could easily have taken her head off had he not pushed her aside.

"Shit!" he gulped, snatching his wife to her feet and shooting a fear-borne glance in the direction from which the cane cutter had come. The two men who had held the young girl were walking toward them with a silent deliberation that was more menacing than had they been running.

Paige was sobbing quietly, oblivious to the approaching danger. Phillip gave her arm a rough tug. "C'mon, we gotta get outa here."

Still pulling her, he darted across the square to seek invisibility in the first dark street he reached. Before rounding the corner, he shot a quick look over his shoulder. Their two pursuers followed, still with a gait so unhurried it implied the futility of flight. Although the darkness made it impossible to determine the features of their faces at this distance, he could see their eyes, which gave off the dull glow of polished stones. He was sure the excitement had caused an illusion, or some errant bit of light, or . . .

He did not look back again.

But he could still see them in his mind, following slowly, because somehow they knew they didn't have to catch them, somehow they knew their mission would be completed by this thing under the bed that was going to keep right on making sounds until he lifted the dust ruffle and took a look. And when he looked, it wouldn't be there. Just like the little man of the child's rhyme:

Yesterday there was a man upon the stair,
A man who wasn't there.
He wasn't there again today.
How I wish he'd go away.

But this was no child's rhyme or fantasy. Phillip was an adult and there *was* something under the bed just as there had been something in the corner and in the bathroom. Until he looked.

There was a thump on the bottom of the mattress, undeniable because Paige mumbled in her sleep and turned over again. It was the snake, of course. That twisting, moving serpent from the church doors, that woman in the churchyard, writhing on the ground. Although he didn't know what the connection was, he was certain there was one. And it was going to slide its scales across the tile, push on the mattress and whatever else until he looked under the bed. He could sit here, shivering in his sweat or get on with it.

Again his feet felt the cool tiles as he walked across the room, picked up the lamp and lifted the dust ruffle gingerly as though the cloth itself presented a danger.

Nothing but brown clay tile, grout, and the wisps of undisturbed dust bunnies.

Returning the lamp to the table, he stretched out on top of the covers only to have the evening's events begin exactly where his memory had left off.

* * *

Staggering, out of breath, Phillip and Paige had stumbled through the empty openness of the hotel lobby. The band Jean had promised was playing in merry contrast to what both were thinking, its steel drum twanging in counterpoint to a guitar and rattle. Paige collapsed on a rattan sofa, panting words between gulps of air, "Shouldn't we . . . notify someone? Jean? The police?"

Phillip was leaning against a mahogany panelled wall, searching the blackness outside. "Sure. Don't know how we get the cops since Jean said there weren't any." He, too, could hardly fill his lungs quickly enough after the long run. "His room's up those stairs. I'll go get him."

She glanced around apprehensively. "I'll go with you."

The hotel keeper had not been asleep, for he answered their frantic knocks fully dressed. His surprised smile faded at the sight of their faces. "Something is wrong?"

Phillip nodded, just beginning to breathe normally again. "At the church, the graveyard . . ."

Paige was now outwardly composed, eager to speak. "In spite of what you told us, we wanted to see a real voodoo ritual. We did. They . . . " Phillip could see her turn white, the blood draining from her face like mercury in a falling thermometer. She swallowed and continued, "They murdered a young girl. Killed her. We thought you should call the police." She finished barely ahead of a shudder that stopped only when Phillip put an arm tightly around her.

"Murder? Police?" Jean glanced past them and motioned them in. "Surely you are mistaken."

Phillip was more relieved than he would have admitted when the door was shut against whatever might be outside. "No mistake. We both saw it." Now that he'd had time to put the facts in sequence, he described what had happened in the terse who, when, and where of his trade.

"And," he finished, "I guarantee you there was no

imagining those machetes. If one had hit us, we wouldn't be here.''

Jean pursed thick lips in thought as he reached for a crystal decanter, its beveled surface twinkling cheerfully as he poured. ''Calvados?''

''Thanks, we can use it.'' Phillip handed a snifter to Paige who tossed it down as though she were accustomed to the burning stuff. She barely gasped before she suggested, ''Don't we need to alert the authorities?''

Jean motioned them toward uncomfortable-looking carved mahogany chairs and took one himself. ''Authorities? Hmpf! In the first place, Haiti *has* no one in a position of authority, as I may have mentioned. Second, I'd recommend you forget the entire matter.''

''Forget?'' Paige asked, her voice arching in disbelief.

Jean held up a hand to ward off the protest he anticipated. ''M., Mme. Owens, I know you are, eh, upset from what you believed you witnessed.''

''Believe?'' Phillip interrupted angrily, ''I've been a reporter and newsman for years. I *know* what we saw.''

The hotel keeper stared at them with placid eyes. ''Do you? It was dark and you say what little light there was came from smoking torches.'' He shrugged. ''What you really, er, witnessed, saw, was the slaughter of a small pig, or perhaps a goat. Besides, there has been no human sacrifice here for over seventy years.''

Phillip struggled to keep his voice even. ''I saw a human being killed, not a pig or a goat.''

Paige leaned toward him to put a hand on his arm. ''Perhaps Jean's right. I couldn't swear what I saw.''

Phillip started to protest until he felt the pressure, a signal not to pursue the matter. Don't argue politics at a cocktail party, don't ask a question that might embarrass a friend. Don't insist we saw a ritual murder. He was well acquainted with the old pressure-on-the-arm trick. He sighed, a counter signal of his reluctance to abandon the matter. "Okay, maybe you're right."

The relief on their host's face was clear. "Of course, I am." He indicated the decanter. "Have at least one more. It will quiet your nerves."

"They could use some calming," Phillip muttered as he helped himself.

Jean settled back into the chair. "You are wise to accept the fact your eyes, er, played tricks." He smiled with the confidence of one who has won an argument. "Besides, even if you should summon whatever police there might be, they would require you to remain in this country while they conduct an investigation only to determine you were mistaken. I think you would not much care to be stuck in Haiti for weeks or even months."

Phillip emptied his glass. "You're right there. Now I guess it's time to go to bed. I've got to fly tomorrow."

Phillip's peace of mind would not have been restored had he known that Jean's smile became the grinding of teeth as soon as he shut the door. *Merde, MERDE!* This filthy, wretched excuse of a country! He should have kept his shop in Rouen instead of selling it to buy an impoverished Haitian hotel. He had grown weary of the lead-gray Norman skies and the summers that never came until July. The idea of Haiti had been seductive and he had come to this land where winter never intruded and spent what little money he had left to fix the hotel up. Even when Anne, his wife, had returned to France, the business was good and he had prospered. There was hope he might persuade her to return.

Now that appeared at an end. The imbecilic revolution had frightened off his guests other than a few Scandinavians who would brave hell itself in preference to their own harsh climate. Now this. It was bad enough to have an American

witness some bloody pagan ceremony, see a human sacrifice, but to have a journalist assaulted! Gloomily, Jean en-
visioned articles in every major American newspaper,
articles that would insure the dearth of American clientele
even when this stupid political situation was resolved.

He refilled his glass. Perhaps, with luck, the woman could
convince her husband they were mistaken. He tossed off his
entire drink, replacing it as he thought. Perhaps he could
ask M. Owens not to write a story that would damage the
hotel's reputation beyond repair. Perhaps . . . the glass
paused at his lips. Perhaps the Owens would never get a
chance to publish the story.

He had heard rumors, tales too fantastic to believe, of
others who had stumbled upon such ceremonies and met
with mysterious deaths, deaths no rational mind could accept. He himself had witnessed the terror in which even the
more civilized natives held this savage religion of voodoo
although he had scoffed at their fears. Maybe there was
something to it all. He was almost ashamed to acknowledge
that the thought had become a faint hope. Well, no one had
asked this meddling writer to come here, certainly not to
witness whatever he had seen, If, and he shivered at the
possibility, there was truth in the stories, there would be no
damning articles to strangle his already dying business. He
gulped down the Calvados, reaching for another.

Outside, Phillip let his eyes become accustomed to a
darkness that was now threatening. Shadows of tree limbs,
grotesquely deformed arms, reached menacingly. The
cheery chirp of tree frogs had become sinister laughs, their
sources invisible. Stirred by a light breeze, the outline of
vines twisted, lifting reptilian heads. He shook himself,
forcing his mind to ignore the imagined horrors of a tropical
night gone rancid with fright. ''You certainly were quick to

admit we were hallucinating,'' he commented, reproving his imagination more than her.

Paige also was staring into the inky black that walled them in. ''It was pretty obvious he wasn't eager for us to believe what happened,'' she said pensively. ''I'd guess he figures a story like that would ruin what little business he has left. There didn't seem any point in getting into a dispute. We can try and find a cop tomorrow.''

''We sure can't stay here for some investigation.''

''Phillip Owens!'' She was looking up at him accusingly. ''A young girl was murdered and those people tried to kill us. We are not going to just walk away from it and pretend it never happened.''

''You're right,'' Phillip said as he led the way toward their room. ''Before we fling ourselves into the sky tomorrow, let's go by the cemetery and take a look.''

''For what?''

''I don't know. Maybe anything that might convince the police.'' They had reached the room. ''Now, do you want to stand out here all night?''

Once inside, Paige glanced around. ''Do you think those people are still looking for us?''

''They would have been here by now if they knew where to look,'' he responded with a certainty he did not feel.

Now, staring into space as he shivered in bed, Phillip realized it would have been better to confront their pursuers than lay here, waiting for the snake to appear—no, not ''appear,'' *sound*—waiting for the snake to evidence its presence by a sound somewhere else. Should he wake his wife? No, let her sleep. What could she do but share the fright that was keeping him awake? He glanced at the luminous dial of his watch: six hours till sunrise and an end to this night. Things always looked better in sunlight.

* * *

The events which were taking place in a hut a few miles away, however, would have dispelled Phillip's good feeling. There was nothing to distinguish this hut from the other occasional dwellings beside the rut down the side of the mountain that served as a road—nothing except that the feet of those passing this way had worn a path through the jungle growth that gave this particular building a wide detour. A stranger to the area might wonder why so many people would have chosen a different route around this hovel that appeared no different from its scattered neighbors. The locals would prefer to avoid the place by an even wider margin, but the steepness of the mountain's slope made that impossible. So, on passing, they satisfied themselves by digging a cross in the dirt with a toe and spitting in the middle, or turning around three times, or a number of other methods commonly known to ward off the evil eye, curses, and a host of other such afflictions.

Inside, the furnishings were not what an outsider would expect to find in a peasant's hut, not unless he was well acquainted with the black arts. Against a wall was an altar which, at first glance, looked like an altar one might see in a small chapel. Closer inspection would have revealed a number of aberrations: on the arms of the cross rested a deck of cards with strange animals on the face of each card. Although the usual array of saints' effigies were arranged across the rear, their hands and faces were painted black, and they carried articles unknown to most devout Catholics. On the altar itself sat a brass bell, a mirror, an ordinary wash basin and pitcher, along with a gourd rattler. On the dirt floor a complicated design had been drawn in charcoal. Strange fish, oddly shaped fish, played among tridents and waterlike ripples.

Between this unique drawing and the door, an old woman sat on her heels, chanting. Her many years had thinned her face, pulling the black leathery skin tightly across the bone structure with that tendency age has of making the nose seem longer and jaw underslung. The general impression of her profile was that of a hawk. Her eyes were covered by the white skin of cataracts. Someone who didn't know better might say she was blind, but they would be wrong. She could not see the interior of her dwelling, perhaps, but she could see faraway places—places she had never visited— and things that had not yet happened. Many said she could see in the conventional sense also. How else would one explain the intricate drawing before her? Or the fact that she lived alone and yet her water jug was always full and the nearest spring was a mile away? At the moment she was seeing the two people in their hotel room and took satisfaction that one of them was already experiencing the power. He, and she, would feel its full weight shortly. This big, bearded white man and his woman had desecrated the sacrifice. The thought of what had happened curled her lips back in a snarl to show toothless gums. The ceremony was sacred to the great *loa* Damballah and now he was angry. Angry because of what had happened and because it had been necessary to kidnap another young girl, something that made the people grumble and question the need of the offering of a human heart. Yes, these two had caused her authority to be questioned, something Damballah would not tolerate. That was why the white man and woman must die. Tomorrow they would travel in the bird machine with the spinning knives on its wings. In that machine, they would perish. She was too weary now, too tired from conducting a second ceremony. But tomorrow, even as the white people left, she would satisfy the *loa*'s demand for revenge. Let them shiver or sleep in their room. Seconds after their machine climbed into the sky, they would die.

Chapter 3

Phillip was still awake at midnight. With only Paige's regular breathing in his ear, he could feel muscles uncoil and
nerves cease their electric tingling. There had been no more
crawling sounds, but his memory insisted on replaying the
scene in the churchyard. And the guys with machetes . . .
They were enough to keep sleep away for a lifetime. To hell
with it, he told himself. Tomorrow, under a bright sun, he
and Paige would get into the airplane and leave this creepy
place where carved snakes moved and children were murdered. Somewhere in mid-rationalization, Phillip drifted off.

"Dadeeee!" The plaintive cry came from a distance only
memory could span.

Becky, her age forever fixed at five, swam into view. With
the futile effort of dreams, Phillip reached desperately for
his first child, now dead twelve years. A halo of her blonde
hair floated around her child's face, awash in the water in
which she always appeared to him. As always, he strained
to touch her as her cold blue lips mouthed the soundless
words that, in dreams, communicated so clearly, "Daddy,
where were you?" Even in silence there was accusation in
the question.

He became desperate. He had to make her understand that it wasn't his fault, that if he had only known . . . But he could not speak. Try as he might to touch her, to speak to her, he could not. He *had* to tell her. She began to fade, the lines of the child's face blurring despite his effort. She was simply dissolving. The last thing he saw were her brown eyes, eyes that wept in spite of the fact that she was underwater.

He awoke, screaming.

Paige was instantly awake, her arms around him. "The dream again?"

He choked back tears that were real and nodded mutely. Had the sound in the room been real or a dream like Becky?

She rubbed the back of his neck reassuringly, speaking in that sympathetic tone she used whenever the subject of Becky's death came up. "There. You can't keep blaming yourself. The child was with her mother."

Phillip lay a finger across his wife's lips. "I know. I know. Logically, you're right. Now if I could just convince my subconscious . . ."

"Maybe you ought to start seeing Dr. Hilsman again when we get home."

"I haven't seen him in years. I'm not sure I'm up to psychiatrists again."

"You said he was a help."

"He was. God knows after . . . after Becky died, I needed somebody. Margaret certainly . . ." He left the phrase unspoken.

"I'm sure she was just as grief-stricken as you were." Paige always defended his ex-wife, even after ten years of their own marriage.

"Certainly showed it, didn't she?" he asked with the bitterness time had done little to diminish. "Stuck her nose right back in the bottle."

Paige gave him a squeeze. ''We all have our own way of dealing with tragedy. Now try to get some sleep.''

He was still debating whether to mention what he had been hearing when the weariness that is the residue of fear dragged him back into sleep. A sleep that the old woman thought would be his last.

Chapter 4

If Haiti has a national bird it must be a rooster. The arrival of each morning Phillip and Paige had spent here had been announced by cocks' crows. Phillip shook his head as though to clear it of sleepy fog. It seemed only an instant since he had dozed off. Stretching before stepping out of bed, he padded across cool tiles to draw the curtain back from the window. A brilliant red tropical sun was edging above the mountains across the harbor, painting a scarlet streak over water still enough to reflect the cloudless sky. He stared at the view a moment, thinking how unreal last night seemed in the day's growing light. Just as the brilliance of a new day denies the existence of night's dark, this morning in its special glory made last night—the ritual in the churchyard, the crawling thing in the room—seem unreal. Before he was aware he had really thought about it, he decided not to mention the sound to Paige. Why frighten her, or, worse, suffer that look of pity he had seen so often when he'd had that mental problem about Becky? Besides, he and she were about to leave—leave Haiti, voodoo, and the rest of it. He was looking forward to getting to the plane.

(*"In that machine they would perish . . ."*)

"Look like a good day to fly?" Paige's sleepy voice came from behind him.

"Couldn't have special-ordered a better one," he replied, heading for the bathroom. His wife would use the extra few minutes he needed for his morning toilet to catnap.

At his insistence she reluctantly burrowed from underneath the sheet and stumbled toward the bath with the measured step of a sleepwalker. While she busied herself in the shower, Phillip packed their single suitcase. She might not be too swift in the mornings, but she was the only woman he had ever known who could make do with only half a single piece of luggage. And look good, too. The events of the evening were taking on a dreamlike fuzziness already.

"Hey," logic said, "let's just drop the whole thing. It's not like that voodoo stuff has anything to do with us, right?"

"Not so fast," the mind argued. "We know what we saw, even putting aside that weird business about the sound in this room, and a bad dream."

"We're going to have a lot more bad dreams if we get ourselves involved in whatever took place in that graveyard," logic threatened. "We're leaving this place today, headed back to the old US of A where shit like that doesn't happen. Why drag baggage like that around?"

The mind was only temporarily stumped. "Because it's our business—the news' business—to know what happened. We're not going to start ignoring facts just because they might be unpleasant, are we?"

And there the argument ended. Not because logic couldn't find a snappy retort, but because Phillip shoved both contestants in this cerebral debate offstage to start planning the flight back to said good old US of A.

They were the only people sitting under the citrus trees around the pool to enjoy the rich Haitian coffee and sweet fruit preserves on croissants. More precisely, Paige was the only person. Phillip was not hungry and Jean was not in sight.

Paige glanced around. "This is the first time I haven't seen our host at mealtime. You suppose there's something wrong?"

By unspoken agreement, last night was being avoided as a topic of conversation. Both knew it would come up soon enough.

Phillip looked up from pushing a piece of bread around his plate. "I guess even hotel keepers get to sleep in once in a while. Why would something be wrong?"

Paige shrugged. "I don't know, but I would like to at least tell him goodbye."

Phillip stood. "Tell you what, I'll go knock on his door while you finish here."

The first brisk raps produced no response. He gave the door a series of solid blows. There was a muttering from inside followed by shuffling, the sound of someone moving. The door slowly opened and Phillip was looking at a face in pain. Jean's usually bright eyes had the dullness of sleep not yet abandoned, and the round face was without color under the veneer of tropical tan. The heavy lips were moist from the tongue that darted in and out. Phillip tried not to show surprise or wince from the stench of stale alcohol. Jean, it seemed, had a hangover.

"Yes?" Was that disappointment Phillip saw flicker across his host's face?

"Er, I just wanted to say 'So long.' We're leaving as soon as we can get a cab to the airport. So long and thanks for your hospitality."

Jean forced a smile. "I regret I cannot be downstairs to see you off, but I had a bit too much Calvados last night, eh? I fear I shall be ill for sometime to come. And, about last night: you surely were mistaken as to what you thought you saw. No point in writing about an error like that, eh?''

Phillip almost snapped with the peevishness he always felt when someone suggested he suppress a story. But continuing the argument was pointless. Instead, he observed that the hotelier must have emptied the entire decanter to look that bad. He extended a hand. "I hope things improve in Haiti so the tourists will be back soon."

"Thank you, M. Owens. Perhaps a few kind words about this establishment in your articles?" The flesh of Jean's hand was cool and damp.

Phillip took an exaggerated step backwards. "Well, time to go."

"Au revoir," Jean replied with a sadness that Phillip could not decide came from either the failure to obtain his promise not to write about last night, or the departure of what might be the hotel's only guests for some time. "The girl at the desk downstairs will figure your bill and summon a taxi for you."

The same ancient car wheezed up the hill to take them to the airport. As soon as they were in the torn vinyl seats, Paige leaned toward the driver. "We want to go to the airport. But first, please, take us by the church."

The driver treated them to a wide-eyed stare that spoke his surprise at the senseless requests of American tourists.

Phillip spoke up, "You're not really serious about going back there?"

"Certainly I am. It was your idea last night."

Phillip sank back into the seat. He *had* come up with the plan, which in today's bright sunlight seemed foolish. "It was only a suggestion."

The cabbie was still looking back at his passengers, following the exchange with interest. Paige shooed him forward. "To the church, driver," she said before turning a determined face toward her husband. "Phillip, you *promised*."

He considered the futility of pointing out that expressing an idea is hardly making a promise. He'd never succeeded in doing so before. With a sigh, he confirmed her instructions, "Just drive us to the church. We'll only be a second."

So the white people were going to delay their trip! The old woman cackled happily as she reached for the bell on the altar and rang it three times. Although the sun was well over the mountain's top, she had kept the door and single window of her hut closed, preserving a dusty night in the interior. At the third ring, a musty odor filled her nose and there was a single soft hiss. She knew she was no longer alone and she resumed her chant from the night before:

> "I will summon the snake
> The serpent who does not speak
> Damballah father of us all you are a serpent."

The words flowed in lilting Creole while her mind reached out to her visitors.

> "If you see a snake
> You see Damballah."

"How does Your Greatness wish this done?" her thoughts inquired.

> "If you see a snake
> You see Damballah."

"The sea." The words were sibilant hisses in her brain. *"Drown them in the sea when their machine falls from the sky."*

"I have your power, Your Greatness," her consciousness agreed. "I shall call upon Baron Samedi."

"Samedi, yesss," the hiss replied.

There was the audible scratch of scales against the mud wall.

For some reason Phillip was not surprised at what he found; there was no evidence of the events that had taken place in the churchyard the previous night. Even the white flowers were gone. The tomb that had served as an altar exhibited the same pristine, white-washed stucco as the others. Paige walked around it suspiciously as though ordering it to give up its secret. Phillip seemed to wander aimlessly through the enclosure until he reached the entrance. There he knelt, running a hand up and down the stone pillars between which the gate hung. He glanced up as Paige's shadow fell across him.

"Find anything?" he asked, turning to squint up at her.

She shook her head slowly. "No. It's like we dreamed the whole thing." She glanced back into the peaceful cemetery. "Do you suppose there is such a thing as group hallucination?"

Phillip shook his head. "We saw what we saw. Look here," he said pointing to the surface of the stone, "that's where the machete struck. See how new that chip is? The rain and wind haven't had time to leach it out. Whoever took the trouble to wash away the blood, remove the flowers, and brush the ground to hide the footprints couldn't hide that—the newness of that nick in the stone."

She stooped to run a finger along the irregular surface.

"For all we know, that could have happened this morning or yesterday afternoon."

He grunted as he got to his feet. "You're right, but we know it didn't."

She was still staring in fascination. "So we don't have anything to take to the local cops, I guess."

Phillip made no effort to conceal his relief. "Nothing at all. Even if we found somebody in charge here, we have nothing but a story for them, no proof that we aren't a pair of loonies."

Still looking back at the spot, she slowly walked toward the waiting cab. "So you're saying just let it go? Forget that a young girl was murdered?"

"You have a better suggestion?" he asked quietly.

She shook her head slowly. "No, but I can't just walk away. There must be something we can do."

Once again, Phillip knew he was beaten. They'd be here all day if Paige wasn't satisfied they'd done everything possible. "Tell you what: we'll go by the police station, see if anybody's there. But if we have to stay for some kind of an investigation . . ."

She brightened. "If what? You and I have both been stuck in worse places and you're always saying how much you love the Caribbean."

His fears were groundless. Other than a few scrawny chickens listlessly pecking at the dirt courtyard in front of the open end of the horse shoe structure, the police barracks were deserted. One of these birds, Phillip was certain, had been his malefactor so early this morning. No doubt calculating the added fare, the cab driver smiled benevolently at his eccentric charges as they went from one bolted door to another. The only sign of recent habitation was the blue

and red of the new Haitian flag that draped limply from its
pole.

"If there are any cops left in Cap-Haïtien, they sure aren't
here," Phillip observed as he wiped sweat from his forehead with the back of his hand. "And it's getting hot. I'd
sure like to be in the air before the daily thunderstorms brew
up."

"Oh, all right, but I don't feel like we're doing the right
thing."

"What else can we do?" Phillip was surprised by the
irritation in his voice.

Baron Samedi. The old woman saw him so clearly that
the sunlight at the airport hurt her eyes even though her
vision was taking place miles away. She would keep watching, though.

("*Drown them in the sea when their machine falls from
the sky. . . .*")

Even though Gulliam had not heard from his superiors in
Port-au-Prince for two weeks now, he had no intention of aban-
doning his post as Commander of Immigration of the Cap-
Haïtien airport. Where else would he go, anyway? Back to
the poverty of the native village he had left years ago? He
winced at the thought. No, even if the President for Life
had fled the capital—as people were saying—he would stay
here. He would remain if his superiors in the capital had
also departed. In fact, he hoped they had. The men from
Port-au-Prince were always complaining. "Gulliam, too
much of the money that passes through your hands sticks to
them," they accused. When they were unable to rake off
their share because too much stayed here, they became ugly.
Now they were gone—or at least quiet—and Gulliam was
living better than ever. If this was revolution, he was all for

it. He had even helped raise the new national flag over the terminal building, not so much for patriotism, but because now he could afford to have a woman wash, press, and starch his uniform, not to mention the women he could pay to perform other, more personal, services.

Yes, this was his reward for faithful government work. He was in a good mood as he watched the Americans arrive in the taxi. There would be many fees to collect. The Americans would protest, of course, but who did not? There was the fee for working on a holiday. (When the government for which you work no longer exists and you are still doing your duty, every day is a holiday, is it not?) And, of course, there would be the radio fee. What did it matter that there was no longer anyone here who knew how to operate the one in the tower—it was there, used or not. Naturally, they would pay an immigration fee also. He almost salivated at the thought of the American dollars he would pocket. This couple would give him no real trouble, he decided. The big, bearded man was actually carrying things out to the airplane while the woman filled out papers. No real man would go about in the hot sun when there was a woman available to do the heavy work. No, this large man would be no problem.

And the airplane! Although he had never been on one of those machines that soared higher above the mountains than the buzzards, he had heard what such things cost—more than everyone in his village combined would make in a lifetime. With that sort of unimaginable wealth, these Americans would gladly pay Gulliam's fees.

Through his reflective sunglasses, he watched the woman prepare the general declaration forms. What would be a good number to require? The answer struck him immediately and he congratulated himself on his cleverness. He would demand at least one more than she had. No matter that few here in Cap-Haïtien could read, the mass of paper he had accumulated since officials from Port-au-Prince had stopped collecting it was large enough to impress them when and if they ever came again.

He stiffened to his full five feet two inches as the woman counted out four copies of the indecipherable documents and proffered two passports for departure stamps. "I think I've got enough," she said pleasantly.

Before replying, he took his time to admire her. Older than he would prefer, but still well-shaped. Her skin told him she had probably spent little time in the fields working crops. No, that large husband of hers could afford to hire others to do her work. He let his hand touch hers as she handed over the papers—it was smooth, smooth as the belly of the fourteen-year-old girl for whom Gulliam had paid almost three dollars, American. He smiled, thinking what the girl would do for him for part of the money he was about to collect.

Then he frowned, the proper expression for all those with official power. "No," he said, proud of the few English words he had learned, allowing him to rise to his exalted position, "five copies."

She was perplexed. "You only wanted four when we arrived."

He held up a hand, fingers extended to demonstrate. "Five."

She shrugged and dug in her purse. He had expected to negotiate the missing copy in terms of additional fees. Instead, she produced a sheaf of the papers, more than Gulliam could have counted, and he could go as high as ten. Reluctantly, he received the additional document.

No matter, the fees would more than compensate. He recited them. Again the American woman fished in her purse, this time producing a wad of gourdes.

He shook his head. "No, pay in dollar."

She smiled sweetly. He was astounded to see such teeth in the mouth of a woman over twenty. She must have all of them. What was that she was saying, something about having only gourdes or American Express travelers checks? There was no place he could change the travelers' checks into dollars. Grudgingly, he accepted the Haitian money at the official exchange rate of five to the dollar. He could get twice that on the black market. Damn. Today was not going to be as profitable as he'd anticipated.

Phillip, with the help of a brigade of volunteers, each carrying one item, loaded the Beechcraft B55 Baron. Not that he needed the help, but he had learned it was easier to accept the service than to argue about declining it. Besides, the few coins each native would receive as a tip would hardly be missed. With Paige's treasures wedged into the backseats and the single bag in the nose compartment, he began a careful preflight inspection of the twin-engined Baron. All control surfaces free. Any potential contaminants drained from the tanks, tanks visually checked to make sure they had been filled. Despite the sun's heat, he was careful and methodical. Open ocean was not the place to discover a problem that could have been easily solved before takeoff.

His final act before departure was to fill out the required flight plan. The fact there was no radio operator here to transmit it anywhere was immaterial. The rules demanded a flight plan be filed and compliance was mandatory. The same moment he finished his useless task, Paige completed her paperwork. She was stuffing their passports into her purse as she walked over to the battered table where an official perused Phillip's plan with great intensity, an intensity only slightly diminished by the fact that he was holding it upside down. "You checked the fuel?" Paige asked, commencing her own preflight quiz, a practice that calmed the nervousness she felt before a flight.

"You bet. Oil, too." He appreciated her questions as a means of backstopping any oversight on his part. It was a definite improvement over the tremulous fidgeting she had shown the first few times he had taken her up in a small plane.

"How 'bout the tires? Static air ports?"

"All checked." She had reduced his walk around to a litany, complete as any checklist. "Control surfaces?" she continued as they walked toward the Baron. "Sumps drained?"

He climbed through the single door, extending a hand to help her into the seat next to him as she finished her questions. She pulled the door closed, checking the latch and slipping into her shoulder harness as he started the engines. He watched silently as the oil pressure and temperature gauges jumped to life before turning on the radios and navigation equipment. Only when he was satisfied all was as it should be did he start a slow taxi toward the far end of the single runway. He ascertained wind direction by the smoke from nearby mud huts, smoke that poured a pungent odor through the open vent window beside him. He would never smell charcoal, he thought, without thinking of Haiti. Since electricity and gas were virtually unavailable outside town and few Haitians could have afforded them had they been, charcoal was used for cooking, boiling water, and whatever other fuel needs the general populace had.

"Look!" Paige's exclamation interrupted his thoughts.

She was pointing to a man striding down the edge of the runway. People and livestock on the airstrip were not uncommon. The Jepps airport diagram and approach plate even noted the likelihood of such a hazard. But this native was different, very different. Taller than any Phillip had seen here, the man wore not the usual shaggy straw hat, but a stovepipe—the sort of thing the history books associated with Lincoln. Despite the heat that was already dancing off the paving, he was clad in a black swallowtail coat, comical in view of the bare feet upon which he marched along, apparently oblivious of the aircraft. A wisp of smoke trailed from the pipe he clinched in his teeth.

"Strange time of day for a costume party." Paige giggled.

Before Phillip could reply, they were abreast of this apparition and Phillip felt the same creeping chill he had experienced yesterday afternoon on the way into town. A glance at his wife told him, once again, she did not share it. He shook himself as a wet dog might.

"Another rabbit?" she asked.

A wave of heat through the vent washed over him and the chill was gone. "I guess so," he answered as he ruddered the plane around to face into the light breeze.

("In the sea . . .")

After running the engines to full power, Phillip began the last check to assure himself all was ready. Gently he released the brakes atop the rudder pedals and the plane surged forward, its momentum smoothly increasing. With the split vision of experienced pilots, Phillip watched the runway slip past as the airspeed needle moved faster and faster. Goats that had been grazing in the adjacent field went by in a single white blur. The strange, tall Haitian stopped to watch. Although the brim of his hat cast his face in shadow, something was shining under the brim. No, two somethings. Eyes! The man's eyes had the same dull glow as . . .

Phillip had no time to think. The plane was light on its wheels, waiting to leap into the air like a ballerina. The ground disappeared as the windshield filled with blue sky.

With the suddenness of most disasters, the throaty growl of two engines became a series of popping coughs and then was silent as the aircraft pitched forward and he was thrown against his harness. Phillip reacted rather than thought. With almost half the runway beneath them, with the landing gear still extended, with a great deal of luck, maybe, just maybe, he could set this five thousand pounds of hurtling machinery down. One thing was certain: he would have to try.

("Drown them . . .")

He heard Paige's terrified scream at the same instant the flightless craft thumped to the ground hard enough to blur his vision. He had his full weight on the brakes and the sound of shrieking rubber filled his ears. The end of the now precious strip of asphalt rushed toward him with a speed that he could not seem to slow. There was a ditch somewhere past the runway threshold, he remembered. If the now powerless plane hit it with any momentum at all, the Baron would flip over like a circus acrobat. There were over a hundred gallons of highly flammable avgas in the tanks. The thought gave extra strength to his legs pressing down on the brakes.

The edge of the ditch was marked by cane, swaying in the breeze as though beckoning the airplane to destruction. He could see it clearly now as the numbers painted on the threshold of the runway also became visible. It was going to be close—he hoped. He clenched his jaws in anticipation of what was to happen. At the same time he could feel Paige's nails digging into the flesh of his arm the same way she did at scary scenes of movies.

At first, he was afraid to believe, then he became certain they were noticeably slowing. There was a jolt that snapped his head back as the Baron rolled off the pavement's end. The tall grass that swished against the wings grew in loose soil that helped decrease speed. He noticed the now windmilling propeller blades that acted as a scythe, sending a fine spray of green strands into the air.

He could see a trickle of dirty water in the ditch now, a small stream, he thought irrelevantly, near panic. There might be one last chance. If it worked, great. If not, so what? He shifted his weight from both feet to only the right foot, lifting his left completely from the pedal.

The effect was immediate. The plane slewed violently to the right, skidding, scraping off speed. It stopped as gracefully and gently as the best landing he had ever made. Light danced from the ripples of the little creek only a few feet away.

"Shit," Paige said without inflection.

Phillip wasn't sure if she was cursing or making an announcement. With a hand he could barely make stop shaking, he turned off the switches. That sharp, biting smell could be . . . no, it was burned rubber. Without speaking, he leaned across Paige and opened the door. She sat stonily staring ahead. Phillip gently unbuckled her harness and peeled her hand from his arm. There were flecks of blood where her nails had bitten into the skin.

"Paige?" he asked tentatively. "We need to get out. If something ruptured a gas tank. . ."

Her head snapped forward and she blinked as though waking from a dream. In the same somnambulant trance, she wordlessly climbed out onto the wing and to the ground where she shivered as though in an arctic wind. He scrambled down to take her in his arms. He started to lead her away but there was no odor of gasoline. Apparently, the tanks were undamaged.

"What? . . ." Her voice was that of a frightened child.

"The engines, both of them, quit. Just like that," he soothed. "I've never heard of both quitting at exactly the same time." The sound of his words, the return to a safe world, were calming him as much as her. "There was a DC 9 that lost both engines, back in '74, I think, but that was due to hail in a thunderstorm." He glanced back at the twin streaks of rubber, black on black, that pointed down the runway like accusing fingers. A group from the airport was running toward them and several curious natives had stopped along the road to gawk, some on small horses, others on foot, but all carrying something: pitcher of water, a bundle of cane.

That's when it hit him: Haitians are always carrying something. But the tall man in the hat had been empty-handed. And the path beside the runway, usually a sea of motion, had been empty. Except for him. And he had disappeared.

Gently, he sat Paige down and surveyed the damage. She watched with wide, frightened eyes. The tires on the main gear were flat-spotted, but serviceable. Small nicks spotted the props, but they were otherwise usable. One gear door had torn loose, but its absence would only cost a few knots of speed in the air. Why was he even thinking about flying when both engines had stopped simultaneously? A million-to-one chance!

"I don't care what you say," Paige said in that level tone that invited no argument, "I'm not getting back in that thing."

He shrugged. "With no engines, why should you?"

"You were thinking about seeing what the problem was and then fixing it if you could, same way you would a car," she accused.

That, of course, was exactly what he had in mind. He had to know. As the pack of natives from the airport puffed up, he climbed back into the Baron, flipped the master switches, and turned the left starter. He was not surprised that the engine caught before the prop blades had swung all the way around. The right engine did the same. Again he shut down and crawled out.

"Guess I didn't drain the sumps thoroughly enough," he explained. "Must have had a little water condense out into the tank and feed into both engines." He was as certain of the unlikelihood of this as he was of the careful attention with which he had, in fact, drained both sumps. "Anyway, everything's fine."

Paige slowly got to her feet among the small throng that had gathered. "I'm sure you're right," she said slowly, "but I'm taking a cab or car to Port-au-Prince and Pan Am back to the States."

"But . . ."

She gave him a level gaze, her coolness somewhat unsettling to him. "Whatever happened just might happen again, this time over the middle of the ocean. You know I'm no coward, no shrinking, hysterical female. I'm not a fool either."

"But the plane . . ." he started to protest.

Her reasoning was undeniable. In fact, it was compelling. Paige could be as irrational as any person, but when she was serious, her mind made a beeline from A to B.

Phillip lifted his arms in a gesture of surrender that was not entirely feigned. "Okay, okay. I'll taxi this thing over next to the terminal and park it. Want a ride?"

She gave the plane the same glare a person would give a horse that had just thrown them. "I'll walk."

The engines didn't miss a stroke on the way. Phillip was tempted to renew the discussion about flying home. There would be no debate. Paige had made her mind up, he knew. He also knew the foolishness of trusting their lives to potentially balky equipment. For the third and final time, he climbed out of the plane's cockpit, motioning for help to unload it.

He could see Paige was already haggling with two cabbies as he opened the nose baggage compartment and handed the suitcase to a young fellow he remembered spoke some English. "That man, the man in the tall hat—" Phillip pointed to where he had been, "do you know who he is?"

His answer was an uncomprehending stare.

Phillip tried again. "The tall man with the tall hat." He circled his hands above his head to indicate the hat. "And the long coat—the man with the pipe in his mouth." This time Phillip stuck his thumb in his mouth and puffed vigorously. "Who is he?"

Non-comprehension vanished to be replaced with widened eyes and flared nostrils—fear. "I know no such person," the boy muttered as he set the bag down and backed away. "I know no one as you describe."

Phillip took a step forward. "Come on! How many people in Cap-Haïtien go around dressed like that?"

The young Haitian did something with his hands, made a cross or a similar gesture, before he turned and fled to the safety of his companions where he chattered incomprehensible Creole.

Phillip picked up the bag and walked over to where Paige had finally made her best deal. "Two hundred dollars," she announced. "That's the best price I can get."

Phillip was about to protest when he noticed the murmuring of the crowd behind him.

"Samedi! Samedi!" One word was clear from the Creole.

The cab driver shouted at someone and someone shouted back a phrase. The driver also made the sign of the cross, cranked up, and peeled what little rubber was left on bald tires.

Paige stared after him in open-mouthed amazement. "What did you say to those people?"

Phillip put down the bag. "Damn if I know, but it doesn't look like we're going to get a ride to Port-au-Prince."

She folded her arms. "If we, I, have to stay here all week, I'm not getting back in that plane."

Phillip thought for a moment. "Tell you what: if the phones work, I'll call Carib Aero in Miami, the place we rented the Baron. I can tell them what happened and they'll have to fly a mechanic down here. We can ride back on whatever aircraft they bring."

It was a logical compromise and the phones did work, more or less. Phillip's call reached the States in only three tries. He explained the problem and was assured another, larger Baron would be on its way within the hour, complete with mechanic. Much relieved, Phillip left the musty smelling terminal building to find Paige seated alone under a papaya tree.

"I thought you'd be negotiating some last minute bargains," he quipped.

She pointed to the few natives still in the area: three officials who had retreated to the most distant part of the building. "I can't get near any of them. Everyone I speak to acts like he's scared out of his wits, makes the sign of the cross, and dashes off. You must have really said something."

"I guess I did," Phillip said pensively. The word (name? place?) *Samedi* echoed in his mind.

The rustling in the hut was an angry sound. The old woman stared sightlessly, the picture of the airport having slowly faded. "I have failed you," she said simply.

Perhaps not. Not yet, anyway. Strange images filled her mind, visions she did not fully understand. She waited patiently. All would become clear in time. She saw a house, larger than any she had ever seen with her eyes, a dwelling in a faraway place where sometimes it got cold, and where white stuff occasionally fell from the sky. Without understanding why, she knew this was the hut of the white man and woman. She marvelled at the number of houses lining a road, more houses than she had ever thought could be in one place. A city. She grinned, spittle drooling down her chin as though she were relishing a meal set before her. In a way, she was doing just that, for now she realized her powers—the powers of the *loas*—could reach this strange and distant location as easily as they could touch someone down the mountainside in Cap-Haïtien. Almost as easily, anyway. She would continue to do the *loas'* will. The man and woman, the desecrators of Damballah's ceremony, could die in their own land. Die at her convenience. Die horribly.

"I will succeed. I swear it," she said.

Chapter 5

ATLANTA, GEORGIA

Phillip stood in front of the full-length mirror and adjusted the cummerbund as he went down the sartorial checklist: studs neatly placed without wrinkling the starched shirt, jacket buttoned, shoes shined to a bright gloss, bow tie . . . crooked and looking as though it had wilted. For the third time, he undid it and started over. "Damn! I don't see why Reid and Sue have to have a formal party. It's not like she doesn't have a birthday party every year."

Paige's disembodied voice came from the closet dressing room. "No sweat, I'll tie your tie as soon as I finish putting on my lipstick."

Phillip shook his head resignedly. The woman either had Superman's x-ray vision or the gift of clairvoyance. Or they had been married long enough for her to know bow ties defeated him every time.

There was a giggle from the bed behind him and he turned to give a comically severe glare to the small boy who sat there in pajamas. "And just what's so funny, Mr. Case Owens?"

Case broke into a full grin, exposing the gap where front teeth had been. "Mom knows you can't tie that thing. She knows without having to see you."

"Hmpf!" Phillip snorted in mock disdain. "And I suppose you and your friend Rhett there can do better?"

The thought of Rhett Butler, the family golden retriever, in a bow tie was sufficient fuel for a snicker. "He couldn't do any worse."

Rhett, from his position at the foot of the bed, opened one penny-copper eye as if to assure himself he was missing nothing, then resumed his rhythmic snoring.

"Oh yeah?" Phillip growled, becoming the Beard Monster who loved nothing more than to rub bristling whiskers across children's ticklish tummies. "Let's see!"

With eyes rolled back as far as possible and teeth exposed, Phillip assumed the shuffling gait that was his own rendition of Dr. Frankenstein's creation. Case shrieked in a mixture of delight and apprehension. In a single movement, he was standing on the bed ready to elude his attacker. Phillip lunged with intentional clumsiness and missed his gleeful victim. "Gotcha!" the Beard Monster snarled.

"No, you don't, no, you don't!" Case bounced to the floor with a thud that shook Rhett awake. The dog joined in the fun by barking joyfully.

"Honestly!" Paige stood in the doorway in a slip, an amused smile on her face. "And people ask why we didn't have another child! I tell them two is enough: Phillip and Case."

Case fled to the sanctuary of his mother, laughing. "He was after me!"

Phillip shrugged guiltily. "Bow ties bring out the worst in me."

Paige stepped across the room and reached for his collar. With deft moves she completed the task he had botched. "There! No more roughhousing, now. If Daddy's tie comes undone, he'll have to miss the party."

Phillip rolled baleful eyes at his son. "And we all know how much Daddy would hate that!"

Case started to laugh again, but his mother continued, "Case, don't you have school assignments to do?"

The thought banished any thoughts of further rumpus. "Aw, Mom," he protested, "I've got all Saturday and Sunday. Doing homework on Friday night's the pits."

Phillip, surprised, asked, "Homework? In the second grade?"

Paige gave her husband that look that said he was on thin ice. "You're the one that was so hot on putting him in private school. They work the kids pretty hard."

Phillip started to speak but changed his mind. Paige had wanted to send Case to the city's public schools. "Let him learn what ordinary people are like," she had said.

Phillip had pointed out that the public school system had one of the poorest ratings in the nation. "Our son's education is too important to make it a social experiment," he had countered. "Besides, with both of us working, we can afford it."

She had relented, but as with so many disagreements, he only *thought* he had won the argument. In fact, it wasn't over yet.

Paige turned to go back to the dressing room. "I only have to put on my dress, then I'll be ready."

Phillip had never understood why a woman considered herself almost ready when she still had to put her clothes on. "I'll go downstairs and see if Jeanette has come yet," he volunteered.

"Fine," Paige's voice floated to him. "Tell her that Case has already had his dinner and that she can help herself if she hasn't eaten."

On cue, the trill of the doorbell announced Jeanette's arrival. Phillip flipped on the porch lights and opened the door to admit the baby-sitter. "Evening, Jeanette."

"Good evening, Mr. Owens," she responded as she crossed the threshold and surveyed him through thick glasses. "Is Case ready for bed?"

"Just about. There's plenty in the fridge if you get hungry."

She nodded as though assimilating vital information. "Thank you, but I've had dinner."

Phillip led her toward the stairs. "So how're your folks doing? I haven't seen your mom or dad for weeks. A shame, considering they only live down the street."

"They're fine, thanks," she announced with that solemnity that characterized most of her pronouncements. "Is it okay if I go on up to Case's room?"

"Be my guest."

From the bottom of the stairs, Phillip watched Jeanette. In a few years, perhaps months, she'd exchange those horn-rims for contacts, shed a few pounds, and her acne would disappear. Then he would have to find another sitter. He frowned. As careful as he was about the teenagers he employed to stay with Case, that wouldn't be easy. Jeanette could be relied upon to make Case go to bed on time, brush his teeth, and get that last trip to the bathroom taken care of. When dating replaced baby-sitting on her weekend agenda . . . Well, no sense looking that gift horse in the mouth just yet.

"Well, how do I look?" Paige minced down the steps in a tight black sheath that left no doubt her figure was as good as it had ever been.

Phillip gave a low wolf whistle. "A ten, for sure. Are you certain you want to wear something like that to Sue's?"

"You think it's too much?" Paige was concerned.

"You know how she is—still the homecoming queen from

twenty years ago, despite putting on weight. She wears her hair the same way she did the day they put the crown on her head in front of sixty thousand. She's the only woman I know who carries a portable, plug-in makeup mirror to restaurants and takes twenty minutes in the ladies' room fixing her face when she's just left the house. Every time the men at a party pay attention to some other girls, Reid has to take her home.''

''Sue's a pain in the ass sometimes,'' Paige admitted, ''but she is your best friend's wife.''

''I didn't say she wasn't,'' he grinned. ''The question is whether you're willing to upset her by looking ten years younger and twenty pounds lighter.''

Paige searched his eyes. ''You're serious. You think this dress is liable to set off one of her pouts?''

He nodded. ''I *know*.''

She spun around, already retreating up the steps. ''I'll put on something else, just to save me a headache.''

''I'll be getting a head start,'' he called after her, ''making martinis in the kitchen.''

Phillip stirred the icy pitcher carefully and poured the contents into one of the frosted glasses he kept in the freezer. ''Damn Sue Letts, anyway,'' he muttered. Although her husband, Reid, was Phillip's oldest as well as best friend, Sue had worn Phillip's nerves thin some years ago. Not only was she obsessive about looks that had long since given way to age and overeating, she was a chronic flirt. Being hugged and kissed by a woman who was both overweight and over madeup was bad enough, but Sue was actually offended if Phillip didn't respond to her unwanted attentions. It was ironic Reid's work as a child psychologist was the main reason Reid encouraged his wife's behavior by tolerating it. Hell, Phillip thought, he condones her childishness because he so desperately wants a kid. He'd been overjoyed to be named Case's godfather. Sue's refusal to have children was regrettable, if understandable. No way was she going to share her husband's affections with the baby Reid would like to have.

"So, how do you like this one?" Paige swooped into the room in a full red skirt. "I look like Little Red Riding Hood, eh?"

"Not quite." Phillip gave her an admiring glance. "But you have to be the only woman in the world that would change her clothes rather than piss another female off."

She removed another stem glass from the freezer, watching it frost in the warm kitchen as she poured. Taking a tentative sip, she nodded her approval before adding two olives. "No dress is worth getting Sue upset. I, for one, don't want to spend another evening trying to convince her that she's . . . well, you know, that she doesn't show her age. She's hypersensitive."

"Tell me about it," Phillip saluted her with his glass before changing the subject. "I suppose Case and Jeanette are squared away upstairs."

Involuntarily, she lifted her eyes toward the ceiling. "From the sound of it, he has Steve the Butler out."

Phillip smiled. "You mean that little robot toy with the tray that he controls with the remote radio unit? God, but kids' playthings are getting sophisticated!"

"That's the one, the toy *you* gave him for Christmas. I expect Rhett will never forgive you."

They both chuckled, sharing the mutual picture of the Noble Protector of the Home in full retreat before a whirring, eighteen-inch toy that resembled a mechanized toadstool carrying a tray.

Phillip refilled his glass. "I thought I'd made a mistake when Case first turned it on, remember?"

She smiled. "And Rhett was in such a hurry to get out

of its way, he nearly knocked the tree over. Case has been terrorizing that poor dog with it ever since. I think, sir, you may have a monster for a son.''

''And you, madame, have a wuss for a dog.''

Paige flicked a glance at the digital clock that glowed green numbers above the microwave oven. ''You're right there, I'm afraid.'' She drained her glass. ''And I suppose we may as well get on over to Sue and Reid's.''

He checked his watch. ''No hurry. It's only next door.''

She set her glass on the butcher block table. ''I promised Sue I'd help her set things up.''

''You mean you agreed to do her job for her, per usual.''

''That's not entirely true,'' Paige said defensively. ''She likes the way I arrange the buffet and I don't mind. Think of it as a favor to Reid.''

Phillip groaned. ''And, of course, you also agreed to help clean up the mess afterward.''

Her silence was answer enough.

''God, Paige, you should charge that woman for the work you do every time she entertains. I'm surprised she didn't ask you to fetch the liquor, too.''

As if on cue, the wall phone beside the refrigerator trilled. Phillip gave it a smug look. ''Guess who?''

Paige shrugged him a chagrined expression as she reached toward the insistently ringing telephone. ''Hello? Yes, Sue, we were on the way out the door. Soda water?'' She looked questioningly at Phillip who nodded in resignation. ''Yes, we'll be happy to.'' She hung up, giving him a guilty look. ''Well, Reid's *your* friend. You should be happy to be able to help.''

Phillip turned to the pine cabinet where the liquor and mixers were stored. ''The most help Reid could get would be from another wife.''

''Phillip!'' Paige was indignant. ''You know he's happy

with Sue. As long as he loves her, it doesn't matter if she's a little spacey.''

''Like the Starship *Enterprise*,'' Phillip retorted good naturedly as he removed two six-packs of soda. ''Shall we beam over there?''

Paige walked toward the hallway, her heels clicking on the clay tiles of the kitchen floor like the tapping of a hammer. ''Let me get my coat.''

''Coat? It's almost the middle of March.''

Her words floated over her retreating back. ''March or not, if you'd gone outside lately, you'd know it was still winter.''

''I thought we lived in Georgia because of its warm climate.''

She returned, holding out a full-length mink. As he helped her into it, she said, ''And I thought we lived in Atlanta because that's where you grew up. You want warm, we should move to Miami. At least there I bet they don't have spring cold snaps.'' She arched an eyebrow at him. ''Of course, when you stay inside all day in front of a typewriter, I don't guess the weather matters.''

He pulled her gently to him, kissing the tip of her nose. ''And I suppose it snows in your law office?''

''Don't start something you don't have time to finish.'' She grinned as she touched his lips. ''Now, let's go. Sue will be standing on her head if I'm not there to get things arranged.''

Reid Letts had no problem with bow ties other than finding one that fit a size eighteen neck. He smiled as he fine-tuned the bow in the mirror. Poor Phillip would hang himself by accident with one of the things someday. The thought of his friend and his imminent arrival widened the grin. They'd been pals for how long? Since their junior year in college? How many people develop a friendship by literally running into each other, Reid mused. Running into each other rather violently, at that. Reid, an All-American in at least one poll, had been a linebacker for Tech, Phillip a much-feared bruising fullback at the University. They had become acquainted with a sudden clash of helmets that was heard in the upper rows of the stadium, a collision that had resulted in neither of them regaining consciousness before the end of the game.

They had awakened in adjoining hospital beds. "So you're the great Reid Letts," Phillip had said wryly. "Looks to me like you've just had your plow cleaned by a mere running back."

Reid had replied, "And you're telling me you're in here for a checkup?"

Despite aching heads, they had shared the first of many laughs they would enjoy together.

Since they both resided in Atlanta, they managed to form a friendship that defied rivalry on the field. Since he was playing elsewhere, Phillip had sent Reid a congratulatory telegraph the next year when Reid's fiancée, Sue, had been elected Tech's homecoming queen. Even separated during military service, Reid and Phillip kept in touch with birthday greetings, postcards, and an occasional, drunken late-night phone call. Phillip had been present when Reid received his graduate degree and Reid had presented Phillip with a framed copy of the first article Phillip had sold. When his former next-door neighbors had been transferred out of state, Phillip insisted Reid and Sue see the house before it went on the market.

"Zip me up, will you? Sue's request ended his thoughts. "Do I look okay?"

With a view distorted by affection, he surveyed his wife. She'd gained a few pounds over the years, true. But she was still one of the prettiest females Reid had ever seen. So her clothes didn't fit like they used to; his eyes still saw the curvacious girl that had been chosen that homecoming day. If she was a little heavy-handed with lipstick and mascara, it was to try to hide those wrinkles, to; look good for him. And she was sensitive to his needs, treated him like a prince or something. She would have to look pretty bad for him not to compliment the appearance she'd been working on for the last two hours. He kissed her lightly on the lips. "You look GREAT!"

She preened at his flattery, turning from one side to the other. "You always say that."

"Because you are always beautiful."

"As pretty as Paige?" she asked with no small hint of jealousy.

"Better," he lied without remorse. The door chime interrupted further discussion. "Speaking of Paige, I'd guess she and Phillip are at our front door now." He blew her another kiss and started toward the front of the house.

"Your tan is disgusting," Reid said as he helped Paige out of her coat with one arm and shook Phillip's hand with the other. "But welcome back to the real world, anyway. Sue's in the kitchen."

Both men watched Paige disappear down the hallway before Phillip proffered the soda. "I hope this is enough. It's all I had."

Reid took both six-packs. "I really appreciate your bringing this. What can I get you to drink? The usual?"

Phillip watched his friend's head pass inches from streamers of gay crepe paper hanging from a chandelier. Reid still had the solid build of a football player. An All-American, to be exact. Yet he walked as gracefully as a dancer, a grace Phillip had come to respect from their frequent racquetball games. One of the many things Phillip admired about this man was that Reid never mentioned the knee injury that had terminated a potentially brilliant future as a professional linebacker. The scar tissue that was visible when Reid wore shorts made Phillip wonder how the former athlete could move so quickly on the court. Equally surprising was the tenderness Reid exhibited toward his wife, his friends, and, particularly, his small patients. It was a trait that Phillip would not have expected from a man whose body-crushing tackles had made him the terror of college running backs.

Reid leaned over the linen-covered table in the living room that would serve as a bar this evening, and fussed with a bottle of gin. "Have a good trip?"

Both Phillip and Paige were reluctant to talk about their experience in Haiti. What they had witnessed was an ominous dark cloud on the horizon of their memory, a dark cloud that seemed to grow more distant until one of them started to discuss it. Ever practical in such matters, Paige had announced that she was going to try to forget such a thing had ever happened.

"Er, yeah. Getting a couple of weeks away in winter is always nice."

Reid handed him a stem glass. "I think I got that the way you like it," he said. "So, what's going on down there now that, that what's-his-name is no longer in charge?"

"Duvalier," Phillip responded automatically before realizing his friend's question was prompted more by courtesy than curiosity. "And it's a hell of a mess. How'd the Hawks do while I was away?"

Mention of any of the local sports teams to Reid was a guaranteed conversation maker. "Won six of their last seven," he replied enthusiastically. "Including beating the Celts in The Garden. My guess is that they're gonna make the play . . ."

The doorbell's sound announced that the party was about to begin.

From his guardian position at the foot of Case's bed, Rhett stirred and was instantly awake, sloughing the fog of sleep with the celerity peculiar to waking dogs. Curious as to what had interrupted his nap, he stood. Something had broken the cycle of two or three hours asleep, two or three hours awake that is the canine's life. Although the room was dark to human eyes, his enlarged pupils could distinguish everything in his small master's room. Almost. There was something here that had no smell, even to his keen nose, that he couldn't even identify with a sense of hearing that could detect the claws of squirrels as they ran across the roof. But there *was* something in the room, he knew it, whether from that sense common to all animals that man gives no name, or because he had heard it in that split second between sleep and wakefulness.

Whatever, it had no business being where it was. There was a malignancy about it, a nastiness that he recognized just as easily as he could tell if some passing stranger was going to throw a rock at him. Had he had a human vocabulary and frame of reference, he would have called it "evil." He checked the bed's occupant to make sure Case was okay.

A move in the shadows jerked his head around and the hair on his neck rose into a mane that stretched down his back. He suppressed a low growl. It was something bad, something he had to get out of this room and he was certain he couldn't chase it, for it wouldn't run. Slinking low as though he had just had an accident on the rug, he lead the way toward the hall. Behind him was a whirring, mechanical sound.

Chapter 6

On the way home, Phillip was enjoying that euphoric high that only a precise amount of alcohol can produce. His steps were only slightly uneven, his voice only a little too loud. He'd had a good time. The food was tasty, the booze plentiful, the company . . . well, for the most part, the company enjoyable. There had been that little asshole of a lawyer, who upon learning of Phillip and Paige's recent trip, had insisted on stating his views on Haiti. He had considered himself eminently qualified since he had spent one day of a Caribbean cruise in the country. Lang, that was the fucker's name, Lawyer Larry Lang. To hell with him.

"You're feeling chipper for so late, or rather so early in the morning," Paige observed. It was only then that Phillip realized he'd been whistling.

"It's cheating the cops, that is what makes me feel so good," Phillip said with a grin.

"Cheatin' who?"

"The cops. You know, we go out, I'm afraid to have more than two drinks, afraid of a DUI. Now, at Reid's, I can get sloshed all I want. Really shit faced, commode-hugging drunk. As long as I don't pass out on the street, cops can't touch me for walking home blotto."

She stopped to smile up into his face. "A perpetual college sophomore: measures what a good time he had by how much he drank." She grew serious. "If I didn't know better, I would have thought you were about to take a poke at that lawyer you were arguing with. Drunk and rowdy, Phillip."

"The idea crossed my mind," he said innocently as he took her hand.

"You get so, well, so belligerent sometimes when you drink. One of these days you really will take a poke at somebody at a party."

"If I do, it'll be at some asshole lawyer like Lang," he grumbled. "Those legal sum-bitches need to learn that they can't mouth off at everybody just because they happened to pass a bar exam."

She stepped in front and turned to face him in the pale light from a street lamp. "*I* happen to be one of those 'legal sum-bitches', remember?"

"Yeah, but I don't hear you starting an argument over something you know nothing about. In fact, you're the only lawyer I know who doesn't wear his ass on his shoulders." He burped loudly.

Even in the dim light he could see her wrinkle her nose in disgust. "How perfectly charming! First you nearly succeed in picking a fight in your best friend's house, then you insult your wife's profession and follow that up by belching loud enough to wake the neighborhood. I suppose you're going to fart for an encore."

Phillip lifted a leg, a male dog marking his territory, and grunted as though straining.

"Phillip Owens, you are auditioning to sleep alone tonight."

He grinned a drunken smile as he reached for her only

to have her step out of reach. "Aw, come on, Paige. You know you love me because I'm an animal."

She shook her head in exasperation. "One of these days . . ."

"Look." He pointed to cold chips of stars glittering through the reaching arms of naked tree branches. "You don't get a night this clear very often." He swung his arm across the western sky. "You can see almost all of Orion."

She squinted to sight along his extended arm. "Our old friend, the hunter."

"Yeah. He doesn't look quite the same in these latitudes, though."

For a full minute the two of them contemplated the constellation he had identified for her so many years ago. The familiar pinpoints of light rekindled the picture of a beach silver in moonlight and the melody of a gentle surf on the sands of a small island in the British West Indies. He had gone there to forget, or at least diminish, the pain of a marriage that had not been strong enough to endure the loss of a child. She was there to escape the pressures a law firm places on an associate. Although a disbeliever in coincidences, Phillip thought life had dealt him a strong hand when he discovered Paige was also from Atlanta. They had left the island in lust, if not in love. That came later in the less romantic circumstances of the real world. Between his assignments out of the city and her determination to become the first female partner in her law firm, they were fortunate to see each other twice a month. Despite his flawlessly logical argument that she should share the four-bedroom house he had inherited in Ansley Park, the city's fashionably "in town" older section, she had insisted on maintaining her own apartment. One humid night in Bangkok, he had awakened, covered with sweat in spite of the humming overhead fan. Pushing aside the mosquito netting, he had pulled on his pants and gone in search of a phone. He had calculated the time difference and placed the call to her office. Pacing the length of the telephone cord in his bare feet while slapping at a swarm of carnivorous insects, he rehearsed his lines.

At last her voice, wavering through the ether, "Phillip? Is that you?"

"It's night here," he had yelled, hoping to make himself heard through the tenuous connection. "But I can't see Orion. Wrong hemisphere, I think."

Her laugh had been tinny-sounding amid the static. "Well, it's daylight here, so I can't see him either. Surely you didn't call halfway around the world to give me your astronomical observations."

"No, no, I didn't," he had shouted, glaring at a curious head poking from a door down the hall. "I called to tell you not to renew your lease. My key's where it always is. Have your stuff moved into my house, arrange things any way you like."

Even the poor connection had not been able to distort the coolness of her reply. "I thought we had that conversation."

"We did," he trumpeted. "But after you get settled, select the preacher of your choice, or J.P. or rabbi. I'll be back next Tuesday." He had glanced at his watch. "Flight from San Francisco gets in around six in the evening, Atlanta time. An evening wedding will do fine."

There had been such a long silence, Phillip had feared the frail connection had finally broken. Then, "And just what makes you think marriage is what I want?"

Phillip had gulped as his heart felt like it had taken an express elevator to the basement. "I don't think anything. It's just the best deal I have to offer."

Another pause before, "I'll see if I can arrange it outside so ole Orion can watch."

It was only after Phillip had hung up that he had realized he had no idea what church, if any, Paige would select.

Rhett was at the front door, letting the growl out now, letting it flow over teeth that had never before been bared in anger. The noise-making thing came closer.

Paige's voice, tender with memory, brought Phillip back to the present. "Damn you, anyway, Phillip Owens! Just when I have you red-handed, guilty of grievous offenses that any other woman would nag you about for a month, you bring up that stupid bunch of stars."

He shrugged. "It's not that, it's because I'm so lovable."

Before she could voice a retort he had her in his arms.

"Phillip," she protested mildly, "anyone looking out a window could see."

"So?" He kissed her long and hard. "Is the Civic Association now on a campaign against public displays of affection?"

She squeezed him. "Maybe not, but if you keep that up, there'll be a display they very well could complain about."

"Promises, promises." He led her toward their home, a shadow against the starry sky.

("I will succeed. I swear it.")

They heard it as soon as they climbed the steps to the porch that crossed the front of the house: a whining and scratching on the other side of the door.

"Jeanette must have gone to sleep without letting Rhett out," Phillip commented as he fumbled drunkenly with the keys.

"She's never forgotten before," Paige answered nervously. "I hope she didn't forget to make Case brush his teeth.

Phillip opened the door into a dark foyer and a furry form streaked past into the front yard. The hair on the dog's neck was erect as he turned and gave a deep growl toward the house.

"Rhett?" Paige called. "What's . . . ?"

From within the dark there was a mechanical whirring and the click of something rolling across the hardwood floors. Phillip was reaching for the switch just inside the door when he saw the flashing lights a foot and a half above the boards. "Apparently Case thought he'd torture that poor mutt with that damned toy," he observed. "I've warned him about that. We'll be lucky if Rhett didn't piss on the rugs."

Rhett was now dashing toward the house, barking furiously. He stopped short of the porch but kept up the racket even though Paige was trying to quiet him. "I expect you to discipline that child. It's way past his bed time, I can't imagine Jeanette letting him do this."

"Case!" Phillip called. "I know you think this is very funny, young man, but you won't be laughing long. Case!"

The lights came on at Phillip's touch but there was no Case snickering at the dog's fright. Phillip walked the downstairs hall. Case wasn't in the living room, library, or dining room and Phillip was headed to search the kitchen and pantry when the strident buzz reminded him to turn off the burglar alarm.

"Mr. Owens?" The voice came from the top of the stairs. "Is that you?"

Phillip punched in the disarm code before striding back to the foot of the steps. "Yes, Jeanette, it's us. Where the hell is Case?"

The harshness of his tone produced a second of surprised

silence. "Case? He's in his bed where he is supposed to be."

"I think he's down here, tormenting the dog with that little robot toy. You can hear Rhett barking."

"No, sir." She was emphatic. "He's sound asleep."

Guiltily, Phillip lowered his voice. "But if he's asleep up there, how . . . ?"

"Phillip." Paige's voice was low but he could hear the tension in it. "The Butler's tray, there was something on it."

("I will succeed . . .")

He turned to make out the object she was holding between two fingers as she might dispose of a dead rat. "What is that thing?" He looked closer. She had a small figure made of rags, a humanlike figure.

"Some sort of a doll," she said slowly. "Not any toy of Case's."

He gingerly took it from her as Jeanette clumped down the steps. It was a crudely made doll, poorly stitched and disproportionate, but recognizable as male. A fringe of hair around the bottom of the misshapen head formed a beard. He held it out to Jeanette. "Where did you get this thing?"

She viewed it curiously. "Get it? I've never seen it."

Although his mind was foggy with alcohol and he could still smell Sue's perfume, there was a wisp of an odor on the thing, sharp and familiar. It smelled like charcoal. He shook his head as though to clear it. "Jeanette, if you didn't bring that doll and Paige and I know it's not one of Case's things . . ." His voice wandered off in bewilderment. His eyes widened as a thought, a snatch of memory drifted into his head like a long forgotten tune. "Paige," he said, his voice brittle with apprehension, "isn't some sort of a doll used to cast voodoo spells?"

She shrugged. "Maybe, but it's absurd to think that's where this one came from."

He wanted to agree how really absurd the idea was, how impossible that such a thing would be here in Atlanta. Then he noticed the little beard. The recognition was intuitive. That doll was intended to represent him. "I have met the enemy and he is me." Phillip almost giggled in his drunken surprise.

Long after Jeanette had gone home, sometime after Paige was asleep, any time in the dark, lonely hours of a sleepless night, Phillip listened. He could hear the familiar groaning of old floorboards as though from the footsteps of ghosts of former residents. He could hear the whisper of a light breeze through the empty trees outside. He could hear a distant siren in the night.

That thing, that doll. It *had* to be Case's. Or a playmate's? There was some normal, rational explanation, he tried to convince himself. And he could hear the gentle scraping of a branch against the shingles that were on the outside of the house, a scraping he had heard most of his life. Never before had it sounded like scales rubbing against the wood. The sounds of night, sounds that were familiar, now became threatening, ominous, as though a malignant force had occupied his home.

Chapter 7

Saturday mornings were usually a special time for Phillip and Case: the two would normally trash the kitchen in preparing a pancake breakfast, a repast they savored amid the wreckage while planning their weekly outing. This Saturday was not normal. Case's small face was screwed up tightly in an effort to prevent tears as Phillip waved the doll accusingly at his son. "Don't give me that, Case. This thing didn't walk in here. And it was on *your* toy."

The boy's voice wavered, "I told you, Daddy, it's not mine. I've never seen it and I don't know where it came from." He wanted to be believed. "Besides, I don't play with dolls."

Phillip sucked in his breath, trying to keep the anger born of a nameless dread out of his tone. "Then where did it come from? Jeanette's never seen it before and neither have your mother or I." He squinted in the sunlight that was painting the room a golden hue as it poured through the sliding glass doors that led to the deck at the rear of the house. Irritably, he snatched a curtain across the glass. Something was wrong, dreadfully wrong about that doll turning up here in Atlanta. There had to be an explanation, *had* to; and he was going to find it.

"I don't know where it came from." Case sniffed with a stubborn refusal to change his story. "I don't see why that old thing is such a big deal, anyway."

"The 'big deal,' " Phillip said evenly, "is that I've told you not to frighten Rhett with that Steve the Butler toy. He wouldn't even come back in the house last night. How would you have felt if he'd run away?"

The thought only increased the little boy's unhappiness. "Daddy, I was asleep when you came home. 'Nette told you. Anyway, you know the remote unit won't work from my room to the front hall."

Phillip knew all right. That was the problem. The stronger his son's denials, the more uneasy he felt. Cross-examination wasn't his idea of pleasant breakfast conversation, but there *was* a logical explanation of how that rag doll had gotten into the house, wasn't there? He gave a smile he didn't feel and tried again. "Okay, so that thing doesn't belong to you. Which one of your friends might have left it? Randy? Charlie?"

Relieved that the inquisition had at least been temporarily focused elsewhere, Case shrugged. "I haven't had any of 'em over here since Wednesday afternoon. We've been at Randy's, mostly. *He* got a new video for his birthday." Case paused to let the unspoken criticism linger. "Besides, they're too grown up to play with dolls."

"You didn't have any girls in the house either?" Phillip was trying to keep the exasperation out of his voice. "Doesn't Charlie's sister come by here sometimes to tell him to come home?"

Case scrunched up his nose, which was a small duplicate of his mother's. "I told you, Charlie wasn't here. Anyhow, his mom calls on the phone when she wants him home. We don't play with girls, 'cept Terry Wynne down the street and she doesn't count 'cause she can hit a baseball as far as anybody.''

''Well, someone's not telling the truth.''

'' 'Nette doesn't tell stories.'' The tone was defensive. ''An' I'm telling the truth, too.''

Under other circumstances, Phillip would have admired his son's loyalty. Continuing seemed pointless. Case wasn't going to admit ownership and there wasn't any other way it could have appeared. Unless, unless . . . He grinned at the obviousness of the answer, an answer farfetched, perhaps, but certainly less disquieting to accept than . . . He forced the alternative to the remotest place in his consciousness where it crouched, ready to return. Standing, he pulled the drape back from the glass and looked out into a yard still winter brown except for the defiant green shoots of Paige's bulbs that bravely pushed through the cold earth to proclaim their message that spring was only weeks away. He opened the sliding door and whistled.

Before he could try again, there was an orange streak heading toward him from the back fence. Of course! How stupid not to think of this! The booze from last night must have clouded his brain. Phillip stepped onto the rear deck, waving the doll above his head. ''Fetch, Rhett, fetch!''

Rhett slid to a stop at the front of the steps leading down to the yard, his tail a blur of joyous wagging. His eyes followed Phillip's swinging arm in happy anticipation that the game was about to be renewed. The small bundle of rag had not left Phillip's hand before the dog was off in pursuit. Phillip smiled as Rhett locked his rear haunches and skidded across the grass to a stop. That was it, for sure. That damn doll was something old Rhett had scrounged up.

The thought, comforting though it might have been, melted as Rhett warily circled the doll, growling, hair erect on his shoulders and neck. Forgetting he was barefooted,

Phillip was down the steps in a single leap, running toward the dog. "Fetch, goddammit, fetch!"

Fetch seemed to be the last thing Rhett had in mind. As Phillip approached, the retriever backed away from the doll, growling louder than ever.

Phillip snatched Rhett's choke collar and snarled, "You worthless mutt! You brought that thing in, now you're going to fetch it!" Rhett just growled even louder.

Phillip let the dog go and stood erect. If the dog hadn't dragged that thing into the house and no one else had ever seen it before . . . He shivered, although not from the morning's chill.

"Don't tell me Rhett won't play ball anymore!" Reid's amiable voice came from behind a budding quince bush just over the fence that separated the two lots. "Or did he break house training? He must have fucked up big time to get you out here barefooted and in your bathrobe."

"Uh, yeah, he did," Phillip said weakly, feeling foolish. "I guess I let him get to me."

Reid stepped into view, his huge, muddy paw dwarfing a trowel. "I didn't expect to see you up and about so early after last night."

"Case has to be fed," Phillip said, wishing he wasn't standing in his backyard, looking like an idiot. "Saturdays Paige sleeps in."

"Not today." Reid pointed with the trowel. "Here she comes. At least she has the sense to wear shoes."

Her robe billowing behind like a sail, Paige was striding across the damp grass with a determined step that matched her expression. "Good morning, Reid," she said with a cool politeness.

"And to you," he answered uncertainly as he glanced from her face to Phillip's. "Well, I've 'bout finished fertilizing the flower beds, guess I'll go get a bite of breakfast myself.'' He retreated toward his house with the swiftness of one avoiding an unpleasant scene.

Phillip stared at his wife. ''I thought you'd still be snoozing away.''

Her mouth tightened. ''How could I with all the yelling out here? And Case starts crying that he's never seen that doll before . . . Only way I could have stayed in bed was to have been deaf. What the hell is going on?''

Phillip pointed to where Rhett was standing, eyeing the couple nervously. ''I was simply trying to discover if he could have brought that rag doll into the house since Case denies any knowledge of the thing.''

''And?''

''Believe me, he won't touch it.''

''So, Mr. Super Sleuth, what conclusion have you reached about the mysterious rag doll?''

''That it appeared in the house by means unknown,'' he said, growing serious. ''And I'm not amused. After what we—After what happened in Haiti, having some sort of voodoo doll show up is a little weird, wouldn't you say?''

She slipped a reassuring arm through his. ''At the risk of sounding like one of those 'legal sum-bitches' you were muttering about last night, let me point out: (a) we have no idea that doll is in any way connected with voodoo, and (b) it is highly unlikely that it flew down the chimney. Therefore, we must assume that if neither Case nor Rhett brought it in, one of the other kids who visit must have.''

''You sound like a lawyer, all right. The only problem with your summation, counselor, is that Case says he hasn't had any of his friends in the house since Wednesday.''

She shrugged. ''So? That little doll could have fallen out of a pocket, a school satchel, maybe, and not have been noticed until last night.''

''And it climbed up on the robot toy by itself?''

"Okay, okay, I admit I don't know where it came from," she said, tossing her head, "but wherever, it's not worth upsetting Case. He's been looking forward to spending time with you this weekend since you've been so busy all week."

He slipped an arm around her waist, leading her back toward the house. "Yeah, I really have ignored him, but I did get that Haiti series in the mail."

They skirted the cement apron around the pool. At the foot of the steps leading to the deck, she stopped. "Those articles. Did you mention . . . ?"

He shook his head slowly. "No. I wrote what I know the editors want—socio-economic stuff. The more I thought about it, the less likely I figured they'd touch a description of a ritual murder. Probably never believe it anyway. Besides, I'd just as soon forget."

She forced a smile. "Probably a good decision. You're writing for a news magazine, not *The National Enquirer*."

If he heard, he didn't respond. Instead he was staring at the tarpaulin that was stretched over the pool like blue wrapping on a present, his face furrowed.

She tugged at his arm, aware of his thoughts. "C'mon. It's too pretty a day for morbid thoughts."

He sighed deeply. "Maybe I should have sold the place after she drowned. I'll never forget . . ."

She covered his lips with her own before drawing back. "You'd be less than human if you did. Now, let's finish fixing those pancakes. I'll bet Case is starved."

He gave the pool one last glance before following her up to the kitchen.

Case greeted his mother's entry into the house with the delight of a child who has found a defender. "Momma! You gonna fix the pancakes this morning?" he bubbled.

Paige sat stiffly in one of the cane-bottomed chairs around the butcher-block table. "Me? On no. I'm going to sit right here and see how you and your father manage to make such a mess every Saturday morning.'' She made a comically grim face and rolled her eyes at Phillip. ''Come on, master chef, I'm watching.''

Phillip forced a grin. ''Okay, you asked for it.''

Reluctant at first, Case joined in, forgetting his father's accusations in his enthusiasm to be a part of the weekly ritual.

In a few minutes, the countertop was powdered white with spilled flour. The slivers of at least one egg shell lay on the floor in a yellow puddle of yoke and a spotty trail of milk traced Case's uncertain path from the refrigerator to the mixing bowl beside the range. With fluid motions, Phillip flipped two pancakes several feet into the air, catching them with the skillet. Case squealed, ''Lemme try, lemme try!''

''Now I know how that gook got all over the stove hood,'' Paige commented.

Phillip gave her a sheepish smile as he pulled a chair next to the range for Case to stand on and handed his son the spatula. ''Okay, show Momma how good you've gotten at this. Don't forget the hot pad.''

With more eagerness than skill, Case lifted the frying pan in uncertain hands that wavered from the weight of the iron pan. ''Use the spatula first,'' Phillip coached. ''Unstick them before you try to flip 'em.''

''Oh, yeah.'' Case sat the pan back on the eye of the range and prodded the pancakes. ''Now they're loose.'' He gave the pan a jerk and watched dully as two pancakes splatted onto the counter.

Paige put a hand to her face to conceal a smile. ''I think you'd better wait till you're big enough to lift that old iron skillet.''

Case snatched the two doughy gobs up. ''Ouch! They're

hot!'' He dropped them on the floor in his haste to blow on his fingers.

"A good try,'' Phillip apologized. "He really does keep them in the pan most of the time.'' He stooped to wipe up the mess. "Shall I make a couple for you?''

Paige wrinkled her nose. "At about five hundred calories per cake? No thanks. Keeping my figure is hard enough. I'll settle for half a grapefruit.''

Phillip took a plate from the oven where he had been keeping his previous efforts warm. "In that case I'd say we have enough.'' He jabbed a fork into the stack and plopped half of it on another platter. "Chow is on.''

Sitting in the cheerful kitchen, only half listening to Case chatter, Phillip took himself to task for his actions earlier. Paige was, as usual, right: Wherever that damned doll had come from, it was unlikely it had anything to do with voodoo, Haiti, or anything more sinister than a child's misplaced toy, right? That night, the ritual, the sounds in the hotel room, along with the panic at the airport and that strange man there had faded, a scar of the mind that had all but healed. He was willing and eager to forget the whole thing here in the safe reality of his home. Whatever its origins, the doll certainly didn't merit ruining Case's Saturday or scaring the hell out of poor old Rhett Butler. Although repugnant to his newsman's inquisitiveness, he'd let the matter drop for the moment. Maybe later today, he could have someone take a look at Case's toy, Steve the Butler, to see what could have started the thing and to make sure it wouldn't happen again. He paused, a forkful of pancake dripping syrup. Steve the Butler. Case had been playing with the thing up in his room when they had left last night. Or at least Paige had said he had. There was no way the little robot could have come down the stairs by itself, and

Jeanette had said Case went to bed after some game with her in his room.

"Question: how did Steve the Butler get to the front hall from Case's room?" logic asked, perversely picking at the mental scar.

"I don't know," the mind admitted, "but it's sure going to stir the shit to start that subject up again."

"You were perfectly willing to start a fight with that lawyer last night," logic sneered. "Over nothing. Now you're avoiding a rather interesting problem."

"It's *not* a problem, not as long as we drop the matter."

"Case," Phillip said as sweetly as he could, "your Steve the Butler toy, you were playing with it last night, weren't you?"

Case's expression changed from the rapture of a small child enjoying his favorite meal to guarded apprehension. "Yes, sir. Up in my room."

"You didn't happen to bring it down for any reason, did you?"

"No." The response was guarded. Case didn't want to be accused again.

"Phillip," Paige interrupted with an edge to her voice, "you've browbeaten the child enough. He doesn't know where the doll came from."

Phillip shrugged, a gesture of misunderstood innocence. "It obviously self-started. I'm afraid it might have a short or something. I didn't want Case to get shocked." He reached over to muss his son's hair. "Maybe we can drop ole Steve off at the store where I got him, have them check the circuitry. The thing's got a year's warranty. Case and I can take it by on our way to Six Flags."

"Six Flags! Wow!" The boy's concern evaporated in whoops of glee. "We haven't been there in forever!"

"May as well get started," Phillip said conversationally. "Go on upstairs and brush your teeth."

For once there was no reluctance as Case dropped his fork and pushed back his chair.

"Case!" Phillip said sternly.

"Oh," Case apologized, and turned to face his mother. " 'Scuse me?"

Paige nodded solemnly. "You may be excused."

He was gone almost before she shut her mouth.

Paige dug at her grapefruit before looking at her husband. "The child's only seven. There's plenty of time for him to learn."

"It's never too early to teach manners."

"You're right, I guess. I'm surprised you're so eager to take him out to Six Flags. The last time you went you said you were through with amusement parks."

Phillip finished the last soggy scrap on his plate and said, "Better now than summer when every kid in five states will be out there."

Paige chuckled. "You're right." She reached over to squeeze his hand. "I've got to admit, you're a fine father. I don't know many men who'd spend almost every Saturday entertaining their kid, and I sure can't think of one who'd insist on driving him to and from school every day when there's bus service available."

Phillip stood, collected his and Case's plates, and began to rinse them in the sink. "I'm not sure I trust those drivers. Every year it seems there's an accident somewhere involving a school bus load of kids."

"There is such a thing as smothering a child with protectiveness, you know."

Phillip stopped, oblivious to the steaming hot water, and gazed toward the pool visible through the window over the sink. "I guess I have reason to be protective. I just couldn't take it if . . ."

Paige rose and quickly crossed the room to stand behind him. She gently kissed the back of his neck. "Of course, you do. I should be delighted."

Case was in the front of the toy shop, fighting the fatigue of three hours of nonstop rides and excitement as he watched a display of miniature cars race around a track. Phillip felt a sudden weariness as his suspicion was confirmed. "You mean there's no way that robot could start without the remote unit turning it on?" he asked for the second time.

The man behind the counter shook his head, the smile of a sales clerk soliciting satisfaction plastered on his narrow face. "No, sir. I checked this unit carefully right after you brought it in this morning. It's working perfectly."

Although he knew the answer, Phillip continued, "And you're certain that the remote unit has a limit of twenty feet or so?"

The man nodded. "Absolutely. And the beam can't function through walls or other obstructions." His smile faded as his eyes met Phillip's. "Of course, if you insist something's malfunctioning, we will be happy to send it back to the factory."

"No, that's okay." Phillip reached for Steve the Butler with the hesitation he might have had extending a hand toward an ill-natured dog. "We'll take it home."

Case appeared at his side. "Dad, have you seen those race cars . . ." His voice trailed off as he peered up at his father's face.

Phillip reached down to take the small hand in his. "Well, yeah, I saw them." He forced a cheerfulness into his voice. "And you'll be happy to know Steve is okay. We don't have to leave him."

Phillip was glad Case fell asleep on the drive home, ob-
viating listening to a replay of each adventure they had
shared at the amusement park. Instead of talk, Phillip
wanted to think, to try to forestall the foreboding that was
overcoming him like inky night as it swallowed the last
cheer of daylight.

Fifteen hundred miles away, the old woman could feel
the fear that was growing in the man like a cancer in his
body, and it pleased her. Even if he had not died of fright
at the sight of the doll as would many in Haiti, he would
die soon enough. This time she would send him another
little gift, this one alive. A gift from Damballah himself.
She cackled at the thought.

Chapter 8

The next Saturday was cloaked in cold drizzle, confining Phillip and Case inside where they listlessly played a series of board games in which neither had any real interest. Paige secluded herself in the bedroom upstairs where she claimed to be looking over a brief due next week. Even Rhett seemed unhappy, asking to be let in and out so frequently that Phillip finally left him on the back deck to whine to his discontent.

Spring arrived the next day.

Sunday erupted with a brilliant blue sky and warm breeze that promised the speedy demise of winter. Phillip was so grateful to be outside, he managed not to grumble at Paige's suggestion that they get an early start on the yard work, a task Phillip usually hated. He stood, leaning on his rake, and looked around, really seeing the outside for the first time since storing the outdoor furniture and covering the pool last October. The cold months had left the lawn in a leprous state: patches of moist earth were scattered among sickly clumps of wilted grass. He sighed heavily, calculating the amount of fertilizer, seed, and effort required to transform this devastation into the crisp, uniform green that Paige insisted upon. She was certainly willing to do her share to get it, he observed as she struggled with a box heavy with twigs, leaves, and other detritus of winter. Case, dwarfed by a rake similar in size to Phillip's, was working as hard as anybody, although with somewhat less result.

"Great day, even if we have to slave away," Reid called from next door with more good nature than Phillip would have thought such labor justified. Reid was also pushing a rake, which he lifted in a jaunty salute. "I can tell summer's on the way."

"Along with cutting the grass, cleaning the pool, and pulling weeds," Phillip added sourly.

"Oh, don't be such a grump!" Paige teased. "You like warm days, baseball games, and drinks on the deck at sunset as much as anybody."

"Doesn't he, though?" Reid agreed. "Besides, not all of us can take off in the middle of winter for a week or so of sun in Haiti. Hell if I could get Sue and me to the tropics, I wouldn't be in such a rush to see hot weather, either."

"Speaking of Sue," Paige asked, "where is your bride this lovely morning?"

Reid grinned. "In the sack, getting her rest. Ever since that bout with the flu a month or so ago, she can't seem to get enough sleep."

Phillip nodded. Ever since he had known her, the flu or some other malady had caused Sue to sleep late and avoid any physical effort more demanding than her weekly beauty parlor appointments. A glare from Paige dispelled any temptation to share the observation. Instead, he said with a dryness he was sure his friend would miss, "Well, tell her we wish her a speedy recovery." He was about to add, "About lunch time," but bit off the words and returned to scratching at the ground with his rake.

Odd that Reid would mention Haiti. Phillip had been covertly examining the yard for the rag doll that had just . . .

Last weekend, wasn't it? Yes, only last Saturday the thing had been lying out here where he had tossed it for Rhett. He searched his memory. When had he last seen it? He shook his head. Well, he was glad the thing was gone, dragged off to one of the oak trees by some enterprising squirrel for use as lining for a nest. Nothing mysterious about that. Except he'd never seen a squirrel nest lined with cloth. To hell with it. It was too pretty a day to fret about rag dolls that seemed to appear and disappear at will.

A foot or so away, blades of grass twitched as though shaken by an invisible hand. With slow deliberation, the trail of movement curved toward the bare ankles above Phillip's sneakers. Then all motion stopped.

(*"Aida-wedo is a snake . . ."*)

"Phillip," Paige called, "can you give me a hand trying to pull up this crabgrass?"

As though choreographed, Phillip's foot moved just as the grass began to twitch again, bending and snapping back into place as though touched by a breeze. But there was no breeze. "Sure," he answered as he walked over to her.

Bending, he pulled a clod of dirt from the soil. "There!"

She pushed a strand of hair from her face and smiled. "At that rate we won't have any top soil left."

He tossed the clump away. "No soil, no crabgrass."

Again the grass was moving as though something was passing through it, a motion no one saw.

No one but an old woman far away.

Case looked up from where he was studying the buds on a quince bush. "Daddy, where do bugs go in the winter?"

Phillip, thankful for an excuse to interrupt his labor, leaned on his rake. "I think some hibernate—go to sleep—until it's warm again. Some die . . ."

"And the smart ones go to Florida for the season," Reid added with a broad wink.

The grass was moving steadily, the swerving motion coming closer.

"Aw, Uncle Reid!" Case protested.

"True!" Reid held up a finger. "How else do you account for the fact that there're bugs down there all year around?"

Puzzled, Case twisted his mouth, thinking of a reply. The grin on Daddy's face told him Uncle Reid was teasing. Finally, he shrugged. "I don't believe you."

Paige sniffed in mock indignation. "You two grown men should be ashamed, teasing a child."

With a sigh of resignation, Phillip started back to where he had been raking. The tremble of the grass turned to follow as though Phillip had a string tied to his foot and was dragging it across the ground. The sun briefly glinted off a line as it slid across a bare spot, a steely black form, essing toward Phillip.

Getting closer.

("If you see a snake, you see Damballah . . .")

In the driveway, Rhett awoke from his first nap in the spring warmth, stood, and stretched lazily. He glanced about to make sure his people were still nearby and saw a motion in the grass. A mole or small mouse to chase? An insect to sniff? Careful not to frighten the object of his attention, he padded over. Case noted the dog's attention directed to the ground a few feet from Phillip and he followed, curious as to what Rhett might have found. His eyes followed Rhett's stare. A low growl began in the dog's chest like distant thunder.

"Daddy! Uncle Reid!" Case's excited voice was punctuated by Rhett's barking.

Phillip glanced up to where the dog was snapping at something on the ground. There was a quality in the child's voice that grabbed at Phillip with icy fingers.

"Come look!" Case was shrieking excitedly. "See what Rhett found!"

From the periphery of his vision, Phillip saw Reid vault over the dividing fence as easily as he would have eluded a blocker years ago. The sight unfroze him and, with an ill-defined terror still clutching at him, he rushed to where his son pointed.

At first he could see nothing except the trampled grass that Rhett had crushed by rushing forward and backward, alternately growling and barking. Reid pointed with his rake. "Is that what all the fuss is about?"

At the end of the rake's tines, Phillip saw movement, a twisting, writhing piece of string—a small snake. Little garter snakes were common in the yard, although this was earlier in the year than he had seen one before. He had also never seen one like this, one that made no effort to retreat to the nearest rock or hole. This little fellow seemed undaunted by the size of the dog. If anything, the reptile was aggressive.

("For Damballah is a snake . . .")

"Ugh!" Paige had come up behind the two men with the expression she reserved for anything that crept or crawled. "That thing looks like it's trying to bite."

"Don't be silly," Phillip replied. "It's only a harmless—" His words caught in his throat as he looked closer. He'd really never seen a garter snake as coal black as this one, whose striking head moved so swiftly as Rhett dodged away.

"Daddy, can I get a jar and keep him?" Case wanted to know. By summer's end, his collection of snakes, insects, and other small fauna would fill his room. Paige swore her son's love for such creatures was in direct proportion to her loathing of them. "I think I can grab . . ." Case was trying to get around Rhett to pick up his prize.

A snake on a church door, a woman imitating a snake,

the sound of a snake in the hotel room . . . Surely not. Surely . . . The thought seeped through Phillip's mind like pus from an open wound.

"No!" Phillip roared, the fear he felt lending volume to his voice.

For a second, two adults, one child, and a golden retriever were startled by the force of his yell. Only a second. But it was enough. The serpent whipped up and forward, like a rope snapping under tension. Its tiny head disappeared into the long fur of Rhett's chest. The dog yelped and jerked backward as the snake's head became visible again. Its eyes, malevolent pinheads of shiny black, seemed to fasten directly onto Phillip's and he felt a jolt of terror as he had the irrational feeling that the creature recognized him. Somehow he knew this seemingly harmless little reptile was not what it seemed and had not come from this yard.

In horrified fascination, Phillip watched Rhett stagger, the dog's eyes wide with surprise. With a choking sound, Rhett began to slobber as his legs crumpled beneath him. He thrashed once, twice, whined, and was still. Events began to move so quickly that, later, Phillip was unsure he could put them in sequence. Instead, his memory of what followed was like a multiply exposed photograph.

"Rhett!" Case cried, moving toward the mound of golden fur.

"Stay where you are," Phillip snarled with a fury born of fear. "Don't you so much as move!"

"Phillip, what . . . ?" Paige began, then realized what she was seeing. "My God! Rhett!" She ran toward the dog before Phillip's voice stopped her, too.

"Hold it! You want to get bitten?"

"But Rhett . . ." she protested.

Phillip's voice was firm, but not firm enough to conceal

the panic simmering below the surface. "Get the car. We'll run him to the vet's as soon as I can kill that thing."

She opened her mouth, about to protest until she saw her husband's face. She turned and raced for the garage.

Reid, uncomprehending, looked from Paige to Phillip. "What the hell is happening?"

"That snake. He's killed the dog," Phillip said slowly.

"That little garter snake?" Reid asked, the incredulity making his voice waver. "There're no poisonous snakes around here."

"God dammit, you saw what happened," Phillip said, aware he was speaking too loudly and not caring. "Whatever that snake is, it isn't harmless."

"Dead?" Case's face began to wrinkle in grief. "Rhett's dead?"

With a furious slice of his rake, Phillip took a swipe at the serpent which still made no effort to escape. Instead, it struck at the wooden handle. On the second attempt, Phillip cut it in half. As he watched its final, flopping death throes, he felt the fear seep from him like water from a bathtub when the plug is removed. Only when both parts were still did he become aware of Case's sobs.

Paige snapped, the disapproval crackling in her tone as she ran from the car. "You don't even know he's dead." She stooped over, struggling to lift the ominously still form of the family's pet. "Instead of talking, help me move him."

"Maybe he's gonna be okay?" Case was wiping his face with his sleeve.

Phillip took the dog from Paige. "You're right. Let's get old Rhett to the vet's. We can talk about snakes later."

"What's all the fuss?" As one they turned to see Sue, clad in a voluminous robe, her face puffy with sleep. "What's going on? I heard the excitement and came right down."

Bravely sniffing back his tears, Case volunteered, "Daddy says a snake bit Rhett an' killed him." He pointed. "That snake right there."

Sue's chubby face sagged as she looked down at her fluffy pink bedroom slippers as though she might be standing in a nest of vipers. "A snake? Here?" She grasped the fence as though for support. "Reid, do we have poisonous snakes loose in this neighborhood? Oh, dear. I think I'm not feeling too well." With this announcement she began to gingerly pick her way back across the distance to her house. "I'm terrified of snakes." The words drifted behind her. "I'll be afraid to be in the yard."

Reid gave Phillip a reproachful look as he quickly followed his wife. "Now, Sue, we don't *know* for sure what happened . . ."

Paige had the car out of the garage and Phillip gently laid Rhett on the backseat. He opened the trunk to remove a box of typing paper he had forgotten until now, dumped its contents, and walked over to the snake.

"Phillip," Paige called impatiently, "we need to get Rhett to the vet's as quickly as possible. What are you doing?"

Phillip squatted, using the rake to gingerly dump each half of the reptile into the box.

"Surely you're not going to put that thing in the car?" Her voice said she knew he was.

"It might help to know what type of venom we're dealing with," he replied, closing the box. "The thing did bite him, you know."

"Well, hurry up. That critter is dead. It's not going anywhere."

Phillip wasn't so sure.

Within minutes they were breathing the heavy disinfectant odor of all animal hospitals, waiting in a room decorated with photographs of dogs, cats, birds, and other creatures. With each bark from behind the closed doors leading off the waiting room, Case looked up, hope fading from his face when his pet did not come bounding in as he had on so many other trips here. Paige tried unsuccessfully to interest her son in a small terrier that snorted peacefully at his owner's feet while Phillip thumbed through well-worn issues of the *AKC Journal*. The woman in white behind the reception desk encouraged them, saying, "The doctor is doing everything possible, I'm sure."

Paige thanked her with a nervous smile.

A chubby man in a white smock entered and all three turned to him expectantly. Although a thick beard obscured the lower half of his face, there was no mistaking the sorrow in his eyes. Phillip stood slowly, a man awaiting a verdict he knew would be unfavorable. "Doctor Semmes?"

The veterinarian nodded. "I'm afraid I have bad news; we've lost Rhett."

The scene could have been one played out in a real hospital: Case buried his head against his mother, sobs shaking his body while tiny jeweled tears glistened down Paige's cheeks. The doctor patted Case's head, saddened by that knowledge his profession has of the special love between small boys and dogs.

Phillip would have wept himself were it not for the anxiety that gnawed at his mind with sharp teeth. "Doctor," he said softly, getting Semmes' attention, "what was the cause . . . What killed . . ." He could not make himself say it. The answer, he feared, would be far worse than the present tragedy.

Semmes shook his head. "I can't say, really. Appeared to be some sort of a stroke, something that made the entire nervous system quit."

Phillip lowered his voice, not wanting Paige or Case to hear. "Could you do an autopsy?"

The doctor regarded Phillip with puzzled, but kind eyes. "An autopsy? Why yes, we could. Do you have any reason to think my diagnosis may be incorrect?"

Phillip moved closer, speaking in a near whisper. "Doctor, the dog was bitten by a snake. I saw it."

The veterinarian became wary. "Snake?" he asked loudly enough for everyone in the waiting room to turn and stare, including Paige and Case. "There aren't any around here that could kill a dog. An occasional copperhead wanders into the city and I have heard of rattlers, but . . ."

Phillip sucked in his breath. He'd come too far to back out now. "This wasn't either of the above," he said a little more curtly than he would have liked. "If you'd just do an autopsy and give me a call. We've brought Rhett here over the years and you have our number."

Dr. Semmes nodded vigorously. "Yes, of course, Mr. Owens." His manner was that of someone placating a potentially violent lunatic. "I should be in touch this afternoon. Now if you will excuse me . . ." He started to disappear through the door from which he had come.

"Wait!" Once again Phillip was the unwilling center of attention. "I killed the snake. It's in the car. Maybe you could identify it."

"I really don't know much about snakes," Dr. Semmes said, nodding his resignation, "but if it will make you feel better, I'll take a look."

"Phillip," Paige asked in a voice husky with grief, "do you really have to . . ."

Phillip was gone and back in less than a minute, proffering the box for inspection. The veterinarian gave its contents a perfunctory glance. "Looks like an ordinary garter snake to me, but then, as I said, I really am not overly familiar with reptiles.''

"The color," Phillip protested. "I've never seen a black garter snake.''

Semmes shrugged. "Probably just shed its skin after a winter of hibernation.''

"Doc, the dog collapsed within seconds of the bite; it killed him almost instantly.''

"Mr. Owens," the vet placated, "I don't doubt what you say, but there're no snakes that poisonous in the whole United States. My guess is the shock of the bite itself caused the nervous system to quit functioning. No, your dog died from a problem he probably has had for years. If it hadn't been the snake, something else would have brought it on.''

"Phillip"—Paige was standing, embracing Case, whose grief was still producing tears—"you really have taken enough of the doctor's time. Case wants to go home and so do I.''

Letting his shoulders slump in defeat, Phillip put an arm around her and led her toward the door. "You're right. I guess I'm so upset, I forgot other people want him to see their pets, too.''

The ride home was mercifully short. Case had reverted to a habit of his infancy, putting his head in his mother's lap. Although he had stopped the weeping that had racked his body, tears still streamed down his face.

Reaching the house, all three trooped in without a word. Case slowly climbed the stairs to his room to hoard his grief. Paige glanced around, wiping at the corner of an eye, "I can't believe old Rhett Butler is gone for good.''

Phillip acknowledged her with a mumble that said his mind was elsewhere.

She turned to look at him quizzically. "You were almost rude to Doctor Semmes. What was so important about an autopsy? I'd like to have buried Rhett here at home. And asking him to look at that snake . . .''

He stared as though seeing something far away. "I want to know if the bite killed him."

"Dead is dead. Why make things worse? Besides, the vet said he died of some nerve problem. The bite just triggered it."

"True. But some venom acts on the nervous system, like a cobra, for instance."

Paige was uncomprehending. "Cobra? Here? Besides whatever that was, it didn't look like a cobra to me. I don't understand."

"I'm not sure I do, either. First, that doll—that voodoo thing—appears from nowhere, then a bite of what should be a harmless garter snake kills . . ."

"You don't know Rhett died from the bite," she interrupted, uncomfortable with where the conversation was headed.

He smiled ruefully. "Even as a lawyer, you'd have to admit it sure looks that way. Maybe we'll know more when the veterinarian calls."

She looked into his face with growing concern. "Surely you don't think that rag doll has any connection with what happened today?"

Phillip saw again the cold, reptilian stare of those merciless eyes, a stare that contained personal malice. He shuddered as though with a sudden chill. "I don't know what to think," he said slowly.

Paige hugged herself, looking at him uneasily. She said nothing.

Despite the miracle of spring that flooded the outdoors, no one even mentioned getting out of the house for the rest of the afternoon. Paige announced her intent to finish a novel she had ignored for weeks, leaving Phillip the opportunity to spend a few unexpected hours working on his novel—a one-time hobby that was fast becoming a passion. He shut the door to his third-floor office and stared blankly at the cheerful sunlight that poured through the window, mocking his dark mood. Once again his mind replayed his eye contact with the snake and he fought the dim idea that was struggling to rise from that place in the mind where we store things best not contemplated. The thought persisted, grew stronger, and finally emerged from the shadows: the snake in the backyard had some similarity, some likeness, to the one carved on the door of the church in Cap-Haïtien.

"Of course," logic sneered, "snakes resemble snakes. You know, beady little eyes, scales, forked tongues."

"It was more than that," the mind replied carefully. "I can't define it exactly, but today's viper and the carved one had something in common besides just being snakes. Something in the way they move, maybe. Besides, have you ever seen a snake make no effort to avoid you, just try to stare you down?"

Logic was slow to answer.

"Besides, that look, that glare," the mind continued. "Whatever it was, it didn't come to kill Rhett. It meant to go for me."

With desperate haste, Phillip fumbled through the drawers of his file cabinet until shaking fingers closed around what he sought—a half-full pack of cigarettes he had discarded (but not thrown away) when he decided to quit smoking. The tobacco was stale and had the crumbling consistency of sand, but he lit one anyway, noting that his hand was trembling. Harsh and dry, the first lungful of smoke burned his throat and nose. Then he saw it: the tiny tape from his first pocket-sized recorder. His vision wavered through tears as he pulled it from its hiding place and turned it over in his hand. He had found it the day after Becky's accident, and it had driven him to try to drown his grief—and nearly himself—in a sea of booze. Just holding it here in his hand sent a blade of sorrow, undulled by time, plunging into his gut. My God, *the tape*!

After Becky's death, in a futile attempt to ease his mind and soul from turmoil, Phillip had retreated up here to his office. Sitting in this same chair, he had noticed the recorder lying atop a stack of paper, its tape half used. Curious, he hit the "on" switch and what he got had been more painful than if he had received a jolt of electricity.

"Daddy?" the little girl's voice asked shyly before unnecessarily announcing, "this is Becky [giggle]. I hope you won't get mad because I'm in your office, 'cause I know I'm not 'sposed to be. But Momma's sick [a euphemism Phillip had used for his wife's hangovers]. But I wanted to tell you I love you, Daddy. When Momma gets well this afternoon, she's gonna let me go swimmin' [giggle]." Becky had apparently turned the machine off and on before continuing, ". . . learned my ABCs in nursery school. Want to hear?" She began to sing, "ABCDEFG . . . That's as far as I can go right now, Daddy. I love you."

He had lowered his head and sobbed uncontrollably.

He had played it only once more, the night Paige had announced her pregnancy. With her usual sympathy where memories of his first child were concerned, her eyes had filled with pity. Her voice low, she had said, "My God, Phillip, you've tortured yourself over Becky's death long enough. Now that there's another child on the way, let go!"

"I'll never forget her," Phillip had said defensively.

Paige's tone had softened even more. "Of course you won't. I wouldn't expect you to. But I don't want you wallowing in grief, either. Throw the tape away," she had pleaded.

Instead, Phillip had secreted it in the back of the file drawer. He couldn't blithely toss away the last communication from Becky, sever the one tangible tie. Now the memory of the small voice reached over the years to prod him. He should go on and dispose of it. But he couldn't. He took another drag on the stinging smoke. He suspected it would take more than nicotine to calm him.

The dog, that cursed animal! The thought of sheer chance defeating her purpose sent the old woman into such a rage she flung her drinking gourd against the hardened mud wall where it shattered with a dry crack. Well, the man was beginning to realize what was happening, nurturing the fear growing within him, a growth that would make her task easier. She watched him staring at the pile of paper, paper that was somehow valuable to him. The thought became an idea and she hobbled to the altar, grabbing for vials of different colored powders. It would take time, but time was something she had in great quantity. The white man and his woman did not. Theirs was running out like the waters of a spring that is drying up.

Soon she would try again.

Two hours later, Phillip had accomplished little other than surrounding himself with wads of paper, tombstones of dead ideas. His plot refused to move forward and his characters resisted his efforts to make them speak in anything other than wooden, artificial phrases. He was overcome by the blankness of the typing paper he could not fill. With stubborn effort, he tore his thoughts from Rhett, from the events of the morning, and from the tape, and tried to force his imagination to create events he had never witnessed and people he had never known. Well, almost never known. One of his minor female characters, a neurotic and selfish bitch, was beginning to bear an unmistakable resemblance to Sue and the physical description of a comical drunk was close to that of a hard-boozing editor he had known. He grimaced. One of the few rewards of the writer's lonely craft was the opportunity of taking a shot at those he knows.

He allowed himself a momentary indulgence as he reached to the rear of the cluttered pub table that served as his desk, typing stand, and depository for anything he couldn't find another place for. Lovingly, he fingered the four hundred–plus typed pages, pages he had read, reread, typed, retyped so often that he could quote many of them. Today might not be productive but there would be other times. He could guess that within a month his novel would be ready. He sighed wishfully and returned his attention to the typewriter before him, glaring as though it alone was obstructing his work.

The ringing of the phone at his elbow, usually a resented interruption, was a welcome reprieve. The smile in his voice vanished when Dr. Semmes identified himself.

"Is there a chance your dog, Rhett, could have been poisoned?" the veterinarian asked, his voice heavy with concern. "Had he caused any trouble in the neighborhood, trouble that might make some disturbed person want to kill him?"

A click signaled Paige had picked up the extension downstairs. No doubt she had guessed who was calling.

"No." Phillip was emphatic. "We know our neighbors and there's no one like that."

There was an audible intake of breath, although Phillip could not tell if it was Paige or Semmes. The latter continued tentatively, "I'm pretty certain your pet died from some sort of nerve toxin. Although I wouldn't have the equipment to say what specific variety, a quick examination of the nerve tissue makes me certain that the nervous system was attacked by something.''

''Doctor,'' Paige asked, ''did the toxin come from the snake bite?''

Semmes' reply was as uncertain as it was slow, ''Frankly, I'm confused. The proximity in time—how quickly your dog died after being bitten—would certainly indicate so. But there are no reptiles indigenous to the area that would have that sort of venom—certainly not your garter snake.'' He paused. ''You see, the only poisonous varieties within hundreds of miles are the copperhead, the rattler and, even more rarely, the moccasin. All three of those have a venom that attacks muscle tissue, immobilizes their prey. If the poison came from the bite, it wasn't from any snake I've ever known to be around here.''

Phillip paused to hear if there would be further explanation before asking, ''If that's true, Dr. Semmes, how do you explain the presence of the venom in Rhett's system?''

Semmes patiently explained, ''I said there was some sort of nerve damage. If I had to guess, I'd say your pet accidentally got a hold of some sort of industrial chemical that may have set up a neurological disorder that the shock of the bite made fatal. If I can be of any further help . . .''

Sunday night supper, a potpourri of the week's leftovers, was usually consumed in front of the television, a time when Case was allowed to abandon table manners for TV watching. Tonight he ate little, staring morosely and uncomprehendingly at the screen. Instead of denouncing the news, Phillip picked at his plate, forgetting he had eaten nothing since that morning.

Paige stood, collecting dishes that had barely been touched. ''Well, at least I'm glad to know that we don't ordinarily have poisonous snakes in our yard.''

Phillip looked up, unwilling to let the statement go un-challenged. "I'm convinced that snake killed Rhett. I don't see how you can believe that gibberish about industrial chemicals."

Paige spoke before she realized the day's tensions were building into an argument. "You heard Doctor Semmes. There aren't any snakes with venom like that. At least not around here. Proximity in time isn't conclusive."

Phillip swallowed a retort about lawyers' hardheadedness in general.

Case stood from where he had been sitting on the floor and rubbed a fist across red-rimmed eyes. "Doesn't matter. Momma says Rhett's gone to puppy heaven." He sniffed loudly and headed for the stairs.

Placing the china on a table, Paige overtook her son to embrace him. "Old Rhett's chasing cats and eating steak bones, for sure." She kissed him, something he had lately resisted with all the determination of young boys who have just begun to equate affection with a lack of masculinity.

When he was sure his son was out of hearing, Phillip frowned at Paige. "What's this 'puppy heaven' business?"

She looked at him levelly. "If a child wants to believe that's where his dog is and it makes him feel better, so what? You want to tell him they burned Rhett up in the incinerator behind the vet's building?" The challenge in her voice was clear.

"No." Phillip shook his head in weary exasperation and rose to help carry the dishes into the kitchen. "I guess you're right. I just don't like teaching him stuff he'll find out is untrue later."

She dismissed his objection with a shake of the head. "Let him be a child. He'll grow up soon enough as it is. Frankly, tonight, I wish *I* still believed in a puppy heaven. It'd make me feel a hell of a lot better."

The next morning, Phillip dropped Paige off at the MARTA station for her ride to her downtown office. She rumpled the hair of an unusually quiet son who sat stonily on the backseat. Neither Phillip nor the boy even acknowledged her wishes for them to have a good day. Case's melancholy lasted most of the ride to school. He finally spoke as Phillip was turning onto West Paces Ferry Road, less than a mile from where his father would deposit him in front of the lower-school doors. "You know, Dad," he began, "Momma feels better about Rhett, thinking he's in puppy heaven."

Phillip raised an expectant eyebrow, managing to keep his mouth shut in anticipation.

"Me," Case continued in that serious, adult way he sometimes had, "me, I don't think there's a heaven for dogs. I mean, God has to take all the good people who've died and gone there. I don't think there's room for dogs, too, do you?"

Phillip gave the spaciousness of paradise the serious consideration the question deserved before answering, "I don't know, Case, but I can't see Rhett with wings on his shoulders."

He was rewarded with the first smile his son had shown in twenty-four hours. "Me neither." Case grew serious again. "We'd best not say anything to Momma. It'd only upset her."

With considerable effort, Phillip kept his face from cracking into a grin. "I think you're right, son."

It was only after he reached the interstate, heading south, that Phillip allowed himself a chuckle. "Out of the mouths of babes . . . " he said aloud.

As he passed the State Capitol, he turned east. Now, what was that man's name, the herpetologist he had interviewed some years ago? Rauch, that was it, David Rauch. Phillip had done an article for the State wildlife magazine on the annual rattlesnake roundup in some place in southern Georgia. Rauch had been eager to help. Hopefully, he still would be.

Grant Park, the location of the city zoo, was empty of humans other than two men leisurely collecting the weekend's trash. Phillip removed the cardboard box from the trunk under the watchful curiosity of one of the residents of the nearby elephant house who snorted in hopes this sole visitor might have a treat. "Not today, old buddy," Phillip said. Seconds later, he shook his head in surprise. He'd actually talked to the elephant. First, a snake with personal malice, then a heaven for dogs. He hoped he wasn't really going nuts.

The path led past the fenced area of big cats. A lion, stretched out in the warm sun, flicked his tasseled tail and yawned with a satisfied grunt. A female paced restlessly along the perimeter of the moat on the other side of the fence.

The reptile building was a contemporary concrete structure without windows that reminded Phillip of a modern public library. He shifted the box to his left hand and tried the double glass doors. Locked. He stepped back and read the sign. REPTILES. OPEN 10:00 A.M.–6:00 P.M. TUESDAY–SUNDAY.

"Shit," Phillip muttered before noticing the small button beside the sign. He shrugged with the indifference of a man with nothing to lose and pressed it. Nothing. Surely reptiles, or some of them, needed feeding whether they were on public display or not.

The buzzer from the door did nothing for Avis Johnson's head which was buzzing like a hive of bees already. A man of his age should know better: staying up, drinking, till past midnight on a work day wasn't worth it anymore. He wasn't getting any younger. In fact, he'd be up for retirement in another year. Good thing, too. Working here around all these nasty, crawling things was enough to drive a man to cheap whiskey or whatever he could get. It was the hooch that had put him here, too, his wife, Martha, reminded him at every opportunity.

"Avis," she'd say, "you had a good, clean job washin' out the monkey pens. If you'da kept away from that whiskey, you'da never got in that ruckus with Missa Smith. But no, you had to have a coupla belts right do'in your lunch hour an' get in an argument with your boss. You lucky they let you stay around cleanin' up snake shit."

And he hated snakes. His charges looked at him with bright, evil eyes, flicking forked tongues like he was a frog or mouse or something else those critters ate. And smell! He'd gotten accustomed to the sharp, sour odor of ape feces, hadn't minded it one bit. But these things with their nasty scales and slithering ways—they had a musty, choking air about them that no man should have to endure. Martha had an answer for that, too, "Snakes 'bout the lowest thing God makes, an' you right with 'em, Avis Johnson. I reckon the good Lord found a place for a sinner like you."

Avis Johnson was not in a good mood, no sir. At the second buzz, he angrily threw his mop against a glass pane, noting with only small satisfaction that he had disturbed a sleeping iguana. Whoever that was ringing that bell, he'd tell 'em the place was closed, he'd give 'em a bit of the anger he had for Martha, the high and mighty Mr. Smith, and all those goddamn snakes, yes sir, he would.

With steps far wider and quicker than one would expect for a sixty year old who was only five feet tall, he stomped toward the entrance, his rubber boots making sucking noises on the wet floor.

He flung the door open, glaring at the tall man with the

beard. "We ain't open on Mondays," he growled, pointing. "The sign on the door says so."

Tonight he'd tell Martha how he'd stood up to this big guy. She always said he was afraid of his own shadow, but here he was, clothed in the authority of the Atlanta Zoological Park, telling this jerk to buzz off.

The man looked at him the way big men always did—sort of amused—before he started to fish in a back pocket. For the first time, Avis noticed he was carrying a box. No matter, this place was closed on Mondays.

"I've got press credentials here somewhere," the man with the beard said.

Avis froze. Press, that meant newspaper, since the guy didn't have a TV camera with him. Or did he? Avis glanced around the area nervously. A warning went off somewhere in back of Avis's mind. The zoo was always whining about how much money it needed, money that he was sure went to pay big shots like Smith. Smith would be real unhappy if Avis, in doing his job, pissed off the *Journal* or *Constitution*. If there was a job worse than being around snakes, he'd wind up with it. Then what would Martha say?

"Here's my card." The man proffered a slick blue card with his picture on it and "Accredited Member of the Press" across the top.

Avis looked at it skeptically. He didn't know about "Accredited," but it looked important and it was one of those long "a" words. Long words that began with "a" had usually turned out to be trouble for somebody. Like that time Avis had helped himself to the watch the clerk left lying on the counter, the store detective had called the police to have Avis *apprehended*. The day he'd had the ruckus, Smith said he *ascertained* Avis had been drinking. Yes sir, those big, mysterious "a" words carried big problems, usually for

Avis. If he screwed up, heaven only knew what kind of animal's shit he'd be cleaning up next.

"I'm here to see Dr. Rauch," the visitor announced.

That decided the issue. Dr. Rauch was a nice guy, always speaking to employees, asking how they were doing, like he cared. Even though Rauch was confined to a wheelchair, he was always pleasant. Still, some caution was called for; Avis was *in charge*. In fact he and Rauch were the only people in the building this morning and the doctor was upstairs in his office. It made Avis proud that the kindly Dr. Rauch would entrust him with the responsibility of the whole first floor, even if the reptile house was closed. "You got an appointment?" he asked just like the doctor's assistant did.

The man in front of the door handed him another card, this one with his name on it. "Please give this to Dr. Rauch and tell him I'd like a few minutes of his time."

So, the guy didn't have an appointment. The decision was Avis's: tell him to go away or disturb the Director of Reptiles. Avis hated decisions. They made his head hurt worse than cheap whiskey. He pondered his dilemma. Why did these things always happen to him? Then, like one of Martha's revelations, it occurred to him that if he announced this intruder to Dr. Rauch, it would be someone else's decision to make. Avis would be off the hook. "Gimme a minute," he said, "I'll see if the doctor can see you."

The old woman's meager morning repast of corn gruel had long since gone cold. Hours ago she had stopped eating and begun to listen to something only she could hear, something other than the gentle breeze's sigh as it stroked the palm trees outside her hut. For that matter, she was unaware of her surroundings. She was concentrating on the hut where the white people lived, reviewing her vision of it as though

studying a photograph. Their home was made of wood, she
noted, not the mud of the huts on this mountain nor the
stone of the finer homes in the town below. Wood. She
moved her head slightly to glance at the fire that always
smoldered in the brazier outside her door. Wood. Fire. She
grinned and began to chant.

("I will succeed . . .")

David Rauch wheeled his chair around the corner of the
desk. "Mr. Owens! It's good to see you again." He extended a hand far firmer than the shrivelled legs indicated.

Rauch was broad-shouldered with a square face to match.
From the waist up, he could have been an athlete. Phillip
had noted previously that the man declined to acknowledge
his disability, making remarks about his confinement in an
offhand manner that had made Phillip comfortable in the
presence of such a handicap. "And you, Doctor, how have
you been?"

Rauch glanced down at the frame of his chair with a
solemn expression. "Well, considering I couldn't get Enzio
Ferrari to custom build a racing wheelchair for me, I suppose I'll survive." He indicated the small office's only other
chair. "Sit down, please."

Phillip did so, grateful that his face was now at the level
of his host's. It was difficult to make conversation looking
down on someone's head. He glanced around the room.
Drawings of reptiles crowded each other on the meager wall
space. The desk was clear except for a triple frame exhib-
iting two handsome boys and a cheerful, smiling woman.

The doctor followed Phillip's gaze. "My wife and two
sons." He noted the surprise that flickered across Phillip's
face before he could hide it. "Oh, yes, I lead a pretty normal life. My kids are as big a pain in the ass as anybody's,
and, since I'm not into golf or tennis, my wife says I have

nothing but sex on my mind, that it's a wonder we don't have *ten* children around.''

They shared a smile. Now Phillip remembered how much he had liked this man who seemed to spit in the eye of adversity.

''Well,'' Rauch said, ''as much as I enjoy company, I suspect you're here after a story. Perhaps a python swallowed the mayor?''

Phillip placed the box on the desk and opened it. ''No, nothing like that. I wonder if you can tell me something about this.''

The herpetologist squinted, reached into a drawer, and placed a pair of wire spectacles across his nose. ''Don't usually wear 'em,'' he explained. ''Vanity and all that, I suppose.'' He frowned as he examined the contents of the box. With a pencil, he gently prodded the half of the snake that had the head before he looked up. ''Where,'' he asked softly, ''did you find this fellow?''

''In my backyard.''

''Here? In Atlanta?'' The doubt was clear.

Phillip nodded. ''Yesterday. It bit my dog and the animal was dead in minutes.''

Rauch dropped the pencil on his desk and stared at Phillip before speaking. ''I'm hard pressed to believe this snake was in your backyard. I can easily accept that your dog died quickly. You're very lucky.''

''Oh?''

''What you have here, Mr. Owens, is a member of the genus *Dendraspis angusticeps*. A mamba, a baby black mamba. Its bite has killed men within minutes. If you or another human had been bitten instead . . .'' He left the phrase hanging in the air like a poisonous gas.

''Mamba?'' Phillip was searching until the name popped up in his mental filing system. ''Aren't they from India?''

"Africa," Rauch corrected. "West coast, mostly. A nasty little relative of the hooded cobra, venom's a nerve toxin. I'd say you have a neighbor who collects unattractive pets. Quite illegally, I might add."

Swallowing in hopes of disbursing the knot that was growing in his throat, Phillip paused before stating, "I know my neighbors. None of them collect exotic snakes."

Rauch stared at Phillip a moment before removing his glasses with a flourish. "I assure you, the only other mamba in these parts is downstairs, safely behind four inches of glass." He pointed to the box. "And this one certainly couldn't live outside. Atlanta's winters are cold enough to kill it. Since these creatures aren't known to wander, I'd guess it came from within a half mile or so of your house. That means someone close by got a hold of one of the deadliest vipers in the world and either released it or let it escape—Not very pleasant possibilities."

On rubbery legs, Phillip stood, extending his hand. "I don't have an answer for you, Doctor, but you've been helpful."

With a grip as strong as his gaze, Rauch held Phillip's hand. "I'd appreciate your letting me know when you find out where it came from."

"When?"

Releasing his hand with a smile, Rauch wheeled himself toward the door. "As a newsman, you're not going to ignore the mystery of how a deadly snake indigenous to another continent found its way to your backyard."

"No, I'm not."

"I'm sure there's a rational explanation."

Phillip wished he was as certain.

On the third floor of the Owens' home, the late morning sun was beginning to pour through the windows directly onto the stack of typewriting paper that was Phillip's manuscript. As though by an invisible hand, the loose papers ruffled and settled back.

("Fire. Wood. Paper.")

A bright light, brighter than the sunshine, slid across the pub table, stopped at the IBM typewriter, and moved on to the manuscript. The light shrunk in size, becoming a pinpoint of concentrated energy, much the same as light focused through a magnifying glass.

Downstairs, the exhibit rooms were illuminated only by light from the aquariumlike cages. Phillip was glancing around when the little man who had let him in appeared around the corner. Good grief, but he looked like he'd been on a lifelong bender! Eyes that were streaked with trails of red peered from a face blotched with bourbon blossoms, the burst capillaries of the hard drinker.

"On yer way out?" he asked.

Even at a distance of five feet, Phillip winced from the stale alcohol stench of the man's breath. "Er, yes. But before I go, could I see the mamba?" He was unsure why he wanted to but there was no denying the desire.

The gnomelike features of the little man scrunched in doubt. "I dunno, the place bein' closed . . ."

Phillip had dealt with bureaucratic mentality enough to seize on the hesitation. "Looks to me like you're in charge here. You could let me take a peek."

The fellow straightened thin shoulders. "You're right, what the hell?" He turned, pointing a bony finger and said, "Should be one o' those over there."

The snake responded to Phillip's light tap on the glass with a flick of its split tongue. No doubt it was the twin of the one Phillip had left in the box on Rauch's desk: same slender black body. But the eyes . . . They had the same shiny beadiness, but lacked the malevolence, the recognition. Phillip turned away and the janitor let him out.

Avis watched the big man's back as he walked away. Seemed like a nice enough fella, the kind Doctor Rauch would know, he mused. Odd, though. Why would he want to look at one particular snake? Maybe Avis should have invited him to share a nip of the half pint hidden in the supply room. Looked like he could use something, the way he was pulling his sport coat tight around him despite the warm sunshine outside.

Phillip hardly noticed his surroundings as he hastened to the car. A mamba! He was far from certain exactly how the deadly viper had arrived in his backyard, but he would have been willing to bet it wasn't somebody's escaped pet. Not with the other things that had happened, like a voodoo doll that came from nowhere. He stopped with the car key in hand, inches from the door. Hadn't he read something about a snake having to do with voodoo? Sure, a month or so ago. Some anthropologist over at the University, a Haitian as a matter of fact. Now, what had been the name of the man? De something. Phillip had been leafing through the magazines at the grocery store checkout when the article had caught his attention. He had wanted to see the man before leaving for Haiti but, as usual, hadn't gotten around to it.

Shit, what *was* the man's name? He checked his watch. Plenty of time since Case was going to a friend's house from school. Glancing around, he spied a phone booth. He'd just call the Anthropology Department to see if he could set up an appointment.

Chapter 9

How had a year-old issue of *People* magazine found its way into the stack of scholarly publications, Peter Devoux wondered. More precisely, how had it wound up between a monograph on Arawak Indians and an even older copy of *Anthropology Quarterly*? He squinted through dusty spectacles at the date of the offending publication and shook his gray-topped head. Miss Harp, this semester's graduate assistant, was clearly implicated. Amazing someone of her intelligence would read such trash. An even blacker mark against her was that she was not to be found today when he needed her help in tidying up the astonishing amount of junk that accumulated in his 10×10 office. He picked up a torn black-and-white photograph of two mud-smeared people knee-deep in some sort of dig. Neither face was familiar, but he was certain the picture had been taken when he had met a group of archaeologists in Costa Rica last year. He turned it over, reading the names he'd written on the back, names he could still make out despite concentric circles of coffee stains. He still couldn't place the faces. With a shrug, he tossed the snapshot onto the growing mound in the overflowing trash basket. Maybe he ought to change his policy of not allowing the janitor to touch his tiny domain.

If half the stuff got accidentally thrown away, he might be able to make sense out of the rest. The thought brightened his mood and he sighed happily. There! At last he could see the top of his desk, a well-worn piece of University issue. It must have been disassembled to get it into this cramped space. Or maybe, he mused, they built the room around it. That would not be atypical of the way Americans attacked problems. Using the stone edge of an ancient dish to scrape cigarette ashes onto a piece of paper, he stepped back to inspect the results of his efforts. The place was now reasonably presentable.

He sat in the chair behind his desk before he realized it was the only one. Why had he never noticed that before? Perhaps because few people visited the office of an obscure professor of Caribbean anthropology. With a distinguished journalist due any moment, he would have to hurry. He dashed into the hall, listing from one side to the other like a ship under full sail in shifting winds. His clumsiness was the result of legs bowed by childhood rickets, a common enough affliction among malnourished Haitians. He knew his students imitated his rolling gait, but he viewed their mimicry as a sign of their affection rather than their malice.

At the end of the hall, he timidly opened the door that entered the sanctuary of the head of the department, Dr. Sammons. Sammons himself was a kind and understanding man, a long-time friend; but Miss Baird, his secretary and guardian of his door . . . Well, it would not be inaccurate to say she intimidated Devoux as well as the rest of the department. From behind her desk, she glared at him over half-moon glasses, the look of a hawk about to swoop on its prey.

"Yes?" she asked in a tone that managed to convey disdain, disapproval, and outright contempt all at once.

When he had first come here, Peter Devoux had believed

this woman did not like him because he was black—dark as midnight at the bottom of a well. He subsequently observed that he had been only partially correct: she also didn't like him because he was a foreigner.

She was peering at him down a nose that did nothing to dispel the image of a raptor. "May I help you?" she asked in a tone that clearly said she had no desire to do anything of the kind. "You wish to see Dr. Sammons? He is out."

"Er, no, no thank you. I have come to borrow a chair only." Devoux always felt he was apologizing to this woman, no matter what he said.

She stared at him as though he had just suggested some perverted sexual act. "A chair?"

Devoux bobbed his head. "Yes, a chair. I have only one and I am about to be visited by a most important journalist, Phillip Owens, the man who wrote those articles on Haiti that I showed Dr. Sammons."

Now she was suspicious. "He's coming to see you, not the Head Of The Department?" Her voice invariably capitalized the title.

Devoux glanced nervously over his shoulder. It would be most unfortunate to have Mr. Owens encounter Miss Baird. The possibility gave him boldness and he straightened up to his full five feet, five inches. "I will require another chair, a place for him to sit." Without further discussion, he lifted a reproduction Queen Anne side chair and retreated down the hall, fearful he would be pursued.

"Be sure to return it!" The command followed him like a threat.

Back in the safety of his own office, Devoux placed the purloined chair in front of his desk and stepped back to study the effect. Too close. He moved it to the side facing the single window. No, that gave a view only of the campus power plant. He frowned at the thought. The anthropology

department was housed in an older building that had somehow been kept standing long past its expected life, not like
those Greek Revival buildings where most classrooms were,
located on sweeping green lawns. He sighed. Even the lowest assistant football coach had a nicer office. Football. Devoux had tried for two falls now to understand this American
contest where gigantic young men tried to pummel each
other to death to move an oddly shaped object up and down
a field. He shook his head. There was much that was strange
about America. But there was more that he understood and
loved.

He had made a chance remark in a classroom back in
Haiti, a trivial thing that he could no longer remember. That
night, one of his students had furtively knocked on his door
and whispered, *"Tontons Macoutes."* He had had no time
to pack, barely the opportunity to get dressed and outside
before four large men had kicked in the door of his small
apartment. From the shadows of a mahogany tree, he had
watched through an open window. He saw them read his
correspondence with his American friend, Dr. Sammons,
letters less than favorable to the present regime. There had
been no doubt that had he been found, he would have disappeared forever into the hell of Fort Dimanche, a prison
where few survived the daily beatings, the human filth and
starvation. The *Tontons Macoutes*, Duvalier's secret police,
were very good at making people vanish without a trace.

Devoux had been lucky. He had a friend with a car who
had been willing to drive him near the Dominican border.
The next morning, he wandered out of the bush, the only
clothes he possessed in tatters, his shoes torn by rocks. He
hitchhiked a ride on a sugar cane truck to Santo Domingo
City where he stayed with an associate at the University
there until Dr. Sammons had arranged for him to enter the
United States.

He arrived with a new suit of clothes, five American dollars, and an offer of a job at the University of Georgia. He had considered himself one of the richest men in the world, but even then he could not believe what went on in this lovable, if sometimes incomprehensible country. Newspapers and television were openly critical not only of the local powers, but of the President of the United States himself. That alone would have been sufficient to have the paper closed in Port-au-Prince. Many people here even kept firearms in their homes—a certain death penalty in Haiti. And the laws! From what he could see, persons arrested not only had a real trial, but had so many rights that the guilty went free as often as not. Where he had come from, trials were rare and acquittals unheard of. Yes, Devoux considered himself a very rich man when he thought of the friends in Haiti he had thought he would never see again. He had his life, over four hundred dollars in the bank, and a car barely three years old. Now that Duvalier was gone, perhaps he could go back, visit for a while during school vacation.

"Dr. Devoux?"

Devoux turned from the window to see a large man with a neat beard. He appeared to be about forty, but his coloring was the pale translucency of a much older person, the texture of wax. Tired eyes darted around the room as if anticipating an attack. Whoever he was, he looked worried, if not distressed. "Mr. Owens?"

Phillip stepped into the cubicle and extended a hand that would hide the professor's. "I'm glad to meet you, Doctor."

Devoux indicated the just acquired chair. "Please, sit." He squeezed behind his desk. "What may I do for you?"

With his bandy legs and round belly, Devoux reminded Phillip of a frog, an illusion that was emphasized by eyes magnified by thick glasses and a wide mouth and little chin.

"I was interested in your article on voodoo."

Ah! Devoux smiled. At last his work was being recognized. This eminent journalist was, perhaps, to review the article. That would be a feather in Devoux's academic cap. "And I enjoyed your series of articles on Haiti," he said politely.

Phillip placed a note pad on the desk. He frowned, wondering how to begin. "Doctor," he said finally, "I need your help."

The tone was so plaintive, Devoux thought he had misunderstood. "Sir?"

"I need your help, I . . . Let me tell you something, something that you may find difficult to accept. Then I want your advice."

"I gather this has to do with voodoo?"

Phillip nodded. "I think so. When I was in Haiti gathering material for those articles, I went to Cap-Haïtien . . ."

When Phillip finished, the anthropologist stared at him silently, masking whatever thoughts he had.

"I know it's asking a lot to expect you to believe me . . ." Phillip began.

"On the contrary, I believe every word you've said."

Phillip jerked erect with surprise. "You're the first person. I mean, everybody else thinks I've lost my marbles when I see a relationship between what happened in that churchyard and the events I've just told you."

"I see a definite relationship," Devoux assured him. "The woman priestess—'*hounan*' we would call her—was undoubtedly Marie deSault, the most feared *hounan* in the Cap-Haïtien area. When Duvalier was in power, such practices as human sacrifice were outlawed, but not even the *Tontons Macoutes* dared arrest her as long as she was reasonably, er, discreet. Now that there is little if any enforcement of the law, she is apparently holding her ceremonies quite openly."

Phillip waited for him to continue until it was obvious he had finished. "Doctor, I'm here to ask for advice. What can I do before me or my family . . ." He let the possibility trail off, incomplete.

Devoux ran a hand through white curls as he wrinkled his forehead. "I would suggest you do nothing."

"Nothing?" Phillip protested. "But there's no telling . . ."

"Let me correct what I said: Do nothing for the moment. She failed with her attempt through Baron Samedi and through Damballah. Perhaps . . ."

"Samedi?" Phillip jumped to his feet. "That's the word I kept hearing after the airplane incident!"

"Yes, so I would think. The *loa* of the dead and of the air.

" '*Loa*' means spirit," Devoux said, noting his visitor's confusion. "If you have the time, perhaps I might explain a little of voodoo. After all, as the saying goes, 'forewarned is a forearm', whatever that means."

Phillip sat down slowly. "Take all the time you need. I'm listening."

"Good," Devoux said with a tight grimace. "Americans are always in such a hurry." He stared at a place on the ceiling. "In the eighteenth century, the French colonists brought slaves to what we now call Haiti. Most of these were captured along the west coast of Africa, particularly Senegal and Dahomey. Understandably, these poor wretches brought with them the only two things they could—their language and their religion. Over the years, the African religion, rich in spirits—or *loas*—both good and bad, began to merge with French Catholicism, producing a mixture of both. For every saint, there is a corresponding *loa* with similar characteristics. Even today, voodoo is as widely, if not as openly, accepted by the Haitian people as Christianity. They practice the religion of their ancestors side by side with that of their former masters. When Haiti won its independence in 1804, it was a poor country indeed, its riches depleted by years of revolution. So poor that it was largely ignored by the trading nations that also exported its forms of worship. Isolated and impoverished, the old ways did not vanish as they did in other Caribbean countries. Much as voodoo, in a somewhat different form, continues in parts of Louisiana and the isolated islands off the South Carolina and Georgia coasts. In a nation like Haiti, where illiteracy is nearly eighty percent, ignorance and superstition flourish. Hence voodoo is alive and well.''

"Superstition?" Phillip asked. "I thought you said voodoo was *real*."

"Please," Devoux, a pedant in mid-lecture, held up a silencing hand. "It is real enough, as you yourself have witnessed. The efforts against you fit parts of a classic pattern: air, land, water, and fire—the four ancient elements. You were, er, attacked by the spell in the air, by a creature of the dirt, a snake. Yes, it all fits: you saw Baron Samedi and, although you did not know it, a form of Damballah, the *loa* who always appears as a snake and who is the most powerful of all.''

"What about fire and water?"

"Ah!" Devoux held up a finger as he might when a student asked a particularly intelligent question. "There is a chance, perhaps a good one, that you will not be visited by those *loas*.''

Phillip sat back in his chair, his face a mixture of hope and curiosity. "Why not?"

Devoux made a steeple of his fingers as he composed an answer. "Samedi, Damballah. They are the male, and hence the stronger of the *loas*. Both have failed. Or rather, deSault failed them. It is entirely possible they have become angry and have withdrawn their powers. *Loas* are impatient. If so, the other loas would do likewise. If that is the case, you have nothing further to fear.''

''And if not?''

Devoux's face became grave. ''The only thing left to do would be dangerous indeed, Mr. Owens. It is best not to discuss it unless it becomes necessary.''

''And that would be?''

Devoux shook his head slowly. ''No, Mr. Owens. I would be doing you a serious disfavor to even mention it to you unless you really needed to know. I would suggest you hope for the best, but be very, very careful around any fire or lakes. Even small ponds.''

''You're holding out on me, Doctor.''

''Holding out? Yes, that is true. I am. It is for your own good.''

Phillip grinned. ''The last time somebody told me that, I was in East Germany. I got escorted to the nearest airport and sent home. I'll take your word for it.'' Standing, he reached across the desk to encase the small black hand with his own. ''You've been most helpful.''

Devoux stood. ''I hope so, but remember: avoid fire and water until you are certain there is no more trouble. Say, nothing unusual happens in two weeks or so.''

Devoux stood in the doorway of his office, watching Phillip disappear down the stairs. Perhaps he should have told the big journalist all. Maybe he should have told him that the mind was the pathway through which the *hounan* was reaching him, that his very thoughts were the danger. But how to explain? Besides, to tell a man not to think of something was to assure it was foremost in his mind. It was reasonable to guess the *loas* had given up and it was Mr. Owens' only realistic hope that they had. The other possibility of survival would be a small one. Very small.

* * *

A brown spot appeared on the top paper where the light was concentrated. Instead of igniting, the next sheet began to brown also. A tiny tendril of smoke grew like a young plant reaching for the sun as the third and fourth pages in the stack began to smolder. At this rate, it would take hours before the whole manuscript was burning. Another hour or so before the wooden table caught fire. Hours. About the time the Owens family was asleep.

Chapter 10

"Obviously, we have some neighbors with a strange taste in pets." Paige put her wineglass down on the deck's wrought-iron table. "Your herpetologist is right. Besides, we don't know everybody within the radius he suggested. There could be all kinds of kooks and weirdos here in midtown."

Phillip sipped at his martini. He was, so far, not willing to discuss his visit with Devoux. If the anthropologist was right and there were no more incidents, there would be no need to be subjected to Paige's skepticism. "You're right, I suppose."

Paige read his mind, an annoying habit formed over the years of their marriage. "But you don't think so." It was a statement, not a question.

He sipped again like a school teacher drinking tea, then said primly, "No, I don't."

A quizzical smile played around her lips, the expression of someone indulging a small child. "So? What's your explanation?"

He set down the sweating glass, staring at the glow of sunset. The fading light silhouetted the tall buildings that surrounded this enclave like an invading army. Someday,

Phillip surmised, mega-dollars and the holy cry of economic development would burst the fragile bounds of zoning and reduce this, the city's oldest intact residential area, to more faceless towers. He supposed that he would be well-compensated for his loss—if money can replace a state of mind. He winced at the inevitable before returning to the present. "I don't have an explanation, but I can't imagine anyone keeping a mamba. Who wants something that deadly around?"

"Tarantulas were a big item a few years ago. Ugh!" She shivered at the thought. "And your own son collects bugs, snakes, and anything else he can catch."

Phillip smiled despite the seriousness of the conversation. "So, he's *my* son when he keeps creepy-crawlies?"

She reached for her wine. "Uh-huh. I can't imagine any kid of *mine* doing it."

He returned to the discussion. "Anyway, tarantulas aren't poisonous, even if they are ugly and I don't think Case catches anything that could kill him, not since he tried to make friends with that nest of hornets."

Paige started to speak, stopped, and sniffed the air. "Do you smell something burning?"

Phillip took a whiff. "No, I . . . Wait, something does smell like fire."

With the concern of anyone who lives in an eighty-year-old clapboard house, Paige stood quickly, testing the air like a dog trying to recognize a scent. "I think it's inside," she announced, striding for the door.

Phillip followed her into the kitchen where the odor was unmistakable. It seemed to be floating down the back steps. "Up here," he called.

Without waiting for a response, he was racing up the stairs, apprehension lending speed to his steps. He reached the top where the upstairs hall led off to the right. To his left was a former sleeping porch which, with the advent of air-conditioning, had been converted to an upstairs sun room. Following the growing strength of the smell of fire, he turned in here. At the back of the room was a narrow set of stairs that was the access to the third floor attic and his office. He could see wisps of smoke reaching ominous fingers down the attic steps.

"Something's on fire on the third floor," he shouted. "Grab the kitchen extinguisher on your way up!"

Two steps at a time, he leapt upstairs. Already he could see billowing, stinking smoke. It came from his work area. Through the choking haze, at the far end of the room where his pub table was, a red glow flickered like a small camp-fire. A hand over his mouth, he felt his way along the wall, ignoring the air that seared his throat and made his eyes water. The manuscript! The neat stack of paper next to the typewriter was blazing cheerfully.

"Shit!" He gulped, reaching for the large unabridged dictionary next to the Selectric. He dropped the heavy volume on the stack of paper, picked it up, and tried again.

"Move." Paige's quiet command came as she shoved him aside. A whoosh of white foam shot past him, covering the tabletop as though with snow. She continued to direct the jet of chemicals until the extinguisher sputtered, coughed, and went empty.

"Well," she sighed, "at least we caught it before there was any real damage."

Phillip thumbed the sodden lump of black ash. "Damage? My whole novel is gone," he croaked. "I'd call the loss of that 'damage,' wouldn't you?"

Paige ran her hand across her face, leaving a white trail through the sooty grime of the smoke. With exaggerated care, she set the fire extinguisher down. "Yes, yes, I would. I meant I was thankful it didn't spread before we could put it out. Your table is barely singed and none of your other books or things got burned, did they?''

He shook his head miserably as he watched crisp black ash float in the air, the cremated body of his labor. "No, but that's enough. Three years' work . . ."

"You don't have a copy somewhere? Surely you . . ."

Why was she asking stupid questions at a time like this? Phillip's sense of loss was turning to anger and, seeking the only viable target, he said, "Why the hell would I make copies until I was finished? Surely you don't think I should have been able to foresee this?"

"No, but at the law firm we always have important documents on word-processing disks . . ."

"I'm not your fucking law firm!" he shouted, his anguish boiling over into rage. "I don't use a fucking word processor! I'm just a stupid writer, not some lawyer who sells his intellect for the biggest buck!"

She could not have been more astonished had he struck her. She bit her lip, straining her face not to weep. Then the shock of what could have happened to their home swept over her and she stiffened. "I know you don't care for lawyers," she said in quiet indignation. "At least I don't try and slant what I write to please the politics of some editor. How can you say I prostitute my intellect?"

"What's a pros'tute?" The small voice came from behind them. The volume of their heated voices had masked Case's ascent to the third floor. An Atlanta Braves cap was sideways on his head, his fielder's glove slung on his belt, and the dirt on his jeans testified he had tried, at least once, to steal second base. He repeated the question, his eyes large with fear from the tones he rarely heard. "What's a pros'tute?"

The rage seemed to flow out of Phillip's toes, leaving him

weak. Paige engulfed her son in her arms. "It's a grown-up word, Case."

He glanced from one to the other, assuring himself the yelling was over. "One of those things I'm not supposed to know about till I get bigger?"

Phillip had to grin at the way Case bridled against this limitation of knowledge, even though the two parents occasionally found it a convenient subterfuge, "That's right. Now, why don't you go downstairs?"

Case nodded knowledgeably. " 'Cause you an' Momma were having a fight?"

"We weren't fighting, Case," Paige protested. "We were discussing."

"When I yell like that at Randy or Charlie, you say I'm having a fight," he protested. Then, with a wrinkle of his nose, "Something stinks!"

Phillip crossed the room to put a gentle hand on his son's small shoulder. "You're right there. We had a fire and Momma put it out."

Case shook his head sadly. "I always miss the exciting parts."

As he descended the steps, Phillip and Paige could not suppress a laugh. " 'Exciting parts,' he says," snickered Paige.

Phillip put an arm around her. "Look, I'm sorry for what I said. You just can't imagine what it's like losing my novel. It was three years of my life."

"Nearly having the house burn down didn't improve my personality either," she said, pecking at his cheek. "What do you think caused it? Something electrical?"

Practical Paige, Phillip thought. "No, if you look, you'll see that the fire started and ended with my literary opus."

"Spontaneous combustion?" The tone was disbelieving.

"Not likely, not with a stack of paper like that."

"Then what . . . ? Oh, Phillip, surely you haven't been sneaking up here to smoke! You quit."

Guiltily, he remembered the few furtive puffs that had done little to calm him yesterday. No, he'd been careful to conceal the evidence until he could flush the butt down the john. He had taken time to make sure he had also disposed of incriminating ashes. "No. I was up here most of the afternoon yesterday and there wasn't anything out of the ordinary."

"Then what could have caused it?"

Phillip stared into her eyes, trying to gauge the wisdom of sharing his thoughts. Why not? He began slowly, "We have this doll, possibly voodoo, appear on a toy gone berserk, a doll that even the dog wants no part of. Yesterday, a snake that lives only in Africa mysteriously shows up in our yard in Atlanta, Georgia. Today, my manuscript suddenly bursts into flames . . ."

"Phillip," she began to protest.

He raised a silencing hand. "Paige, take a breath, a deep one, and tell me what you smell."

Puzzled, she did it. "I smell smoke."

"Not merely smoke, not even burnt paper. You smell a charcoal fire."

She sniffed experimentally. "But there wasn't any charcoal up here."

"Precisely. Now, where were we when we last smelled it?"

She looked at him blankly. "Haiti?" she finally said in a tiny voice.

"Right. That odor was everywhere."

She wrinkled her forehead, still not grasping what he was saying. "And?"

"Paige, think. First, both engines on the airplane quit, not one but *both*, for no ascertainable reason. They started back up and when the mechanic arrived, he couldn't find a problem either, remember?"

"You said it was water in the gas, I thought."

He waved a dismissive hand. "Maybe, maybe not. If it hadn't been for the other things . . . ''

"Other things?" She was not happy with where this was going.

Counting on his fingers, he recited, "That doll shows up, apparently out of nowhere." He continued, ignoring her attempt to interrupt, "Next a snake that has no business on this side of the Atlantic is in our backyard. Now this. My manuscript mysteriously catches fire, nothing else, just the most important project in my life, almost a part of me." He thought a moment, trying to decide if he should continue. "Paige, I know this sounds nutty, but that snake, it knew who I was. I mean, I got the clear feeling he actually was there to attack *me*."

Paige's face tightened in apprehension. "Phillip, all of what you say can be explained and I don't believe you can tell if a snake knows you."

He put his hands on her arms, withdrawing them immediately as he saw fright in her eyes. "Paige, I tell you, all this has to do with what happened in Haiti—that ceremony!"

Taking a step out of his reach, she surveyed him critically. "I admit there's been a string of unexplained circumstances, things out of the ordinary, but you can't really believe that, think we're under some sort of curse. You've been reading too much Stephen King."

"I *do* believe it, it's the only explanation that ties all this together."

She inhaled, her eyes still playing across his face. "You're serious."

"As a heart attack."

They were silent, each searching the other's eyes, before she said softly, "If I asked you to do something for me, something really important to me, would you do it?"

Phillip had fallen into that soft trap too many times. "I love you and I'd do almost anything other than another blind agreement. The last time you hooked me like that, I spent almost a year writing a history of the DAR of Atlanta, not to mention having to interview every old bat in the city. For free."

She smiled at the memory. The task had been onerous and Phillip's contempt for those who measured their worth in lineage had been ill-concealed. "Pedigrees are for dogs," he had snorted. The privately published book had accomplished the goal Paige had set for it, though. Wealthy blue bloods had paid dearly to see their names in print. Some had even purchased two or more copies. The proceeds had financed the acquisition of much needed equipment for The Atlanta Historical Society.

"I promise this won't occupy more than an hour or so of your time," she said.

He was still reluctant. "If you thought I'd agree, you'd tell me what you want."

She sighed. "Very well, I want you to make an appointment with Dr. Hilsman."

He gaped, unbelieving. "You think I've got a screw loose!"

"A logical mind has trouble absorbing the illogical, and you have to admit, believing in some voodoo curse isn't exactly normal." She stood her ground.

"Neither is witnessing a human sacrifice," he retorted. God, he could never tell her about what he saw, or thought he saw, on the church door—or that sound in the room. Not now. She'd have him in the laughing academy for certain.

She persuaded gently, "I, for one, am not prepared to accept that a series of coincidences have a supernatural basis. Normally, you wouldn't either. You've been under some pressure. First Rhett, and now your book. *Please* call Dr. Hilsman. He helped you before, you said so.''

"When Becky died, I admit I couldn't handle it. So now you think I'm off the deep end again, is that it?'' His tone was getting angry again.

"Tell you what,'' she offered. "You spend one session with the shrink. If he says you're okay, not emotionally upset or something, I'll accept your curse theory, or at least I'll accept the possibility you may be right. Deal?''

Another row with Paige was not something he wanted and he knew her well enough to realize she wouldn't give up until he visited the psychiatrist. Once she was convinced any family member's welfare was at risk, she was impossibly stubborn. "Okay, deal. I'll phone him first thing in the morning.''

Paige smiled relief she did not entirely feel. Any connection between these events had to be in Phillip's mind. *Had* to be. She was fighting a growing concern he might—just possibly, mind you—be right. It was as though if she could make him stop believing in a supernatural explanation, it would not be true. Her mind, her soul, her being protested that witchcraft and curses could not co-exist in a world with science and realism. Could not. Should not. Determined, she slammed down the gate of the world she knew to keep something out, something dark, ugly, something she feared might break through that gate.

Phillip wanted to call Devoux, but there was no opportunity to do so under Paige's watchful gaze. This was no time, he thought, to tell her, not after her insistence he see Hilsman.

Becky came to Phillip again that night.

"Dadeeee,'' the anguished voice called. Again, she was

immersed in the water in which she had drowned, her small face contorted in fright. "Dadeeee . . ."

The paradox of the dream world allowed him to call out to her, although he, too, was underwater. "I'm coming, Becky, I'm coming." He reached for her, but no matter how hard he tried, he could not touch the little girl with the blond hair that swayed around her face like seaweed in a current.

His limbs made lead by his nightmare, Phillip kept moving toward her, reaching vainly to touch her beseeching arms. No matter how hard his futile efforts, she seemed farther away, her tearful eyes imploring him to save her. With terrible omniscience he knew she was aware of her own impending death. He struggled harder with arms and legs that seemed restrained.

"Phillip!"

In that instant between sleep and wakefulness, Becky's face faded into Paige's. His wife was sitting upright, her concerned expression spotlighted by the bedside lamp. Phillip strained against the bedclothes in which he was tangled, a fish in a linen net.

"You were dreaming about her again," Paige stated, sympathetically. "I was afraid you were going to fall out of bed, you were thrashing around so."

Phillip squinted in the light and grunted with a mixture of relief and sadness. "Yeah, it was the dream again."

"Another good reason to call Dr. Hilsman."

Wearily, he nodded before rolling over in hopes of going back to sleep. It was no use. He saw the pearly gray of dawn before he dropped off again.

The only sound in the hut was the choking sputter of a single candle as it drowned in its own tallow. She did not need the light, but the dwindling flame cast shadows on the mud walls, shadows of creatures half human, half animal or fish or reptile, creatures that existed only in shadows. And in her sight. She paid them little attention tonight, for she was angry and puzzled. Three times now she had failed. Although she had no doubt of her eventual success, she had never failed before.

The white woman. She did not believe. Perhaps that was the reason for the failures. Her husband did, with increasing terror. The old woman could see what he saw, but she could not see through the eyes of his wife, and somehow, the wife's disbelief could be weakening the power of the *loas*.

The man and his wife had been lucky. Lucky that the bird machine did not fall into the sea, lucky that the stupid dog had taken a bite intended for the man and the woman had smelled the smoke. At least the papers with the man's marks on them had been destroyed, causing him anguish. But now a plan must be found to make the woman believe. The old woman would think about how that might be done. She never doubted it could be.

Chapter 11

Although Freud may have used a couch, Dr. Samuel Hilsman's was mainly for show. It was tufted and buttoned red
leather. And rather uncomfortable. It did, though, match
the two wing chairs in which he conducted most of his ses-
sions. They, along with the mahogany coffee table and
bookcase which housed his collection of leather-bound volumes, gave his office more the appearance of an Edwardian
men's club than a room for psychiatric treatment. That, he
felt, made patients much more comfortable than the cliché
of stretching out on some bedlike sofa while he scribbled
in a note pad. He didn't use one of those, either. Instead,
concealed microphones relayed every word to the tape recorder in the base of the bookcase. Some of his patients
were disturbed enough without the trappings one associated
with the headshrinkers of old films.

He didn't even look an awful lot like those stern-faced
actors in white jackets. Eschewing the stereotypes of his
trade, he was clean-shaven and wore well-tailored three-
piece suits. The total effect, instead of doctor and patient,
was of two people sitting in a well-furnished office and talking like two rational executives. Rational, that was the key,
of course. Many of those visiting here were far from ra-

tional, if not already having crossed the border of insanity, a word Dr. Hilsman loathed both for its lack of precision and for its pejorative connotation.

Like this man, Phillip Owens, whose file the doctor was reading. Some years ago, Phillip (he always called his patients by their first names and insisted they do the same to him) had been enmeshed in a marriage that, in retrospect, had been doomed to failure. The woman . . . He searched his neatly typewritten notes. Margaret, that was it. Phillip had suspected his wife was something of a boozer, irresponsible. In fact, Phillip had claimed to have known it all along, but Hilsman believed that knowledge came only with the benefit of hindsight. That was the basis of the problem. Phillip, a journalist, had been on assignment some place when the child, Becky, had drowned in the pool. The next-door neighbors had found the child and had tried CPR without result. They had also found Margaret, passed out inside. Understandably, Phillip had blamed himself for leaving the child to be supervised by a drunk, even if she was Becky's mother. The self-inflicted guilt, combined with grief, had driven Phillip right to that undefined border. He had been unable to work and unable to sleep because of the re-occurring dreams, dreams the doctor viewed as a not entirely unnatural reaction under the circumstances. But not after this much time had elapsed. Hilman's round face squeezed into a frown, bringing sculpted eyebrows together in a single line. Something in his patient's life, stress of some sort most likely, had started the problem of the dreams again.

A discreet tone from a hidden buzzer announcing Phillip's arrival in the reception area interrupted any further thoughts. Tugging down the skirt of the coat of his pinstripe suit, Hilsman opened the door. The man who stood before him had the appearance of a person carrying his emotional problems like a load of rocks. He seemed bowed under the weight. He wore his sports coat and slacks with the air of someone beyond caring about his personal appearance, a supposition borne out by the wrinkles in pants and shirt. Bloodshot eyes were a clue that Phillip hadn't slept well lately and the way they seemed to dart around indicated the man was agitated, to say the least.

The psychiatrist extended his hand. "Phillip, good to see you again." He reached what he intended to be an assuring arm across the man's broad back. "C'mon in."

Phillip glanced around the familiar room with a sense of déjà vu. Easing himself down into one of the wing chairs, he noted that little had changed since he was last here.

Hilsman tugged at the knees of his trousers before sitting in the chair opposite, and, as always, came directly to the point. "You said the dream had come back, the one where Becky is calling to you and you can't reach her."

Phillip ran a hand across his bearded chin. "That's only part of my problem. My wife thinks I'm going crazy."

A frown flashed across the doctor's face—he disapproved of the word. "Your wife, the two of you are getting along?"

Phillip smiled wanly. "That's one of the few things that's going right."

"She thinks you're, er, disturbed in some way? How do you feel about that?"

"Disturbed? I'd say she's right. I am."

Hilsman made a steeple with his fingers. "Tell me about it."

"Sam, I'm afraid you're going to think I'm nuts."

"Try me."

Phillip did. When he had finished, the psychiatrist stood and stretched. "Paige witnessed this, er, ceremonial murder also?"

"Yes. She's the one that insisted we report it to the police. Only there weren't any to report it to."

"And you never mentioned to her what you thought you saw on the church door, the movement of the carvings?"

With a shrug, Phillip explained, "That early on I figured I was mistaken, bad light."

"And now?"

"Now I'm not so sure."

"And that crawling noise in your hotel room. You didn't wake her up, tell her about it?"

"We were leaving the next morning. No need to frighten her."

The doctor pressed a finger to his lips. "The first time you've had that dream in quite a while was within hours of that scene in the churchyard, right?"

"Yes."

Hilsman stared at a point some place above Phillip's head, a man putting together a complex scenario. "Seeing what you did and then being attacked would be traumatic for anyone. Stressful, to say the least. Although we don't know the exact effects that stress might have on the mind, I'd say it triggered your dream. That opinion is strengthened by the fact that the dream re-occurred right after your work literally went up in smoke. When I first saw you years ago, you were suffering considerable stress and certain guilt feelings related to the death of your child. Seeing that young woman ripped open in the graveyard, being unable to do anything about it, brought the same emotions to the surface again. It would be my opinion that if additional related stress is absent, the dream and the distress it caused will fade away." Hilsman's face tightened in disapproval. "And I definitely recommend you *not* have any further contact with Professor Devoux."

Phillip shifted in his chair. "All that sounds logical but the dream isn't the worst of it. I mean, I'm frightened over what may happen next."

"Who says anything will?"

Leaning forward in earnestness, Phillip explained, "Sam, even if I believed in coincidence, which I don't, how can you explain *both* engines on the plane quitting at the same time, a doll that nobody has ever seen before, a snake from Africa, and a fire that started itself? Whatever this thing is, whatever is causing these things, isn't going to quit. At least, I don't think so."

Hilsman shook his head. "Obviously I can't explain those events any better than you, but let's try this: Every time one of those things happened, you were, or had been, discussing what happened in Haiti. Or you were thinking of happenings that you related to it. I'd say those thoughts triggered an actual subconscious recollection, bringing on the same stress and making you see things in a somewhat unusual light."

"Sam, I'm a professional journalist. I observe and record facts, not make-believe."

"You're also a human being subject to the same frailties as the rest of us."

"So, what I hear you telling me is that my problem is in my head." Phillip was frustrated. But what had he expected? For Sam Hilsman to perform some mystic incantation to dispel evil spirits? "I tell you, what I said happened. I didn't make it up."

"I have no doubt you believe that, but you'll have to admit that seeing a doll as some sort of evil talisman or being recognized by a snake are somewhat subjective. No, I think if you can put this Haiti incident behind you, forget it, you won't take life's accidental misfortunes as quite so personal." Phillip started to protest, but the doctor continued. "Like yesterday—I couldn't get my car started. It cost me thirty bucks to have someone come jump it off. I was in such a hurry to get here, I hit the garage door, bending a fender. I was two blocks down the street before I realized the bent fender had stuck into the tire, causing a flat. I left the car at the curb and took a cab to work only to find my first appointment had cancelled. I can tell you, if I'd had someone or something to blame, I could have been convinced that some power didn't want me here. It's normal to blame our troubles on forces out of our control. Combined with the shock of what you saw, you've just carried that a little far afield.''

In one last effort, Phillip tried to make him understand. "Sam," he pleaded, "don't you see? The things I've described don't happen. Having a dead battery isn't the same as finding an exotic snake in your yard. Any one of them would be peculiar, maybe impossible. Together they form a pattern and I don't like the shape that pattern is taking. Next time, somebody could get killed.''

"Try starting over on your book, take an assignment that will keep you and your mind busy. I think you'll see that things that go wrong don't seem to be pointed quite so directly at you.''

Standing, Phillip said, "At least you don't think I've gone bonkers.''

"No more so than the rest of the world, no. Please don't hesitate to call. You still have my home number?''

"Yeah. Thanks, Sam.''

Hilsman watched his former patient close the door behind him. The doctor always spaced fifteen minutes between appointments to enjoy a smoke while he dictated his still fresh observations and conclusions into the tape recorder. Selecting an unfiltered cigarette from a silver box, he lit it with a disposable lighter and inhaled deeply as he sat back down. He watched the smoke reach blue fingers toward the ceiling before he exhaled a perfect smoke ring that shimmered across the room. "Paranoid," he said toward the microphone in the bookcase. "With some delusion. It is hoped that Phillip Owens' mental state will prove to be self-healing, for, should it be exacerbated, he might well revert to the deep depression he exhibited when I first treated him. In this case, it is thought that confinement for treatment may become necessary.''

Far to the south, a practitioner of a more sinister art watched. The man was getting out of an automobile now, walking to his dwelling that could have held ten Haitian huts. Now he was passing by the spring, or pond, he kept in his yard. Although she had never seen him draw water from it, he did stand around it and that would be enough. She would get him there, and then the woman would believe and all would be easy. Yes, the pond was the way to reach him. The man was stopping, calling to . . . Who? She could not see, her access to him was fading. Before she could see no longer, she had a brief image of the child running to meet his father.

Behind her there was a rustling, the sound of dry leaves stirring. He was angry, impatient with her failures. ''I will succeed this time,'' she said aloud, speaking the Creole that was her only language.

Undisturbed by the presence that had joined her, she resumed her chant in a voice surprisingly mellow, as unlike her speaking voice as a young girl's is from her grandmother's. If the words had been put into English, they would have been something like:

> Simbi of the springs and ponds o
> Call this *loa*, O father Damballah
> The great Damballah
> The great *loa* Simbi is in the spring.

When she finished, she was alone.

Chapter 12

Case boiled from the school's door with the glee usually reserved for Friday afternoons. He carried no books.

Leaning across the seat to open the car door, Phillip tried to look as stern as possible. "No homework tonight?"

With a smile and a shake of his head, Case climbed in. "Nope. Tomorrow's some kind of teacher's workout."

"Workshop?" Phillip grinned.

"Yes, sir, workshop. Anyway, there's no school and Miss Sweet gave us the time off with no assignments to do."

Phillip cranked the car. "Maybe I ought to go complain, I mean, with what we pay to get you educated, I might not be getting my money's worth."

Case's gaiety was temporarily subdued before he realized his father was kidding. "Aw, one day won't make that much difference. Besides, I can help you around the house."

Phillip rolled his eyes. "Help" from Case produced more work than the task at hand required. Once, when he had his son's assistance, he had been painting the steps to the front porch. The predictable results were that he had spent nearly an hour scrubbing a fidgeting little boy with turpentine to remove the gray splotches that covered small hands and face like some malignant fungus. "What about Randy and Charlie? I'd think the three of you would want to get up a ball game in this beautiful spring weather,'' he suggested hopefully as he pulled out onto Paces Ferry.

Case turned to watch the pillars that marked the entry to the school's grounds disappear around a curve. ''Randy has to go shopping for clothes with his Mom.'' He made a wry face. ''What a pain! And Charlie goes to public school. They don't have the day off.''

Great. Even if Phillip avoided a home project with his son, tomorrow would be a total waste as far as writing was concerned. Although well intentioned, Case's frequent visits to his father's office made any attempt at creative thought futile. And no telling what trouble a seven year old would get into if left alone for a day.

It looked very much like housework was going to be the activity for tomorrow, Case's aid included. Now what task could he find . . . ''Okay,'' he said slowly, ''we'll start getting the pool ready.''

That seemed to carry the least risk. With Phillip close at hand, the worse Case could do was fall in and the child was an excellent swimmer. Phillip had insisted upon his son taking lessons as early as possible.

Devoux's warning sounded in his ears. But the pool? It wasn't much larger than a bathtub, anyway. Besides, on a gorgeous spring day such as this, who could think of witches and evil spells? He had, however, called the Haitian earlier today only to be informed by some haughty woman in the Anthropology Department that Dr. Devoux was out.

''Super!'' Case's enthusiasm was genuine. The uncovering of the pool meant summer (and no school) was near, or at least in sight. The spring ritual of making the pool ready was an event in Case's life second only to the erection of the Christmas tree. In joyous overtones, he asked, ''Any chance we can stop at the McDonald's on the way home?''

"You're pushing your luck, buster," Phillip said with good humor. "Your mother would skin both of us when you didn't eat your dinner. Don't they feed you lunch at that institute?"

"What's an ins'tute?" Case wanted to know. "Is it like a pros'tute?"

Phillip reached over to rumple his son's hair. "What a mind! You can't remember the capital of Canada on your geography test, but you have no trouble with a word you've only heard once."

"Well, is it?"

"Not exactly. An institute is, well, a school, an organization."

Case absorbed this information for a few seconds. "Is Little League a ins'tute?"

"I suppose so. Say, isn't Little League about to start up?"

Case's face wrinkled in a frown. "Not till the last of April."

"That's only a few weeks away."

With the elongated view of time held by the very young, Case shook his head. "Aw, Dad, that's *forever*." He glanced around with sudden attention. "Where're we going?"

"I ordered some books from the main library downtown. They called this morning to say they found them and they are at the branch. I thought I'd pick 'em up on the way home."

The thought of books sapped Case's interest as Phillip parked in front of the modern building. It *did* resemble the reptile house, Phillip confirmed as he cut the ignition. "You want to come in or stay in the car?"

A tough choice. There was nothing to do in the car and Case had been to the dumb old library before. The lady behind the desk always told him how cute he was. Cute!

Like a dumb old girl! Almost as bad, she would show him a bunch of dumb old books about things that he didn't care about, stuff he had to learn in school anyway. The only books he really liked were comics, but she made him feel that if he didn't act interested and take one of the real books home, he would be doing one of the worst things he could, Being Rude to an Adult. Once, though, the stupid book had turned out to be about baseball, or at least a big kid who played a lot of it. Maybe there was another book like that. If she wanted him to take one home, he'd ask. "I'll go with you," he said with sudden good cheer.

While the woman was gone to fetch his father's books, Case glanced around the familiar room. "Dad," he asked, "is a library an 'ins'tute'?"

"Here you are." The librarian deposited four volumes on the countertop.

"Thanks," Phillip said to her before turning to his son. "Yes, I guess a library is an institute."

It was then that Case had an inspiration. "Do pros'tutes work in ins'tutes?"

The lady behind the desk did not ask Case if he wanted to take a book home or even tell him he was cute; she didn't have a chance to. He could tell his dad was trying hard not to laugh, but was in a hurry to do it outside. Case had done it again: he had said something that he would hear Dad and Mom repeat over and over to their friends. And they would laugh just like Dad was now and Case would still not know what was so funny. He decided not to ask about pros'tutes again.

When they got home, Phillip sent Case to change into the oldest jeans he could find. No point in getting good clothes soaking wet or covered in chemicals, two very likely possibilities. Phillip was wrestling a fifty-pound drum of pool chemicals out of the garage when Reid called across the fence, "Looks like you could use some help."

Gratefully, Phillip set the container down. "I'm amazed you're around when I need you. What're you doing home so early?"

"Such a pretty day, I didn't go back after lunch."

Phillip gazed at the fiery azaleas along the fence and noted the pregnant buds on the dogwood trees that soon would become snowy blossoms. Even the sunlight had added that special, gold-green hue of new leaves to this season. He savored the earthy sweet fragrance of things about to come to life again. "Well, come on over here and put your back to the job with me."

"Seems fair enough since Sue and I will enjoy the pool this summer as much as you." Reid vanished into the house so that he could walk out of his front door and across to Phillip's yard.

Phillip was looking at the now barren stems of jonquils, those early promises of spring. He supposed this fall he would have to dig up the bulbs and separate them. His back was to the pool where the cover rippled briefly as though something beneath had brushed against it, something large.

("I will succeed . . .")

"So," Reid said as he walked down the driveway, "I suppose we're going to have Case's much valued assistance?"

Phillip nodded ruefully. "Not only in getting things ready to do the pool tomorrow, but he'll be around to help then, too. No school."

("The great Simbi is coming out of the spring . . .")

With a chuckle Reid stooped to lift the chemicals. "One time he helped you out, you were setting out a rose bush. If I remember correctly, he had half the dirt in your yard on him before the two of you were through."

Phillip grunted as he lifted the other end of the container. "Not only was he a walking sod farm, he managed to turn the hose on himself, too. He was one big mud pie."

"You're a real sport to let him participate, you know? It's good for kids, though, working beside their parents. Builds not only a sense of responsibility, but a bond between them, too."

("Simbi in the spring, o . . .")

"I'm glad to know there's some benefit in it," Phillip puffed.

"Here comes young Mr. Helpful now," Reid noted as Case exploded through the back door.

"Uncle Reid!" Case shrieked in delight, nearly falling down the steps from the deck. He was so intent on his favorite grownup (next to Mom and Dad, of course) that he didn't see the edge of the pool cover lift briefly, ballooning as though a gust of wind had lifted it. But there was no wind.

("She is all wet . . .")

Reid straightened up, setting his half of the burden down. " 'Lo Case. I understand you're paroled from school for the day tomorrow."

Case snickered. " 'Paroled,' like outa jail."

Reid continued in the adult-to-adult tone he preferred to use with children, "How'd you like to spend tomorrow with me? There'll be a lot of kids your age . . ."

Case looked beseechingly at Phillip who protested, "Reid, I can't let you waste a day to entertain . . ."

"What waste? I work at a children's hospital, remember? For the kids that can be up and around, we've got a supervised playground. I have a few patients to see tomorrow and while I'm tending to them, Case will be well cared for. He can help me make my rounds, too, meet a lot of youngsters he'd never get to know otherwise."

"Oh, Dad, please!"

Visions of finishing up an article on the air traffic control situation danced through Phillip's head. He'd completed his research several days ago and the deadline for the piece was moving inexorably closer. "Well, if you're sure he'll be no trouble . . ."

"That's settled, then. Case, I want you ready to roll at eight sharp. We'll eat breakfast in the hospital cafeteria, or at McDonald's, your choice."

"McDonald's." Case didn't have to choose even though he had never been exposed to hospital food.

Phillip shook his head. "Honestly, Reid."

"That's what favorite uncles are for, right, Case? To spoil their nephews?"

Phillip grasped the drum again. "In that case, we won't be using this."

"Hey," Reid said. "To show you what a really good guy I am, I'll help you get the cover off the pool right now."

("Simbi . . .")

On the far side of the pool, out of sight from where the three stood, something reached from under the cover to explore the edge, something black and glistening from the water, something almost like a hand. Almost. As the two men moved towards the pool, it slithered silently back under the cover.

("Simbi in the spring o . . .")

Phillip surveyed the task at hand. "Let's start by pulling the weights off the edges." Rectangular plastic sandbags were used to hold the cover in place so winter rains and winds wouldn't cause it to collapse into the pool. He glanced to where Case was stooping. "Case, you can help with putting the chemicals in once we've got the tarp rolled back."

"Aw, Dad, I can help now."

"You can help by not falling in."

"Tell you what, Case," Reid offered. "You stand at the far end. When your dad and I fold the tarp back, you hold it so it doesn't get in the water. Just be sure you don't, either."

"Wait a minute," Phillip suggested. "Case, would you please get me something long-handled, a shovel or yard rake or something, from the garage? It always helps to have something that will reach if a corner falls into the water," he explained.

Happy to be included, Case bounded for the garden tools in their locker in the garage.

Phillip lifted the corner. "Okay, Reid, if you'd just peel your side toward the other end . . ." He glanced up. "An ax? Case, I asked for something with a long handle."

Reid laughed. "An ax has a long handle, Phillip. Cut the kid some slack."

"Okay," Phillip capitulated, "but be careful, will you, son? I sharpened that thing just last fall and I'd hate to be rushing you to the hospital without an arm or leg." He turned his attention back to his neighbor. "Ready?"

Case carefully put the ax down on the pool's cement apron. "I'll get the other end," he volunteered as he ran to the side opposite his father and Reid.

What happened next occurred in seconds, but Phillip would always see it in the deliberate slow motion of a film, each detail clear. Case slipped and fell. Strange, since the child had been standing still. From where Phillip was, Case seemed to be sliding under the blue tarp, although the little boy was twisting, attempting to find a handhold on the smooth concrete.

It could have been a call for help, it could have been a terrified shriek. Either way, Case was frightened and struggling to pull away from something as though being drawn toward it. Reid moved first. With charging steps, he was behind Case, his huge hands under the child's arms, pulling.

A second cry brought Phillip to Reid's side. He reached an arm around his son's waist and tugged. "What th' fuck . . . ?"

"He's caught on something," Reid gasped, blue ridges of veins on his muscular neck bulging from the strain. "Something that's dragging him under."

Phillip could feel the strength of it. Despite the efforts of two large men, Case was being pulled forward into the water. For a second he had a vision of his son being torn in two. Then he saw another mind picture, Becky, lying on the bottom, her blond hair swaying around her child's face. The thought gave extra power to his efforts. This pool had killed Becky, now it was . . .

He became aware that Reid was screaming in his ear and Becky faded. "Can you hold on while I pull the tarp back, see what's got him?" Reid was shouting.

Phillip nodded and grunted through clenched teeth, "I'll try."

"Daddy," Case was groaning, "Daddy, help me!"

Phillip fought his mind's effort to replay Becky at the bottom of the pool and felt his sneakers slip across the concrete, closer to the edge, closer to . . .

"You're hurting me," Case moaned.

"Shit!" Reid yelped.

Phillip looked up through the sweat that was stinging his eyes to see Reid gaping into the pool. He forced himself to follow that astounded gaze. At first he saw nothing in the water made opaque green by months of untreated algae. Slowly, his rational mind fighting him, he made out a form in the murk. Something vaguely human was roiling the water, something with arms that were extended to grip Case's foot. In dazed fascination, he watched a fishlike tail break the surface and slap downward, giving Case another snatch forward, this time jerking the frightened child knee deep into the water.

Instinctively, Phillip heaved backward and he saw what was holding his son: a hand, black and glistening. Before it slipped back into the scummy water, he thought he'd seen scales and webbing between fingers. He shook his head as though to clear it and swallowed down the terror that filled his throat. "The ax, Reid," he shouted. "Get the ax!"

Reid needed no further coaching. With two giant steps he was beside Phillip, a medieval headsman about to do his duty. "Where? I mean I don't want to cut a leg off."

Another tug on the now listless Case brought Phillip's feet to the edge. "I'll pull, you take a cut at that, that, whatever it is," Phillip panted. "Get ready."

Throwing his full weight backward, Phillip gave a pull he feared would dislocate every bone in his son's small body. He heard the swish of the ax blade above his own frantic grunt. His lunge carried him to the cement, knocking the air from his lungs. Before he could breathe again, he was forcing himself upright. Beside him, Case, eyes fixed in a limitless stare, moaned. He appeared intact.

"Is he okay?" Reid was bending over both of them, concern knotting his broad face.

Phillip drank in air like a man stranded in a desert might gulp water. "Yes, I think." He clasped the still form next to him, gratified to feel the shallow breathing. "Case, Case?"

The child clutched him with a strength far out of proportion to his small size, his eyes still wide.

"Case?" Phillip was fighting the warm numbness that is the aftermath of total panic. "Case?" He shook the small body gently.

Reid hurried over to examine the child. "I'd guess he's

having some sort of shock reaction,'' he suggested. ''Not to mention the possibility of some real physical injury from being nearly pulled apart. Let's get him to the hospital.''

Phillip staggered to his feet, never lessening his hold on the still burden in his arms. ''Everything's gonna be okay,'' he murmured. ''No sweat, Case.''

''I'll go get my car—'' Reid stopped in mid sentence. ''Jesus!''

Reid was staring at the pool's apron, at an object black and slimy. Despite his rush to get help for Case, Phillip was transfixed by the scaled, webbed appendage that was oozing a puslike liquid from the severed joint. Reid gingerly flipped it over with the handle of the ax he still carried. ''What in the hell is *that*?''

''It's part of whatever had Case,'' Phillip moaned with the horror of one realizing his nightmare had not been a dream. ''You chopped it off that thing in the pool.''

Reid gave Phillip a searching look. ''I'd hoped I was just seeing things—a shadow in that murky water. Are you telling me that you saw . . .''

''Let's get Case to the emergency room. I'll tell you a few things on the way.''

As she often did in good weather, Paige elected to walk the two blocks home from the MARTA station down 15th Street. On such a beautiful afternoon, she had expected to see Phillip and Case playing catch in the backyard. Instead, Reid and Phillip were grim-facedly watching the water being pumped out of an open pool. Odd. Phillip had explained to her that cleaning the pool's water by chemicals was both easier and more economical than draining it empty. Even more peculiar, Reid had an ax on his shoulder and Phillip was cradling the double-barreled shotgun he used for duck hunting. Both men seemed intent on the receding level of green water. Men! And they said women were irrational! Here were two adult males staring into the family swimming pool, prepared to do battle. "Hello, boys," she called cheerfully, "I don't think you're going to find the Loch Ness monster in there."

She was greeted by stony stares. They were not amused. She sighed. Phillip had probably seen another snake, one that had somehow gotten into the pool, and, with typical male overreaction, had decided to take no chances. Put a firearm in a man's hand and he's convinced there's no problem he can't solve. A sex of John Waynes and Clint Eastwoods. Still, two grown men, armed for war with some small creature that had the misfortune to fall into the pool . . . But where was Case? Her hand stopped midway in removing the pin that held her long hair in a chignon and she quickened her stride up the driveway. If there was any excitement, her son would at least be spectating from the safety of the deck. Reid and Phillip didn't look very happy, either. The panic hit her in the stomach with the force of a physical blow. Case! What if they were looking for Case!

Her voice cracked with repudiation. "Where's Case?"

Both looked at her with expressions that did nothing to calm her as she glanced from the one to the other before Reid spoke up. "He's all right, Paige."

She was far from satisfied. Reid was using the same tone he employed when Sue had one of her emotional wackouts. And she didn't feel any better when Reid slipped an arm around her elbow and led her to a seat on the back deck. "I want to see Case," she said. "Where is he?"

"Upstairs asleep. He had a little accident." He put a hand on her shoulder, pushing her gently back into the metal chair. "He's got a couple of fractured ribs and a dislocated hip. The doctor sedated him."

She could feel the anger flowing in to replace the panic,

an emotional changing of tides. "And what the hell were you and Phillip doing while my child was breaking ribs and dislocating a hip?"

Reid stood quietly for a moment before he spoke. "I'll let Phillip tell you, but let me point one thing out before you get harsh with him: he lost one child in this pool and he came damn near to losing another today. If I were you, I'd worry a lot more about what sort of effect this afternoon's going to have on Phillip. We already know Case is at least physically okay."

"At least physically?"

"After Phillip tells you what happened, I think you'll understand why, as a child psychologist, I am concerned about Case's emotional reaction. I'll drop by tonight to check up on him." He turned to call to Phillip. "You want to tell Paige?"

"You tell her. She won't believe me. I've tried."

"Now look," Paige began, "if this is some more of that voodoo hocus-pocus . . ."

Reid regarded her solemnly before he reached for a newspaper bundle on the nearby table. With a tug on a corner of the wrapping, a dull black object rolled in front of her. She smelled a sour, fishy odor that made her wrinkle her nose before she inspected it closer. It seemed to be a crude replica of a hand.

"What is that thing?" She started to touch it and then drew back.

"Listen to what I'm going to say," Reid urged in his most clinical, Sue-soothing voice. "Listen and I'll explain."

"I want to see Case first," she insisted.

"Fine. I'll be right here."

The child looked somehow smaller in his bed, Paige thought. Maybe it was because he was doubled into the fetal position or because he had his thumb in his mouth, two postures she had not seen in several years. The regular rise and fall of the covers assured her he was breathing, a reassurance made necessary by the pallor of his face. Leaning over the bed, she ran a loving hand across his cool cheek. She leaned over to rearrange the bedclothes and stopped with a sudden intake of breath. There was an angry bruise on Case's left ankle, already as dark as a thunderhead against the white skin. She let the sheet hover softly as it settled back into place. Mr. Phillip Owen had some explaining to do, all right. While he and Reid were playing soldiers, Case had gotten hurt. She felt the anger start to rise again as she left the room. No, wait. Phillip had been the most responsible of fathers, frequently too protective of Case. He had even been reluctant to let the child sign up for Little League for fear of inadequate supervision. No, if Case had been injured, she'd bet it had not been because Phillip had been negligent. There was something strange going on, for sure. And Phillip's fixation on voodoo didn't help. Well, she'd listen to what Reid had to say. Surely *he* would have a logical explanation.

"You don't expect me to believe . . ." Paige sputtered when Reid had finished.

He shrugged. "Believe whatever you want. I've told you what Phillip and I saw." He poked at the thing on the table gingerly, noting how it had already shriveled to half its original size. "And this didn't exactly fall off a tree."

Paige shuddered. Logical, orderly life in twentieth-century America wrestled with that dark corner of the mind where strange things lurk, things so old and so desired to be forgotten that there are no longer words for them. She glanced around her now as though half anticipating she would find something creepy peering at her. "What do you make of it, Reid?"

Again he shrugged. "I don't. I just know what we saw and what almost happened to Case. You know Phillip thinks it has to do with—"

"But Case wasn't in Haiti with us," she insisted.

The conversation was interrupted as Phillip called out. "Pool's empty. Nothing, just like I guessed."

Paige still couldn't accept what had happened, but somehow she was disappointed the full proof of it had not been found—the natural preference of a known horror over one not seen.

"Hi, neighbors!" The call came from Reid's driveway where Sue was getting out of her car. "Having a party? I'll be right over!"

Reid stood, his face weary. "I hope you don't mind, but I guess I ought to go. I don't want Sue to . . ."

Paige nodded. "You can count on it. We won't mention any of this to her."

Reid smiled without humor. "You know she's easily upset."

"Thanks." Phillip came up to the deck to shake his friend's hand warmly with a tenderness that always seemed out of place between big men. "I can't thank you enough."

A flicker of a twinkle sparked in Reid's eyes. "Then don't try. I'll be over here after supper to check on Case. With a little luck, he'll forget the whole thing in a couple of days."

Phillip started to ask if Reid really believed that but settled for, "See you then."

Phillip and Paige watched their next-door neighbor until he reached his front door before Phillip said, "Well, do you believe me now?"

Paige hugged herself against a chill that was not entirely due to the early evening's cool. "I . . . I don't know what to believe. I grew up where things were taken care of by rules. If there was a problem, you went to somebody—a doctor, a lawyer—who understood how those rules worked. Now you're asking me to accept something that those rules say can't happen. That's a tall order.''

"You promised that if I saw Doctor Hilsman and he didn't put me away, you'd at least listen to me.''

She reached for his hand and squeezed it. "I'm doing more than listening. Phillip, I'm scared.''

"Scared'' wasn't exactly accurate. She was terrified. Her defenses were crumbling about her, the blocks of her beliefs no longer held by logic's firm cement. All the other incidents could, possibly, be explained away. But this slimy, foul-smelling hand came from a creature out of a world that was not hers, where the rules she knew didn't apply. It was as though she had been transported somehow into a realm of witches and demons. She could no longer doubt, she must believe. A rational mind could not deny the physical evidence, no matter how irrational that evidence might be. Her only hope was that she was dreaming. And she knew she was awake.

He put an arm around her. "I'm scared, too, but you've given me a good idea. You said something about going to someone who understood how the rules worked. That's what I've done.''

She looked up at him quizzically. "Oh?''

He told her about Devoux, finishing with, "And I've been trying to get a hold of him today. Whatever the next step is, he'll know.'' He noted her skepticism. "What else would you suggest, stringing garlic and crucifixes around the house?''

"No,'' she whispered, "I don't have any suggestions. I'm just frightened. At first I was frightened because I thought the man I loved was coming loose at the hinges, now I'm frightened because I don't think he is. You've been right all along . . .''

Phillip didn't sleep that night. Instead of submitting to the dream he knew was awaiting him, he sat at the bedside table, reading there because logical, rational Paige insisted he not leave the room. He read the major parts of three volumes on Haiti, voodoo, and those who purported to understand it. He read with an intensity as though his life depended on it, pausing only once when a groggy Case stumbled into the room on the crutch the doctor had given him and climbed into bed with his mother without opening his eyes. The practice had been forbidden since the child was two, but tonight Phillip said nothing. He simply returned to his reading.

Failure again? No, not exactly, the old woman told herself. She could feel the white woman's fear as though it were twisting, writhing in her own chest. *The woman believed.* Now all that remained was to find the opportunity to destroy both man and woman, a task much simplified by the terror that the sight of Simbi's hand had planted in the white woman's breast. A terror that would grow and flourish like a weed. There would be no more failures now, her senses were certain.

Chapter 13

Reid Letts was worried. Whatever that thing was in his neighbors' pool, it was enough to scare anybody, but it had disappeared or, perhaps, managed to squeeze into the drain and flow out with the water. That was hardly a comforting thought: having that creature swimming around the city sewer system was more frightening to him as an adult than all those alligators he'd believed were down there when he was a kid. The tale some older child had told him about the people who bought souvenir live gators in Florida and then flushed them down the john had made him wary of taking a shit for years. Now he'd be thinking almost the same thing every time he went to the head. Whip it out for a quick leak and that black hand reaches up and grabs you where it really hurts.

But that wasn't what was disturbing him this golden spring morning. Earlier, he'd called Paige and renewed his offer to take Case with him today. No, she'd said, the little boy wouldn't let her out of his sight, breaking into almost hysterical crying (her word, not his) when he was left alone even for a minute or two. Reid could believe it. Last night, Case had stared up at him from the bed with glassy eyes that held little recognition. Could have been the pain killers.

Reid hoped so. As soon as he finished the cup of coffee he was drinking, he'd go back over there and form an opinion as to whether therapy might be in order. Anyway, Paige was taking a day off from her practice to stay with her son. Reid peered toward the Owens' house. Even in this dazzling sunshine the old house had an ominous appearance. The Victorian architecture featured a roofline that ran at fifty different angles, giving the building a wild, disheveled appearance. It missed being hideous by a narrow margin, a perfect setting for a murder—or a horror story. Christ, maybe the place was haunted. It looked the part, and yesterday had certainly made him think something weird was going on to say the least. Haunted or not, he would be on his way over there in a few minutes.

But what about Sue? He heard the shower upstairs being turned off. Now she would begin the hour of makeup application and fooling with her hair. He could burn the house down and it wouldn't tear her away from her set of mirrors until she was satisfied. For once, he was thankful for her obsessive vanity. She wouldn't notice he was gone, thank God. If he had to explain that his services were needed over there, she'd keep at him until she found out what had happened yesterday. That would do it—she would *freak out*. He paid enough in shrinks' bills now. No, he'd be real careful getting out of the house this morning.

His thoughts returned to his small patient. God, but he loved that kid, the son he would never have. The very thought of a figure thickened by pregnancy sent Sue running to the toilet to throw up. Case. With any luck and a great deal of love, the child would get over the incident with that astounding resiliency of the very young. The memory of that thing trying to drag him into the pool would probably hang around in his subconscious, waiting for a chance to bubble up, sewage from a ruptured mental septic tank; but it could possibly fade and evaporate. In Reid's experience, the thing kids never seemed to get over was abuse from those they loved and trusted. A violent beating from a parent could fuck up a young mind more than all the weird things the world had to offer.

No, Case wasn't what worried Reid. It was Phillip. He'd seen the wild, almost demented gleam in his friend's eyes last night. And the man wasn't acting rationally. And now Paige was acting strangely. First, there was this gory murder in Haiti, then this illogical connection between events that had no correlation without an impossible hypothesis. Admittedly, having some black, malevolent mermaid, or whatever, appear in your family swimming pool wasn't comforting, no. But there had to be some explanation. A healthy mind demanded one. Modern, rational people didn't believe in voodoo spells, and definitely not in one that reached all the way from Haiti. But Phillip did. He was busy researching the subject with the fervor a college student might have in finishing a term paper on time.

A wounded mind, like a torn muscle, never regained full strength, and Phillip's mind had been wounded severely. As though the glass window were a TV screen, Reid saw himself making the phone call that Margaret had been too incoherent to make herself. Phillip had been . . . Where? New York? Chicago? It didn't matter. Reid had been the one who'd had to tell his best friend that his daughter had drowned, the one who'd had to meet the flight. Not likely Reid would ever forget Phillip's face as he came through the gate: eyes that were webbed with red set in a face that had aged twenty years. Phillip had demanded to see his daughter, despite Reid's insistence that tomorrow would be soon enough. The sight of Phillip's tall frame collapsing to its knees before the pitifully small casket was devastating. And the anger! At Reid's suggestion, Margaret had stayed with friends while her husband's near homicidal fury dissipated in a sea of whiskey. Reid had tried to comfort his friend, only to have the door literally slammed in his face. And then he knew the dreams had begun. Although Phillip had not witnessed it, he began to see his daughter drown, to suffer the agony and guilt of being unable to save her. That was when Reid had suggested, then demanded, Phillip consult Sam Hilsman.

Now Reid was afraid, frightened not of some water monster his brain was already trying to deny existed, but that the sight of Case almost drowning in that same pool could really fuck up Phillip's head. This morning Reid would not only give Case a good looking over, but Case's father, too. Reid wasn't going to lose his old racquet ball partner, no sir*ee*. Nor was he going to risk Paige being around if Phillip *really* flipped out. He'd look for the signs his training had taught him and he'd . . . He glanced at his watch. Shit! He'd best get on over there if he was going to be back by the time Sue got downstairs.

Paige was on the telephone, its coiled spring cord tethering her to the phone, limiting her to pacing the width of the clay tiles of the kitchen floor as she gestured to an unseen audience. Reid had to tap on the window twice before she looked up from her conversation and gave him a tired smile. Opening the door without skipping a word, she pointed to the wheezing Mr. Coffee beside the range top. Reid nodded his thanks before circling the butcher block table to reach for the cabinet where he knew cups would be neatly spaced like china tombstones.

". . . and today's the deadline for filing the answer and motions in McCarren. They're on my desk." Paige stared into space, checking her mental list. "I hope I'll be back in tomorrow, but if not, you'll have to handle the GM brief. The draft should be finished . . ."

Reid lifted the pot and poured a black stream into his cup, savoring the robust, almost bitter aroma of the Brazilian coffee Phillip ordered specially. It would be sinful, Phillip often said, to dilute such strength with sugar or cream. Well, Phillip wasn't here, was he? Feeling slightly guilty, Reid helped himself to the refrigerator, rummaging around until he found a plastic milk carton. Christ, the oily black stuff in his cup could dissolve a spoon unless he cut it with cream, milk, anything. First blowing gently, he took a sip and felt his mouth squeeze into a wince. He was drinking battery acid, for Chrissake! As Paige continued to instruct the anonymous lawyer on the other end of the line, Reid glanced at the framed menus that hung in a line above the cabinets. Phillip bitched about the travel requirements of his profession, but from where Reid stood, it looked like old Phillip ate pretty well while abroad. He squinted at the neat block letters on heavy paper that listed the offerings of the Grill Room at the Savoy of London. To one side, indecipherable script detailed a lunch at Roger Verge's Moulin Mouges, on the other, a bilinqual page from Raffles of Singapore.

Paige placed the wall phone back on its hook with a determined click. "Sorry. I had to get some things done since I'm not going to work today."

Grateful for an excuse to leave his coffee undrunk, Reid glanced at her. She was wearing one of Phillip's shirts over a pair of jeans. With no makeup and her hair in a ponytail, she could have been mistaken for a college sophomore, and a very attractive one at that. Hell, Sue couldn't have gotten one leg in those pants and he couldn't remember the last time she came downstairs before completing the daily makeup ritual. Not coveting thy neighbor's wife wasn't always easy, he thought before he forced his mind to the reason he was here. "How's the patient?"

She looked at him with solemn eyes. "If you mean Case, he's in his room asleep. He had a pretty restless night. Phillip's in his office on the third floor, talking to some expert on voodoo over at the University. I can't even get him to come down for breakfast."

"Sounds serious." Immediately, Reid regretted the flippant remark.

She sighed. "Reid, I'm worried about him. He's obsessed with the idea that there's some sort of black magic involved in all this. Remember, I met him right after his divorce. He was still in therapy because of Becky's death. He seems more, more distant, like his mind is somewhere else, than he did then." Whether to preserve a veneer of normalcy or because the words would stimulate her own fears, she decided not to mention that her husband had every reason to act abnormally. The admission that she knew Phillip had been right all the time would somehow bring that dark world of voodoo closer, lend it strength.

"Since Case is still sleeping, I won't bother him, at least not right away. Since I'm here, I'll go see Phillip."

Phillip turned from his desk to survey Reid through red-rimmed eyes that peered out from a haggard face. The man looks like he's been on a drinking binge, Reid observed, but he said, "Find any answers from your witch doctor?"

Phillip ran a hand across his bearded chin. "Surprisingly enough, yes. He's hardly a witch doctor. He's got a Ph.D. He's Dr. Peter Devoux, an anthropologist teaching over at the University. I've called for an appointment and he'll see me this afternoon."

Reid studied his friend's face. "You think that's wise, leaving Case right now? I mean, the kid had a hell of an upsetting experience."

Phillip stood slowly, the effort of an old man. "Reid, I've *got* to see this man Devoux again. He came from Port-au-

Prince, apparently got on the wrong side of Duvalier. I can read on the subject all day, but I've got to find out what to *do*. If I can't end this, this curse or whatever it is . . .'' His voice trailed off and his expression was that of a mendicant.

"You're certain there *is* some sort of hex or curse?" Careful here, Reid thought. An argument could send him off the deep end.

Phillip collapsed back into the uncomfortable-looking chair. "I'm not certain about anything other than the fact that I've got to fight this thing. Devoux knows the subject. I know leaving Case and Paige right now might not sound like a hot idea, but what choice do I have?"

Reid bit back the urge to suggest psychotherapy. You didn't tell a deeply disturbed and frightened man he was nuts, particularly if he was your best friend. "Tell you what: I'll take Case with me just like we planned. I know he's still sore and he'll have to hobble around on that crutch the doc gave him yesterday, but he'll enjoy it. Besides, I can observe him all day, make sure that, er, incident isn't disturbing him abnormally. Hell, I'm giving him thousands of dollars worth of psychological treatment for free, how can you pass up a deal like that?"

Phillip managed a smile that looked out of place. "You're a true friend. With Case gone, Paige can go to work. She should be safe there." He grew serious. "Reid, I know you think I've gone round the bend with this thing, but there's so much in what Devoux says that dovetails with what's happened." His tone quickened with excitement. "Remember my telling you about that guy at the airport in Cap-Haïtien, the one with the Abe Lincoln hat? He's Baron Samedi, the *loa*, or spirit, of the dead, complete with hat, cutaway coat, and pipe!"

Without thinking, Reid took a step back. "You're telling

me you saw some sort of evil spirit?'' This was worse than he had thought.

"Ask Paige," Phillip said defensively. "She saw him, too, right before the engines stopped."

"I remember you mentioning it," Reid admitted, "but that doesn't mean some native wasn't parading around in costume."

Holding up his hands in a gesture of capitulation, Phillip declined to argue. "Have it your way. You could be right. All I know is that if there is an answer, a solution, this guy Devoux warned me about fire and water, and look what happened: my manuscript mysteriously catches fire and would have burned the house down. And that thing in the pool. I'm telling you, Reid, if anybody knows what to do, Devoux does."

So Phillip had already been consulting with this Devoux guy about black magic or whatever. Not good. What Reid thought and said were not the same. "So now Case and Paige are taken care of for the day. Go see your man."

Jesus, Reid thought, I hope this Devoux character isn't some sort of a witch man, part of the lunatic fringe college campuses draw like flies to honey. If the man was a straight shooter, maybe he could convince Phillip that all this voodoo bullshit doesn't really exist, but it doesn't sound like it. "I'll go wake Case up and give him his marching orders. Why don't you come down and show Paige you're still alive?"

Case came awake with a start, glancing around his room with the frightened eyes of a small animal sensing a nearby predator. When he saw Reid, he smiled tentatively. "Hi, Uncle Reid."

Reid tried to ignore the small face pinched in fear and pain. "Hi, yourself, you lazy blob! We're supposed to leave here in fifteen minutes and I come over here to find you still in the sack! Get in gear!''

Case pulled himself to a sitting position. "You mean I can still go?''

"Why not?''

Case stared at him blankly as though searching for the answer. "I—I thought I'd have to stay in bed all day . . ." His small voice trailed off.

Reid turned toward the door. "I'll be downstairs.''

"*No*! Er, Uncle Reid, would you mind staying while I get dressed?'' Case was fighting back tears, determined to be a man in front of Uncle Reid. Only girls cried when they were scared.

With two steps, Reid was across the room, ripping open the curtains to let sunlight probe every corner with merry, golden fingers. He sat down on the side of the bed, studying Case carefully. Now was the time to get a good reading of the child's mental state. "I need to go downstairs to talk to your mother.''

Again Case cast a frightened look around his room. "*Please!* I'll be ready real quick, I promise.'' With an effort, he put one foot on the floor, dragging his stiff leg behind him as he reached for the miniature crutch leaning against the wall.

Showing an unusual interest in the array of Walt Disney drawings above the head of the bed, Reid asked casually, "Case, why do you want me to stay?''

Case turned clumsily, pivoting on the crutch. Its rubber tip squeaked on the wooden floor. He stared at the floor. "I dunno, I just don't want you to go.''

"Afraid, maybe?''

The small boy hesitated for an instant, embarrassed that anyone, particularly Uncle Reid, would think he was a scaredy-cat. "Maybe,'' he admitted in an almost whisper.

Reid smiled warmly. "Case, everybody is afraid of things once in a while, including me. It's nothing to be ashamed of."

Unconvinced, Case wanted to know, "What're you scairt of?"

"You didn't know I'm terrified of spiders? Ugh! When I see one, I want to get as far away from it as possible." Reid managed a realistic shudder.

A tiny smile tugged at Case's lips, became a full grown grin, and matured into a snicker. The thought of tiny little spiders, like the ones he collected in jars sometimes, scaring Uncle Reid was funny. With the imagination that brightens childhood, he summoned up a picture of Uncle Reid—maybe the biggest, strongest man in the world—cowering in a corner as a daddy longlegs made its way indifferently past on its way to the market or wherever daddy longlegs go. The vision disappeared to be replaced with the very real memory of that black, slimy hand around his ankle, trying to pull him into the pool, and he felt his lower lip begin to quiver. "You're not afraid of that thing in the pool?"

"Case, we all tend to be frightened of things we don't understand, don't know about." Reid searched for an example and found one. "You don't like to go to the doctor's, right?"

Puzzled, Case nodded agreement.

"Now, why do you suppose you'd not want to see a nice man like Dr. Stein? I'll tell you: sometimes he has to give you a shot and it *hurts*. The reason you get, er, nervous about going to his office is because you don't know whether he's just going to look you over and kid with you or if he's going to get out that big long needle. If you knew ahead of time there wouldn't be any shots, you'd be willing to see him every day, I'll bet. Now, we don't know anything about what that was in the pool, whether or not it was trying to hurt you, really, do we?''

If Uncle Reid said it, it must be true. ''No, sir.''

''If we knew what that was, it might be like a lion or a tiger, something we're not going to get near because it's dangerous, but not something to be afraid of.''

''But you're scairt of spiders,'' Case protested. ''An' you know what they are.''

''Aha!'' Reid lifted a finger to signal his point was made. ''So, I make sure there aren't any around.'' He made an exaggerated search of the bedclothes and, on mincing tiptoe, went to peer into the bathroom. Holding a finger against his lips to signal silence, he stooped to peer under the bed, in the toy box, and behind two chairs. By now, Case was giggling. Lifting his brows to make his eyes large with discovery, Reid announced, ''Guess what! No spiders, lions, tigers, or critters from the pool!''

Case maintained a precarious balance on his crutch, shaking with laughter. ''You didn't look in the closet,'' he gasped.

Reid scowled. ''You think there's a spider in there?''

Case shook his head, his merriment dissolving into hiccoughs.

With a snatch, Reid opened the closet door. ''Nothing here either!''

Case became serious. ''I guess I'll just have to look around not to be scairt.''

Reid agreed. ''Case, grownups only stop looking under their beds because they're more afraid of what other grownups will say than they are about what might be under there.''

''You're certainly philosophical for so early in the morning.'' Paige was standing in the doorway with a smile wrinkling her face.

Reid pointed to the bathroom. "Go on, Case, we've got to get this show on the cotton-picking road!"

The two adults watched the small figure hobble to the bath before Paige spoke. "I heard him laughing! Reid, you're marvelous!"

She brushed his cheek with her lips and he got a faint whiff of her musky, woman smell. It didn't do a thing to keep those unneighborly thoughts out of his head.

"Like Jimmy Buffet says, 'That's my job.' By the way, Case's going to work with me today so I can keep an eyeball on him. Phillip's driving over to Athens to see some anthropologist, so you may as well go to work."

The smile vanished. "An anthropologist? About . . ."

"Voodoo, yes."

"It may help," she said noncommittally.

Reid became serious. "Maybe it's time we all started thinking about it. Whatever that was in the pool wasn't anything I've ever seen before and it sure wasn't there for a swim."

"You believe that there's some sort of . . . of supernatural force?"

Shaking his head slowly, Reid said, "You saw that hand, claw—whatever it was. There's no denying Case's injuries. I'm scared."

"You're not alone," Paige said with a shudder.

Chapter 14

Peter Devoux leaned across his desk, dragging the sleeves of his linen jacket and leaving snakelike tracks in the dust that always seemed to cover the desktop. "Although I am, of course, delighted to see you, Mr. Owens, I am truly sorry to hear what has happened. I hope your son will be all right soon."

Phillip nodded wearily. "Thanks. I just don't understand. You guessed that we—Paige and I—committed some sort of sacrilege by interrupting the voodoo ceremony and that's why all these things keep happening, right?"

"That is indeed my opinion, yes."

"But neither Case nor poor old Rhett, the dog, had anything to do with it."

Devoux hesitated. To explain all could be dangerous, but to withhold all now would be disastrous. It was clear deSault was not going to give up. "I find that significant and will address it shortly. Even more significant is how this woman is managing to exercise her powers, something you must understand if you are to rid yourself of her curse or spell. She is using your mind. It is only through your mind that she can touch you."

"That's what my psychiatrist told me, it was in my mind."

"Not *in*, but *through*. There is a great difference. Each time you experienced one of these, er, happenings, voodoo was apparently in your thoughts. You were still thinking of the ritual murder when your plane's engines quit. Was it in your mind when you came home to find the doll, the gris-gris?"

Phillip nodded. "As a matter of fact, yes. I'd just had a discussion on the subject. And I *was* thinking about that weird doll, what did you call it?"

"A gris-gris. A *hounan* uses such a thing to announce that he has placed a curse on his victim. It's frequently sufficient in itself to cause such terror that the victim dies on the spot."

"Yeah. Well, I was still wondering where the gris-gris came from when the snake appeared. My wife and I were discussing that when my manuscript caught fire, and I had just checked out some books on voodoo when that thing tried to snatch my son. Are you telling me this woman can funnel all those things through my mind?"

"Precisely. Only when you are thinking of some related subject, though."

The idea of a Vulcan mind-meld with some sort of a demon was unsettling, to say the least. "So my only defense is not to think about that stuff, like turning something into gold by not thinking of a hippopotamus."

"That's it."

"You could have told me before." There was accusation in the tone.

"Would it have done any good to try to force her from your thoughts?"

"No," Phillip admitted, "but what about my son and the dog? Like I said, they weren't in Haiti and I doubt either of them were thinking about anything related to it."

"You misunderstand. It is only necessary for *you* to open your mind to her. It is the vehicle through which she can operate."

"But why did she attack them?"

"As I said, I find that significant. I don't think she would go to the trouble of harming either intentionally. I would guess she meant to strike at you or your wife. Perhaps at this distance her abilities are not as strong as they would be in Haiti where everyone believes in them, hence giving her total power."

Phillip ran a hand across his chin. "You mean, if I were in, say, New York, she couldn't reach me?"

Devoux nodded. "Perhaps. I do know that had you stayed in the area around Cap-Haïtien, she could have destroyed you."

"Then why didn't she, before I left?"

Devoux smiled. "I suspect a strong spell, like a strong stew, takes a while to get together. She would have had to summon whatever *loas* she needed and *loas* do not always come immediately when summoned, even by Marie deSault."

Phillip was silent, forming the question he had to ask. "If I do nothing other than try and move out of her range, as it were, do you suppose she would finally give up?"

"Would you be willing to take that risk, waiting for her to strike again?"

Phillip slowly shook his head. "No, I guess not. But what can I do now?"

Poor Mr. Owens. He could certainly use a night's sleep. He would lose many more. "You must destroy her," Devoux concluded.

Phillip wiggled himself straight in his chair. "Destroy? How? A stake through the heart?"

"I said 'destroy,' not kill." Devoux inhaled deeply, wondering if this big man across the desk had the courage to attempt what he was about to suggest. "In theory, at least, there is a way."

Phillip had a feeling he wasn't going to like what he was about to hear. "And it is?"

"Confront her, stare her down with your mind firmly set on other things. If she cannot harm you face to face, the *loas* who do her bidding will no longer respect her, nor will they serve her again. She will have lost her power entirely."

"Has anyone ever succeeded in doing that with one of those *hounans*?"

"I've heard of such a thing happening once, I believe in Jacmel, but that *hounan* did not have nearly the power this one does."

Both men were silent, alone with their thoughts. Finally, Phillip sighed deeply. "I guess I don't have a lot of choice, do I?"

Sadly, Devoux shook his head. "None that I can see."

Phillip slowly rose, extending a hand. "Thank you, Dr. Devoux. You've been most helpful once again."

"Good luck," Devoux replied softly. "And remember: you must totally close your mind to her, like shutting off a pipeline. One stray thought about anything related to her or voodoo and . . ."

"I understand." Phillip turned and walked down the hall.

Sadly, Devoux watched him go. Phillip Owens was a nice man, a talented writer. Devoux liked him, and what was going to happen was something Devoux would not have wished on even the hated *Tontons*. Just before Phillip started down the stairs, Devoux called out, "Wait, Mr. Owens!"

Phillip turned, a questioning look on his broad face.

The two men continued to look at each other, each seeming to expect the other to say something, until Devoux spoke. "Er, Mr. Owens, perhaps I may be able to supply a small portion of help."

Taking a step closer, Phillip cocked his head. "Oh? How is that?"

Devoux swallowed hard, rethought what he had in mind, and spoke with that courage possessed by so many men of small stature. "I have some time off now that spring break is here. I would like to go with you."

Phillip was unsure he had heard correctly. "Go with me? Why? The thought of meeting that woman scares me shitless."

Another American idiom, "shitless." The prospect of facing Marie deSault had the exact opposite effect on Devoux. He glanced up and down the hall. If Miss Baird heard what he was about to say, she would trumpet it all over the department, if not the entire campus, as proof he was unfit to teach kindergarten, let alone college. "If you don't mind returning to my office . . ."

When the two men had reseated themselves, Devoux made certain the door was closed. He gathered his thoughts and re-organized what he was about to say. "I could tell you that witnessing a *hounan* at work would be such a coup that any anthropologist would leap at the opportunity."

"But that's not the real reason?"

The professor shook his head slowly as though denying the existence of an unpleasant fact. "No, it is not."

"Why, then? Why would you risk that woman's anger? You've just heard my story."

"I'm not sure, Mr. Owens, but I must go with you. For one reason, I could not, in good conscience, allow you to face such power, about which you understand little, alone. I feel that because I am Haitian, I have a better chance to defeat her."

Phillip's journalistic insight told him he was not hearing everything. "And that's not the whole reason, either."

"No, it is not. If I tell you the rest, you will only think

less of me. I have observed that Americans tend to distrust those who claim to be acting from unselfish motives."

Sitting back in his chair, Phillip stretched out his legs, a gesture of one preparing to listen at length. "If we're going to face that woman together, I'd just as soon know why you put yourself there."

Devoux's eyes, magnified by his glasses, narrowed. "Very well. Stop me if I bore you, Mr. Owens."

Phillip put up a hand. "And make that 'Phillip,' if you please. I'll call you 'Peter,' or would you prefer 'Pete'?"

Devoux thought for a moment. Peter. Pete. These Americans participated in ritual slaughter of formalities, those sharp edges that most of the world insisted on keeping in its relationships. Still, this *was* America and he was going to be travelling with an American. Best to do it the American way. Besides, no one had called Devoux by his first name in a long time. The idea had a certain warmth of camaraderie about it. "Pete. Make it Pete, Phillip. Now, I was . . ."

"Telling me why you're willing to enter the lion's den with me."

The small black face wrinkled in pleasure, looking very much like a prune with glasses. "Well, now, I shall begin at the beginning. I was born near a small town on Haiti's south coast. We were poor as was everyone else. Never enough to eat, wrong diet, no time to do the things most children do, for we had to work to eat. At four, I was wielding a machete in our small cane·field, my brothers and sisters the same. But there were two things we feared more than the hunger and disease that took so many Haitian children: the government, particularly the *Tontons Macoutes*, and the local *hounan*. The Tontons periodically collected 'taxes,' taking whatever they could find of our meager goods. Those who hid the produce or animals were beaten or shot. The *hounan* was worse, for he enslaved our souls and minds with fear of the supernatural which he, alone, controlled. To anger him was to face the anger of the *loas*, something you have experienced. To illiterate peasants, a cross look from this man was terrifying.''

Curious, Phillip interrupted, ''But you, Pete, you're far from illiterate.''

''Bear with me, Mr. O— Phillip, and I shall come to that. When I was sixteen, my father got into an argument with a neighbor about who owned a certain piece of land. This neighbor went to the *hounan* and purchased a spell. Within a day or two, my father's machete apparently slipped and he cut off his left hand. He bled to death before we found him. The next day, I stumbled into a bees' nest and was stung many times. I have an allergy to such stings, and my whole body swelled within hours. I was also becoming unable to breathe. My mother was able to get me to the Catholic mission clinic before I suffocated.''

''Now wait.'' Phillip sat up. ''You don't mean to tell me that the *hounan* . . .''

''Please, Phillip, you yourself have seen what one of these people can do. Anyway, I stayed at the clinic for three days until the doctor said I could leave. My mother was frightened. She wanted me to stay out of the *hounan*'s sight, away from our village. I began to do small tasks for the healing fathers in exchange for my keep. Then they discovered I had taught myself to read and write. This was so unusual, one of the fathers took me to a mission school in Les Cayes, where I was able to work in exchange for more education. Kitchen, laundry—anything I could do at night to earn the privilege of attending classes during the day. When I finished the mission school, I won a scholarship to the University; but I never forgot that *hounan*. I wanted revenge for what he did to my father and my family. I understand he is dead, but I feel, in a small way, I will get my revenge by helping to destroy this Marie deSault.''

"Revenge?'' Phillip was fascinated. ''You're going to risk your life for revenge?''

"Perhaps there is also a more altruistic motive, if you will indulge me. My country has just shed a dictator. It is said there will actually be elections. It is hard for you, as an American, to understand, but I wish to return to my country and I want that country to be as free as yours. We can never be free as long as there is fear. The first Duvalier, 'Poppa Doc,' came to power by using voodoo, or at least the threat of it. 'The dogs and cats in the street tell me who my enemies are,' he said. And the people believed him.

"Dictators, *Tontons Macoutes*, *hounans*, voodoo, all must go before Haiti has a chance to be more than the destitute and hopeless place it is today. I would be proud to have a small part in ridding my homeland of at least one of its burdens. I have fled like a timid rabbit from the *Tontons* and I hid at the mission school to avoid the *hounan*. I have been a mere teacher most of my life. This is my chance to be brave, perhaps a hero, to myself and my countrymen. In short, Phillip, I want to go home and I want that home to be a better place than when I left it. Does that make sense to you or do I sound like I'm being, er, sentimental?''

Phillip was silent a moment. ''I'm impressed and I thank you for volunteering to go with me. When can you leave?''

After speaking so long, Devoux seemed to shrink in his chair. ''If I am to miss no classes, I must return in ten days. I can depart any time before then.''

Phillip stood slowly, extending a hand that enveloped the small black one. ''I'll call as soon as I make the flight reservations. Again, thank you. You have no idea how much I appreciate your agreeing to come along. Between the two of us, Marie deSault hasn't a chance.''

"I hope so, Phillip," Devoux said quietly as he watched the broad back descend the stairs. "I certainly hope so."

"You're nuts!" logic screamed at the mind. "Go back there? She'll probably turn you into a fucking toad!"

"And what's the alternative?" the mind wanted to know. "Wait around until deSault finally succeeds in killing you? Or Paige? Or Case?"

For once, logic had no answer.

Two girls, water jugs balanced gracefully on their heads, exchanged frightened glances. Although the hut where the old woman lived was still a good way down the steeply sloping path, they could hear her cackling laugh, a sound that meant no good for anyone. The younger of the pair set her burden down long enough to face all four points of the compass, her fingers making a cross at each. When she stooped to retrieve the vessel, her shaking hand slipped, spilling the contents. Both girls shrieked, the one dropping her jug as both fled down the mountainside. What they had seen seeping into the dirt had not been the cool clear water of the spring but blood, shiny and red.

Inside the mud hut, Marie deSault was oblivious to anything happening nearby. Instead, she saw the big bearded man as he drove a car along a highway. His thoughts echoed in her head as clearly as though he were speaking to her. He was coming here, here where she was strongest. And he imagined he could defeat her with the help of one of her own people. The very idea sent her into another fit of brittle laughter. Stooping, she began to draw charcoal and powder designs on the dirt floor. She knew when he would arrive with the little Haitian and she wanted to be sure she was ready to meet them, she and those she would summon to join her.

Chapter 15

Paige crossed her arms in unmistakable body language that said there was no chance of her changing her mind. "If you go, I go."

Phillip admired his wife's tenacity when they agreed and was awed by her stubbornness when they did not. Now he was trying to keep his tone patient rather than angry. "Look Paige, I'm going to have trouble enough just taking care of myself . . ."

That was not the right thing to have said, he realized as her mouth tightened. "No one's asking you to 'take care of' anyone else! I assure you I am perfectly capable of looking after myself," she said coldly. "I am *not* some fragile southern belle who faints at the first opportunity. Besides, your Dr. Devoux is going. I can look out for myself as well as some college professor, you know."

He knew. Other than small planes (which she endured) and the things she described as "creepy-crawlies" (which she did not), Paige was rarely frightened of anything. He remembered returning from an assignment in Beirut to have her greet him, discuss his trip, and mix drinks before announcing she had to testify in court the next morning. Why? Oh, no big deal. Just that a burglar who had broken into the house during Phillip's absence had found himself staring down the twin muzzles of Phillip's shotgun. Would she have shot him had he not surrendered? A moot question, she had said calmly over the tinkle of ice cubes. She had had no idea where the shells were and had no time to load the thing anyway. No, Paige was hardly the type to swoon if the going got rough. Still, he would feel a lot better facing this witch without her. "You don't seem to understand. It's going to be hard enough meeting that woman and keeping my mind closed to her."

"I don't see you having any difficulty in keeping your mind closed," she snorted. "It's hardly receptive now."

"Very funny. We're not going to discuss this further. I believe Dr. Devoux and I can handle this best alone and that's what we're going to do."

"What I'm *not* going to do is sit here, waiting to find out if you've been turned into a zombie or something. Besides, if what your professor said is true, I'm in as much danger as you. I was in the churchyard, too, remember? She could use my mind as well as yours."

"Paige, I don't think you understand. In fact, I don't think you're taking this whole thing seriously enough."

"If you mean I'm not as certain as you are that there's some sort of voodoo curse involved, you're wrong. I've got as much interest in destroying that deSault woman as you do."

He ran a hand across his face, more to give him time to quell rising anger than to wipe any sweat caused by the warm setting sun that was bathing the deck in unseasonable heat. "Let me see if I understand," he started slowly, holding up a single finger. "One: you insist on going with me because we are in danger. Two,"—he raised a second finger—"two: you want us to expose ourselves to more of that danger. Is that about it, counselor?"

Paige glared at him, diamond chips of anger in her eyes, before she nodded. "That's about it."

"Okay. Ignoring the illogic of that argument for the moment, what about Case? Somebody needs to be with him, or are you suggesting we take him, too?"

"Jeanette has always been more than satisfactory keeping him when we're out of town and you know it," she said frostily.

"Damn it, Paige!" Phillip exploded. "You haven't heard anything I've said! That creature in the pool could have drowned him if Reid and I hadn't been right there. We can't leave him with Jeanette!"

"You don't have to raise your voice." Her tone was level, a sure sign she, also, was angry. "And I will *not* be cursed at."

"Hope I'm not intruding." Reid's voice startled both of them. He stood at the bottom of the steps, Case sitting happily on his broad shoulders. "I mean, you guys don't fight enough for me to be able to interrupt very often."

"They weren't fightin'," Case announced, "they were discussin'."

Phillip was unable to suppress a smile at the sight of his son on Reid's shoulders, flourishing his crutch gaily. "Right, Tiny Tim."

"Who's Tiny Tim?" Case wanted to know.

"Somebody in a book," Reid answered, swinging the child lightly up onto the deck. "So you wouldn't be interested." He addressed Paige, "If he isn't hungry at supper tonight, don't be too hard on him. I confess, he dragged me, kicking and screaming, into a McDonald's on the way home. I let him have a burger. For medicinal purposes only, of course."

Reaching out her arms, Paige squeezed her son. The happy face he exhibited contrasted so sharply with the child she had seen this morning, she didn't care if he'd eaten a hundred Big Macs. She was smiling when she glanced up. "Whatever you did, Reid, it looks like he enjoyed it."

"I did, too." Reid smacked his lips. "You wouldn't have an extra beer lying around, would you? I gotta admit, spending the day with Case is thirsty work." He peered toward his own yard. "And I see Sue's car isn't here yet. No point in going home to an empty house."

Phillip opened the kitchen door. "I bet we could find a brew or two. C'mon in."

As the two men went inside, Case was babbling happily about his day at the hospital.

Phillip took two frosty bottles from the refrigerator. "So, how'd it go? Case about normal?"

Reid accepted the sweating bottle with a nod of thanks. "Seems to be. With kids you can't always be sure; but I'd say as soon as the doc takes him off that crutch, he'll be close to good as new. How'd it go with you? That guru of black magic tell you anything helpful?"

Phillip composed his answer as he took a long swig. "I think so. At least *he* doesn't think I'm crackers." Between slow sips, he recounted his conversation.

When he had finished, Reid gave a low whistle. "Talk about bearding the lion in its den! Going down there to confront the deSault woman doesn't sound like too good an idea. Voodoo or not, those guys who were throwing machetes at you could send you home literally a head shorter."

Phillip winced to acknowledge the pun before he became serious. "So what's the alternative? I can't just sit around with my thumb up my ass, waiting for her to have better luck next time. I've got to go."

Reid stared reflectively at the bottle's label. "And Paige insists on going with you and Devoux."

"You know Paige."

"That's an even worse idea. It doubles the chance of one of you getting hurt."

Phillip nodded ruefully. "You try telling her that."

A wicked grin spread across Reid's face. "If you're willing to play dirty pool, I'll bet you could manage to leave without her."

"Oh?" Phillip took a quick look out of the window. "How?"

"Easy. Sneak a peek at that little appointment book she always carries in her purse. I've seen her pull it out a hundred times. Announce your plans to go to Haiti when you know she's on trial. She won't like it, but at least you don't have to worry about her getting killed."

Phillip was momentarily tempted, but finally shook his head. "Paige and I are under enough stress. I'm not going to try to force her to choose between her work and what she sees as some sort of obligation to stand shoulder to shoulder with me. Fact is, I've already told her when I plan to leave and I've got airline reservations for me and Devoux."

Reid finished his beer with a gulp. "If you two are going to continue this fight, I guess I'll mosey on home."

"You could try convincing her."

Rolling his eyes at the ceiling, Reid belched with the exaggerated volume of men in the absence of women. "Catch your flak, you mean. No thanks."

"Some friend in need you are."

"Let's just say I'm prudently chicken shit. I know how determined Paige can be."

Phillip emptied his bottle. "Determined? Like granite, when she's convinced she's right. Remember when her firm passed her over for partnership?"

"*Do* I! Jesus! She had a piss off against anything male for two years."

"No, she was just determined to prove that a female lawyer didn't have to be stuck in real estate or trust work instead of trying cases. Rather than quitting to find a firm that wasn't so hide-bound, 'sexist,' she said, she doubled her hours, or so it seemed. Hell, I was lucky to see her before nine in the evening or on Saturdays and Sundays, she was so intent on showing those old bastards she was as good as any man they had. It nearly broke up our marriage. I'm surprised we had enough time together for her to get pregnant with Case."

"Love has its ways." Reid smiled.

"Thankfully. Anyway, she hung in there, first female litigator to make partner in her firm. Yeah, I'd say she's determined, all right. I'd also say I'd be an Olympic quality asshole to do something like you suggest, put pressure on her where her career is involved. I'd rather scrap with her until the moment I step on the plane."

Reid shrugged. "Best idea I could come up with on short notice, but I think you're right." He reached for the door. "Well, keep your head down in the trench and hold on to your helmet. You're on your own."

By mutual, if unspoken, consent the subject of Haiti was not discussed until after supper and Case's reluctant obedience to curfew. ("It isn't *really* a school night, Daddy. I didn't go to school today.") They were side by side at the sink as Phillip stooped to put a plate in the dishwasher. "Okay" he began, "let's put on the gloves for the next round."

The corners of Paige's mouth started to twitch, the way they always did when she was about to say something likely to start, or renew, a fight. She paused, thinking better of it, before she spoke slowly. "You win. I just want you to understand something: the only reason I was so adamant about going was because I love you."

Ready for more heated discussion, Phillip gaped at her in surprise.

She treated him to the old familiar smile that put soft light into her eyes. "Close your mouth. You look demented," she scolded good-naturedly.

Phillip found his tongue again. "And the reason I didn't want you along was because I'd be so worried about something happening to you, I couldn't take care of myself. But what changed . . ."

She laughed a low, throaty sound that Phillip had always found very sexy. "You forget: on the deck, you can hear every word spoken in the kitchen." Amusement danced across her face. "That sneak, Reid! Suggesting you check my schedule!" Serious again, she said, "I heard what you said, too. If you're willing to, what was it, 'scrap with her until I step on the plane'? Well, if you're that intent on my staying here, maybe I should do as you wish, although I can't say I like it. Hell, I guess it's about time for you to win one, anyway. You didn't want me going to Haiti in the first place."

Phillip was relieved his beard covered the flush he felt creeping into his cheeks. "I really don't want you to be there when I meet that deSault woman," he said lamely. "There's no need to put you . . ."

The rest of his words were muffled by her lips.

Their lovemaking that night was frantic, almost desperate. Afterwards, Phillip rolled over onto his back to stare into the darkness while Paige wiggled into a snuggle beside him. Women, he mused, change from snarling anger to passionate love in an eye blink. When he was a teenager, he'd figured he'd grow older, wiser, and learn to understand women. He had certainly aged, perhaps learned a few things, of which understanding the other sex was definitely not one. His best guess was that Paige had realized her work

would not permit her to go and she had surrendered gracefully, or hearing his proud description of her tenacity had
made her realize his going without her was no slight or put-
down. Or there was another reason, something feminine
he'd never understand and knew better than to ask about.
Whichever the case, he felt relaxed, more at peace than he
had since Steve the Butler had whirred across the floor with
its improbable burden. At last he was going to do something, strike back at the force only he had seemed to recognize, he and Dr. Devoux. There was comfort in having
decided on a course of action.

Phillip would not have felt quite so comfortable had he
been able to follow the stumbling progress of Stephane La-
groux at that moment. Stephane grew a small field of sugar
cane on one of the mountains above Cap-Haïtien, enough
to make a few gourde to spend on the whores in the town.
That was where he had been tonight. His wife, Lorgina,
had her own opinion as to how the money should be best
used: clothes, food, and milk for the five children, perhaps
the first new dress she had owned since she married him.
Stephane had other ideas, and what did a mere woman
know, anyway? It was Stephane who bent his back under
the tropical sun to produce cash. It was only fair he should
use it to purchase an occasional pleasure. Besides, Lorgina
grew enough yams and corn to keep the children's bellies
from swelling in hunger. And milk! Milk was for rich children from families who could afford to feed a goat! With
the stoic servitude of Haitian peasant women, she had
watched him take the wrinkled bills from their hiding place
under the bed and set off down the mountain for an afternoon of entertainment. He had even stopped at the turn in
the path to wave good-bye at the same time he screamed at

the children to tell them they could not come along. He would be back by dark, he promised them.

But the *rhum* at the bordello had been plentiful and the girl after which he lusted had been occupied until nearly sunset. The haggling for her services had taken far too long, but once a bargain was made, he was not about to rush to finish the delight. Now it was dark and he had to make his way up the steep slope by memory rather than sight. He tripped over an exposed root. *Merde!* He burped loudly, tasting the sweet burning of the liquor on the back of his tongue as he pushed himself back to his bare feet. He peered into the inky darkness, punctuated with stars, pinpricks of light in the black velvet dome of the sky. He was late and Lorgina would be angry. She would say something that would force him to beat her, a task he simply wasn't up to tonight. A man had to beat his wife if she became impertinent or soon she would be the boss in the family. In any event, he had best hurry home.

Here was the detour around the old *hounan*'s hut. He stared into the dark sullenly. He could save a good ten minutes if he kept to the main path. Besides, he wasn't certain legs wobbly with pleasant fatigue could be trusted to negotiate the steep alternate. *"Merde,"* he said again, this time aloud. The witch was probably asleep by now, anyway. Taking no chances, he spit in four different directions and plowed straight ahead.

Rounding a bend in the path, he stopped and stared. Light, sunlike in its brilliance, poured out of the open door and single, unshuttered window, painting the surrounding brush bloodred. Stephane had not seen such light even in places that had electricity. It hurt his eyes and he looked away only to notice something else strange: the trees and bushes around the place were rustling as though in a high wind, a wind Stephane certainly could not feel although he was only a few yards away. Then he heard it, a wailing, high-pitched scream that seemed to also be laughter. He had never heard such a sound from human or animal. Despite the coolness of the night, prickly sweat began to run down his neck and stick in his armpits. What was that? Another sound, this one of thrashing, slapping water, the sound of an angry sea. But the ocean was four miles down the mountainside.

Stephane's feet began to move before he was aware of their decision. He stumbled, caught himself, and half ran, half crawled uphill. He sensed, rather than saw, something in front of him. Pausing to the accompaniment of his own thumping heart, he waited, staring at the shadows from the house's light. He gasped as a form materialized on the border of the darkness and he felt the warmth of urine trickle down his leg. A snake, the largest he had ever imagined, let alone seen, slithered toward him slowly, its red eyes never leaving Stephane. He heard it hiss and his sweat turned to ice on his skin. It wasn't just hissing, it was calling him by name, a low, rasping sound. "Stephane," it said, he was certain of it. Stephane jerked fully erect, so he could flee, but his legs would not obey orders. He struggled vainly before he realized the reptile was wrapped around his ankles, slowly winding itself above his knees. With terror-widened eyes, he looked into the thing's open mouth. The wavering light reflected from fangs the size of Stephane's machete. He would have fallen in paralyzed fear, but he couldn't. The snake was winding tighter around him as it reached his waist, tighter, squeezing the breath from his laboring lungs.

Chapter 16

Phillip and Dr. Devoux walked slowly toward the small terminal building, the sun's heat reflecting off the tarmac. A light breeze, hot and gritty, drifted listlessly across the airport's single runway, barely moving the faded Union Jack that hung limply on its pole. Squinting through sunglasses that were unable to dilute the glare, Phillip noted the aging sign, its paint peeling as though each letter were weeping. WELCOME TO GRAND TURK. He didn't feel very welcome, not by the shabbiness of the building he saw, not by the hot sand that burned his feet through his shoes. Two stunted and thirsty palm trees guarded the entrance with fronds that rustled with the sound of dry paper. A whining roar from behind caused him to turn and watch the Pan Am 737 on which they had arrived bore into the cloudless sky, trailing a smudge of oily smoke in its wake as it banked gently to the right and streaked for the more hospitable shores of the Dominican Republic, only one hundred miles away.

Devoux also had watched the plane's departure. "Well," he said with a cheeriness that seemed misplaced, "now we are committed, eh?"

Inside, the shade was marginally cooler. They stood under a wheezing ceiling fan in vain hope of drying the sweat

that plastered their shirts to their backs. As Phillip's eyes
adjusted, he saw the TCNA counter. Turks and Caicos National Airline, the only airline that flew into Cap-Haïtien.
Although Eastern and Pan Am had scheduled service to
Port-au-Prince, the drive from there to the north coast one
hundred and fifty miles away usually occupied a full day in
the best of times. Now, with the government nonexistent,
Phillip had decided to take the direct flight. A suit bag, his
only luggage, over his shoulder, he crossed the concrete
floor, the diminutive Haitian trailing behind, and stood at
the counter waiting for the young black girl to look up from
the tattered magazine she was reading. When it became
obvious she was ignoring him, Phillip cleared his throat
loudly and proferred his ticket envelope. "Flight six to Cap-
Haïtien," he announced. "Supposed to leave in . . ." he
checked his watch. "In about twenty minutes."

A fleeting look of annoyance at the interruption crossed
her face before she smiled, exposing straight teeth made
whiter by the contrast with the dark face. Her reply was as
disappointing as it was predictable. "Flight six, mon, I
dunno. He be in the hangar with mechanical trouble." She
grinned even wider. "You two sit in the bar, I call you when
he be ready to go."

"You think that'll be today?"

With infuriating indifference, she shrugged, her grin wid-
ening. "Don't know. He be ready when he be ready." She
pointed toward the end of the building. "You go have a
cool drink in the bar. I call you." She handed him back his
ticket and returned to her reading.

Wearily, Phillip headed for the few formica-topped tables
that sat forlornly in front of a rough wood bar. They were
on island time for sure now and how well Phillip knew that
drill: two o'clock meant probably before dark, today meant
sometime this week, and next week was a time measure-

ment incomprehensible anywhere south of Key West. Annoyingly, his companion's adjustment had been immediate. Devoux had not only taken the delay with a smile, but had not been surprised. Things moved slowly, if at all, in the Caribbean and getting upset about it only served to raise the blood pressure. Besides, it had been in the Turks and Caicos Islands that he had met Paige—Pine Cay. The easy lifestyle had contributed as much to the initial romance as the chalk white sand and the winter blue-sky waters. He smiled at the memory, wondering if the evening would reveal Orion, forever hunting the night. The tiny island of Pine Cay was fifty or sixty miles from where he stood. Sometime in the next few months, he'd bring Paige back to the small resort that was the only amenity on the island. They'd recapture some of the fervor of new lovers, lying on the beach at night, listening to the song of a gentle surf in counterpoint to the dull roar of the reef offshore. Fuck Marie deSault, anyway! No *hounan*, witch, sorcerer, or other magic-maker was going to deprive him of a return to Pine Cay.

"The sentence is at least postponed, eh?" Devoux piped. "No worry, deSault will be there when we get to Haiti."

Phillip suppressed a retort, but his companion's good humor, bravado false or genuine, improved his own mood.

By the time they reached the bar, Phillip was humming a Jimmy Buffet tune, a song he had referred to as an anthem for all Caribbean countries, a song about the unpredictability of air service in this part of the world.

He leaned against the bar and woke up the napping bar-keeper, actually smiling, a mood that improved further with two Barbancourt and tonics. Devoux seemed delighted to find Haitian beer, a touch of his homeland, Phillip surmised, as he noticed no two bottles of the stuff were the same shape. It was good to be back in the islands, even this one. Why not relax? With him away from Paige and Case, the deSault woman couldn't use his mind as a conduit to strike at them, right? And he would face her soon enough, assuming TCNA could produce a serviceable aircraft. In the meantime, he had nothing to worry about.

The heat drilling through the fly-specked window felt good on Peter Devoux's skin, the feel of the tropical sun he had almost forgotten. The lightly bitter taste of the Prince Beer reminded him of his days at the University, both as student and teacher. He let the liquid lay on his tongue before it coursed lazily down his throat. Americans gulped beer, swigging it down as though it were water. Of course, they could afford as much as they wanted, too. Unfortunately, gulping deprived the beverage of its taste. Longingly, almost sexually, he let his mouth recall the spicy Haitian foods he had missed so much. Lambi, the tiny conch that was sundried, then served in a blazing sauce of the hottest pepper. Chicken stuffed with mango, roasted over an open fire. The first thing he would do after they disposed of Marie deSault was eat Haitian food. If there was an after.

He gave Phillip a furtive glance as though fearful the American could read his thoughts. Phillip must never suspect how terrified he really was. The big American would lose all respect if he knew of the fear that was constricting Devoux's throat like a lump of unchewed food.

Phillip had assured him that he had a means of closing his mind to the *hounan*, something he carried in his shirt pocket, but Devoux was not sure of himself. Years of poverty had taught him to ignore the broiling sun, the chilling rain, and the pains of an empty stomach. But could he turn off the *hounan*'s spell like a light bulb? He was not sure and this uncertainty was the mother of the fear that was choking him. Of two things he was certain: he, as a human being, could not let Phillip face that woman alone, that creature that embodied so much that was wrong with Haiti. Second, his teachers at the mission school, the Jesuits, had convinced him that once resisted by good, evil must fail. Admittedly, he had been slack in the practice of his religion since coming to the States, rarely attending mass or confession, but a just God would understand. As if to confirm this, he touched the rosary under his shirt. Nothing Marie deSault did would distract him from his "Hail Mary's." He would concentrate so hard on becoming a good Catholic again, he could ignore her. The thought made him feel a little better.

Quincy Stubbs creased his round black face with a rare frown as he mopped his Afro with an oily rag. Although TCNA's best mechanic, he was stumped. When the Tri-Islander had landed earlier this afternoon, its pilot, Quincy's cousin, Joe Stubbs, had complained that the number-one propeller, the left, refused to synchronize. The resulting sound was reminiscent of uneven strokes across a washboard and the problem could be indicative of a potentially dangerous situation. In the oven heat of the tin hangar, Quincy had supervised the removal of the offending prop before he personally inspected the oil veins that, by alternating pressure, controlled the pitch of the blades. Nothing. With the patience of a man comfortable with his work, he had followed those lines all the way to the pitch levers in the cockpit. Again, nothing.

Years of experience had taught Quincy that the gremlins that frequented sophisticated machinery often disappeared as quickly and as inexplicably as they manifested themselves. He had hoped this to be the case, but a run-up in the confines of the hangar served only to temporarily deafen him and the two other mechanics. Synchronization of the recalcitrant prop still eluded him after a second thorough search of the entire blade feathering system. Now it was about time for the sun to fall into the sea and he knew Joe was going to be unhappy. Joe

would have to make the entire round trip to Cap-Haïtien
at night, missing not only time with his family, but worse—
supper. Well, there was nothing Quincy could do but subject
his and his assistants' ears to another blast of engines.

He touched the ignition switch just as, through the open
door, he saw darkness touch the western horizon. The roar
vibrated from the metal walls in waves of deafening sound.
Gritting his teeth, Quincy gently manipulated the prop lever,
his eyes fastened on the synch indicator for any defect his
battered ears could not hear. Perfect. The props were as
finely tuned now as a concert piano. He cut the switch and
tried again with identical results. Stretching, he yawned
through his smile. Although he had no idea how or why,
the plane was ready to go.

In the tropics, night swallows the day so suddenly there is
no time for twilight to intervene. The effect is as if a giant
hand draws a blanket across the sky. Darkness had already
chased after the sinking sun when Phillip saw the tug pulling
the Tri-Islander from the hangar. With long, nonretractable
landing gear extending from high wings, the aircraft reminded
him of a stork awkwardly pecking its way across a marsh.
Awkward, yes. But he knew the ungainly configuration made
the aircraft ideal for short, often rough runways. With its two
wing mounted propeller engines and a third on the tail, the
plane could lift tremendous loads from spaces inaccessible to
other aircraft of its size. Like Cap-Haïtien, Phillip thought
grimly, his good mood having vanished.

With their fellow passengers, mostly Haitians, Phillip and
Devoux walked across the tarmac. Dim yellow puddles of light
cast by two stuttering electric lamps marked the way, stepping
stones across a river of darkness. Far away, its color roseate
from the distance, lightning blinked against the sky.

* * *

Marie deSault chortled with glee, her bare gums glistening despite the gloom of her hut. Delaying the arrival of the white man and the Haitian man had been clever indeed. Now they would come at night, she was sure of it. Darkness gave her an advantage over those with normal sight, those who were blind in the dark. Her bony figure shook with mirth. There was yet another reason to be pleased: now that the white man was over the ocean, closing the gap between them, his woman was alone and, she now believed, vulnerable. The man would never return home, so why wait to destroy the woman? Would Marie deSault be diluting the powers to do so now?

Nonsense. Disposing of the woman would take no real effort, a task that would be long completed before the men got here.

Her cackling laughter stopped abruptly, the ensuing silence punctuated by the chirp of tree frogs outside. The woman. For some reason, the *hounan* had been unable to see her as clearly as the man. The image was blurred. Lately, though, the vision had been getting clearer. Saliva dripped from the corners of deSault's scowl. She would watch the woman until the opportunity came, the chance to send the instrument of death. Then the woman would truly believe; with her last desperate breath she would know the power of Marie deSault, power of the *loa* of voodoo. But what instrument? She needed all she could command to thoroughly terrify the two men before they died. A beatific smile crossed the wrinkled face. Of course. Perhaps not all. Perhaps she could spare those of Baron Samedi. In fact, the death *loa* could do what she had in mind without leaving her. Sprinkling brightly colored powders in a design upon the floor, she began to chant. The rough English equivalent of her song was:

> Baron Samedi: keeper of the grave,
> Keeper of the new and long dead,
> I ask you to release one of your minions,

Do let him walk tonight to serve.
Oh, Baron Samedi, the Dark One.

Paige stooped to remove the pan from the oven as Reid sniffed appreciatively. "Great idea, having you and Case over for dinner. Particularly since you volunteered to do the world's best cheese souffle."

"I'm doing the veggies," Sue pouted. "You always love my veggies."

Reid hastened toward the kitchen door. "And I better check the chicken on the grill. It should be about ready."

Sue's voice had an undertone of petulance. "He likes vegetables done the way I cook them."

Gingerly, Paige set the pan down on the countertop. "I love the way you prepare them, too, Sue. It's pure luck this souffle didn't fall." Luck and trying not to worry about Phillip. The thought of what might happen had made her hands tremble enough to flatten the stoutest souffle.

"It never does," Sue said sniffing. "Reid and Phillip always make such a big deal over it." And it isn't fair, Sue thought. I hate to cook, anyway. The damn pots and pans chip my nails and the heat makes my face all sweaty. I'd much rather go out every night, some place with candlelight that flatters me instead of working like a slave under these harsh kitchen fluorescents. Some place where the waiter flirts, or pretends to. Instead, my husband is out there fooling with that nasty charcoal grill, paying it more attention than he does me. And that fucking cheese souffle. Paige whips it out and the men go gaga. Just once, I wish the damn thing would come out looking like a cow pie, the way it did the one time I tried. It isn't fair!

"Dinner ready yet?" Case stood at the entrance between the dining room and kitchen, his crutch squeaking on the tiles.

Paige untied the borrowed apron. "Hungry? It'll be on the table in a minute or two."

"There's nothing good on TV," Case complained. "Just the dumb old news."

"Why don't you go out back and help Uncle Reid," Sue suggested, glancing around to make sure there was nothing that might get knocked over on the way.

Between Uncle Reid and Dan Rather, there was no choice. Case started across the kitchen, dragging as much as using his crutch, and stopped, wrinkling his nose. "Something stinks!"

"Case!" Paige reprimanded, giving Sue an apologetic glance. "There is nothing in here that smells bad!"

"My stir-fried vegetables smell wonderful," Sue huffed. Damn Reid for insisting on having that rowdy child and his souffle-baking mother over here, anyway. She was sure the kid would break something before the evening was over.

Case sniffed the air, insistent. "Can't you smell it, too?"

Now that he had mentioned it, Paige did detect an odor, sickly sweet, the barely discernable stench of rotting flesh. She could tell Sue had also detected it. "Maybe a squirrel died under the house."

Holding his nose with an exaggerated motion, Case went outside where the glow of the charcoal silhouetted Uncle Reid like one of those monsters he'd seen on the tape Randy had snuck out of his folks' room and shown on his new VCR, a film Case's parents would never have let him watch. He ran a tongue through the gap where two new front teeth were making discernable bumps in the gum. That was some movie. Not only did it have monsters, but lots of blood and women with nothing on. Case had seen his mother like that, but the sight of other girls . . . Well, that was different, real different.

"Well, I can sure use the help." Reid's voice shattered

the memory. "Hand me that fork there, would you, please?"

Obediently, Case picked up the twin-tined fork from the outdoor table, giving it to Reid who all but disappeared in the ensuing cloud of smoke. There it was again, the stink. Uncle Reid wouldn't get mad like Mommy if he mentioned it. "You smell that?"

Reid stepped back, wiping his forehead with his sleeve. "I can't smell anything except this chicken cooking . . ." He paused, testing the air. "Yuck! Somebody must have run over one of those stray dogs in the alley."

Rhett's memory was still too clear in Case's mind for the thought of a dead dog not to be disturbing. He fidgeted uncertainly for a moment before pivoting on his crutch. "I'll go find it, Uncle Reid. Then we can have a funeral."

Reid grinned as he thought of the solemn ceremony that followed the death of each bee, spider, or other creature Case collected. "I don't think that's a good idea . . ."

The small boy was already gone, his shape vanishing into the darkness with a wobbling gait. "Case," Reid called, "stay inside the fence. Don't get out into that alley. You hear me?"

"Yes, sir," floated out of the night.

Case followed the chain link fence that marked the property line along the unpaved pair of ruts that had given access to the rear of the houses on the street when garbage men hefted tin, ten-gallon cans onto garbage trucks. Now sanitary engineers used mechanical lifts to dump specially designed trash containers into refuse removal units in front of the houses and the alley was unused other than as an occasional shortcut to the rear of their homes by those who knew the neighborhood. Grass and brush had grown unmolested, making it a favorite place for little boys to play jungle games. Tonight the alley looked quite different from the last time Case and his friends had stalked tigers there. In fact, all he could see now were the tops of weeds and unkempt trees; the alley itself was obscured in the night, scary and invisible. Case's enthusiasm to find the dead dog declined as he noted just how spooky the place was.

To his relief, Uncle Reid was calling him, announcing that supper was ready. Case gratefully turned, facing the house. Something moved, something that was illuminated for an instant in the pool of light spilling from a window. Case felt a surge of joy. Daddy! Then he looked closer. No, whoever this was standing outside the window was as big as Daddy, but not the same. It was a man, though. Case was fairly certain, a man who evaporated into the shadows with a lurching, stumbling movement more clumsy than Case on his crutch. Case stopped, waiting for him to become more visible again.

"Case!" his mother called out, "are you coming or not?"

He could hear the irritation in her tone, but something told him not to reply, to get to the house as quickly and quietly as he could. He stepped into the light that flooded the back stoop where the grill was smoldering, its smoke paving a filmy path toward the overhanging oak limbs in the breezeless night.

Paige was framed in the bright rectangle of the open back door. "Case, I turn my back for a minute and you're off hunting dead animals!"

Both Case and his mother stopped, testing the windless air. The smell, the stink. It was undeniably closer now and it didn't come from the alley. "Whew!" Paige said, contorting her face.

Case stared into the dark at the side of the house at the place he had seen—or thought he'd seen—the man. The smell was coming from there.

(*"Do let him walk tonight to serve . . ."*)

Chapter 17

The Tri-Islander shook in the storm like a terrier with a rat. Hail smashed against the window at Phillip's elbow like the sound of gunshots. Pillows, bits of loose clothing, and packages levitated to the accompaniment of screams when the aircraft dropped as though it had fallen from a cliff. The plane stank of vomit, sweat, and, most powerfully, fear. Devoux, seated next to Phillip, clinched his eyes shut while he muttered something Phillip guessed was a prayer. A streak of lightning split the sky outside and danced across the underside of the wing, illuminating the clouds like some heavenly pinball machine.

"Shit," Phillip muttered for the umpteenth time as the aircraft shuddered and yawed. As a pilot, he knew what the raw fury of a thunderstorm could do to an airplane unfortunate enough to fly into one. Christ, even the big jets avoided this sort of thing, planes far larger than this twenty-seat puddle jumper. He guessed that weather radar was either never installed in TCNA planes or the one on this flight had been out of order. Trying to stay calm, he reasoned that since these flights were usually conducted in daylight, and in areas of normally good weather, the airline had decided the expense of airborne radar could be spared. He mentally cursed the unknown policymakers for their penuriousness at the moment he was driven forward against his seat belt. He hoped to hell the bastards who had made that decision hadn't had any other ideas how to save money. The violence of the shearing winds in these storms could rip the metal frame apart if overstressed. Happy thought. His life was in the hands of a crew whose experience and abilities were unknown. One abrupt maneuver, one overly strong yank on the control yoke, and . . . A roar of thunder sounded as though it came from inside his own head, loud enough to make thought impossible.

The Tri-Islander surged straight up, driving him into the seat with what he guessed was at least a full G, the force of gravity. Behind him, a woman began to shriek and Phillip wondered with detachment if his own sanity would prove less air-worthy than this damn plane.

Devoux opened one eye. As he had guessed, his companion seemed the calmest person on board, more interested in marking each violent maneuver with curses than being frightened. Of course. Phillip had said he was a pilot, so he had probably experienced this sort of thing many times and knew there was no danger. Devoux managed to keep quiet rather than have the big American think him a coward. Just to be on the safe side, though, this seemed a most appropriate time for Devoux to renew his faith by practicing his rosary.

In the cockpit, Joe Stubbs was managing to exhibit calm— a thin veneer over the panic that was trying to claw its way up from his stomach. Beside him, his copilot, Ernest, was not doing as well. "Shit!" the younger man grunted, "I shoulda stuck to conch fishin', 'stead of goin' and learnin' how to fly." He made a futile grab for the cap that went sailing off his head with a life of its own.

Joe managed a grin he didn't feel. Ernest's eyes were

wide, twin moons in the dark sky of his face. "Hush, 'less the passengers hear."

"I don't care if they do, mon. I want outa this here storm!"

Joe snorted derisively. What the hell could he expect from a kid who grew up on Salt Cay? "This here ole thunderstorm, he ain't much. We be done with him in a minute."

Ernest was holding onto his seat with both hands. "Mon, you crazy, you think this ain't much! I never—" The thought was interrupted by a blinding flash of lightning and a particularly severe pitch of the aircraft that reduced Ernest's conversation to low moans.

Cold sweat trickled down inside the open collar of Joe's starched white shirt, making his neck itch. He dared not take a hand from the control yoke to scratch. Just remember what they told you at Embry Riddle when they taught you to fly: the quickest way out of a thunder storm was straight through it. You'll make it okay as long as you go easy with the controls and try to simply keep level. Make an abrupt maneuver and you'll snap the wings off the bird like a kid popping a candy stick in two. Above all: keep calm. Easy advice to give in a quiet classroom. He checked his power gauges to make sure he had slowed to the air speed recommended for severe turbulence, the speed that would minimize stress on the air frame. Another flash of lightning seared his vision. Hell, he thought, I'm blinded—just like having a flashbulb go off in my face. The plane's left wing pitched from a downburst of air, a movement indistinguishable amid the rest of the turbulence except for the violent tug at the yoke. Joe waited for his sight to return, for the artificial horizon to become visible again before making a correction. No chance of doing it visually. It seemed like an eternity and he knew that without action on his part, the plane's bank would increase in steepness, corkscrewing into a deadly spiral. He blinked, trying to will himself to see.

Rain whipped the window beside Phillip as though someone were playing a powerful hose on the glass, reflecting the brilliant flashes into thousands of shiny slivers of light. Without seeing, Phillip felt the steepness of the bank, a feeling confirmed by the sound of an empty drink can rolling across the aisle and half way up the cabin's wall. It suddenly occurred to him: could Marie deSault command the weather also? Perhaps this was her way of dealing with him before he ever had a chance to confront her, strip her of her powers. He touched his breast pocket, taking small comfort from what he felt there. He might never have the chance to use it. The unfairness of it all! He was grateful to feel an anger almost strong enough to replace his fear, fear he would succumb to the *hounan*, fear he would never have the chance to face her. Fear won out as another blaze of lightning illuminated the black sea. *God!* The aircraft was at a crazy angle and barely a hundred feet above the wind-foamed water! Pull up, he willed the pilot, pull up, or the wing will hit the ocean, sending the plane cartwheeling into a crash. If the weather were another product of the *hounan's* power, the only way to survive was to force her from his mind. He willed himself to think of Case and Paige.

Reid put down the carving knife and gazed quizzically around the table. "Something stinks like sh— er, something sure smells bad." His eyes fastened on Case. "Did you find something out back and drag it up by the house?"

Case shifted uncomfortably in his seat. "No, sir." Should he tell the grownups what he thought he'd seen? If he did, they'd probably say his imagination was at work again. Like the time he just knew something was hiding in his closet.

Daddy had gotten angry when Case had awakened him to tell him about that. Of course there hadn't been anything in the dumb old closet but Case's clothes and junk. But that was before the swimming pool thing. Case hadn't imagined that, and both Daddy and Uncle Reid had seen it. And Case was using a crutch because of it. Maybe he'd better speak up. "Er," he began with the timidity of small children about to say something that might be received skeptically, "I think that smell is coming from the man outside."

Sue, a handkerchief theatrically over her nose, groaned, "Case . . ."

Reid gave Paige a glance that told her Sue was still unaware anything unusual had happened. Then he turned to the small boy, his tone earnest rather than patronizing, "You saw somebody outside?"

Case nodded vigorously. "Yes, sir, at least I thought I did. By the side of the house. It was too dark to be sure."

"Reid," Sue began in protest, "you don't really . . ."

His glance told her more forcibly than words to hush. He returned his attention to Case. "Tell me exactly what you think you saw."

Case shifted his gaze from Uncle Reid to Aunt Sue. He sure didn't want to upset her, but now that he'd started, he couldn't stop. "He looked big, like you or Daddy. And he was looking in that window." He pointed. "There . . ."

All eyes followed the pointing finger to the window behind Sue.

"God!" Reid gasped.

Sue shrieked as the entire window, frame included, exploded inward, sending glass showering across the room, each fragment reflecting like a tiny golden dagger. Dropping her handkerchief, she fled around the table to the far wall.

* * *

Sam Dothan had been on the Atlanta police force nearly twenty years and he was tired. Murder, robbery, rape—he'd seen the seedier side of human nature, all right. Not to mention the politics. Jesus, but he hated the damn politics involved in police work. His short stature was getting flabby and he had acquired that expression people sometimes get when they realize things really aren't going to get any better. But they had. For no reason Sam could understand, he'd gotten this cushy part-time job patrolling Ansley Park twenty random hours a week to supplement his wages. Just cruising around on the police Kawasaki, enjoying the scenery on quiet streets. This was a nice neighborhood. Lawyers and doctors with attractive wives and small children. Yep, this was the place to be, where the residents smiled, even waved sometimes when he went by. Here he was addressed as "officer" rather than "pig." Hell, he'd had to patrol neighborhoods where a man on a bike was a moving target for bricks, or worse, from anonymous tenement windows. Here, he dealt with runaway dogs and an occasional juvenile prank. And for this he got paid a better hourly rate than he got for his regular beat. Yes, sir, old Sam Dothan was doing okay for himself, he thought as he belched, resurrecting the taste of dinner, the two tacos he'd mooched from the Mexican place. He grinned. Twenty years of fast, usually greasy foods, hadn't done his stomach a lot of favors, but he still had a digestive tract that worked pretty well despite the abuse it had taken. Gas would be the worst problem he'd have tonight. He farted contentedly.

On his right was the Henderson home, on his list of residents out of town. Pulling to the curb, he lazily swung a stubby leg over the seat, turned on the blinking warning lights, and leaned the motorcycle over on its kickstand. Walking with a jaunty, bowlegged step, he approached the house, playing his flashlight on the windows and doors. Not that he expected to find anything, but it made the neighbors happy to see him doing his job. After all, that was what they were paying him for, private security patrol. He paused to admire a snowy tower of flowering dogwood, yellowed by the streetlight. People in this area sure have a good life, he mused without rancor. They have a lot to lose, so no wonder they're so generous with their security arrangements.

The squawk of the motorcycle's radio interrupted his inspection. Now why would the central operator be calling his number? He was off duty, officially, and there sure as hell wouldn't be an emergency here in Ansley Park. A new operator. Of course. Some green kid had gotten the unit numbers scrambled. Still, he'd best answer. Taking his time to return to the Kawasaki, he lifted the mike from its hook under the windscreen, sighed, and responded.

It was no mistake, the disembodied voice informed him. Neighbors reported the crash of glass and screams. Sounded like a domestic squabble. Sam noted the address. Domestic fracas, my ass! The last husband-wife bout around here had probably been over the size of the bill from Neiman's, he thought. Still, he had no choice but to investigate. He wheeled a U-turn, and, as an afterthought, switched on the flashing blue light.

The thing, the creature that had crashed into the dining room was unlike anything Reid had ever seen, yet resembled the human form enough to be more terrifying than some alien shape. In the panic that freezes sight pictures like a photograph, Reid saw a man (a cadaver?). Flesh around one eye was rotting, hanging loosely from the skull to reveal an eye socket empty except for a beetle that scurried back into the darkness of the cranium. Greenish corruption drooled from jaws held by stringy tendons as the intruder shook itself free of the splinters of the window frame, filling the room with the putrid stench of meat long since gone bad. The thing was caked with mud, dirt alive with worms, clay that hid whatever clothes it might be wearing. Like a corpse from the grave, Reid thought. The one remaining eye, dead and listless, moved until it found Paige. The thing extended a hand, a claw of bone protruding through flesh toward her, swiping as a bear might attack an elk. With a sound that was half squeak, half scream, Paige grabbed Case's hand, snatching him with her to join Sue on the far side of the room.

"Who the . . . ?" Reid spluttered, his hand tightening on the carving knife. "If you think this is funny . . ."

The eye rolled briefly toward him and in that instant Reid knew he was facing nothing living, nothing from the world he knew, anyway. Before the terror of the realization could slow him, the brain telegraphed action to his body. It was the same impulse that had told him where a running back would hit the line, a language too quick for words to be of use. He filled his lungs with the fetid air, drew back his arm and sent the knife shimmering across the room. With the sound of a cleaver striking a side of beef, the blade imbedded itself to its hilt in the thing's chest, quivering with a metallic hum.

The strike of the knife might as well have been as inconsequential as a fly landing on the body. Instead of recoiling from the impact, the intruder took a halting step forward, striking the table, still reaching toward Paige with a single-mindedness that left no doubt as to its intentions. With a sweep of that bony claw, china and silverware went smashing to the floor in a shattering crash that was oddly reassuring amid the unreality Reid was witnessing. Case and the women were pressed against the far wall, only the bare table between them and the thing.

Sue gave a mewling whimper. *"Oh, God, oh God!"*

In a step, Reid was beside the thing, swinging his fist in a roundhouse right that should have stopped anything smaller than an ox. It didn't. Reid's hand struck cool mushiness with a slapping sound, like bare feet on a wet floor, knocking the jaw from its few tendons. Now the rotting face ended in a black hole through which Reid could hear the scattering of tiny legs, the rustling noise roaches make at night when the light is turned on in the kitchen. The jaw bone clattered to the floor, where its few teeth seemed to form a detached, malevolent smile. Unaffected, the eye turned toward Reid again, the stare of a dead fish. Before he could move, Reid felt the cold hand grasp his arm with a strength he could not resist. A split second later, all two hundred–plus pounds of him were flying across the dining room like a ball tossed for a dog to retrieve. Impact with the wall knocked him breathless and nearly senseless. Through the wave of pain, Reid saw the dining room table flipped aside as though the massive mahogany piece were made of cardboard. Fighting the darkness of unconsciousness, he sucked enough air into his lungs to grunt, "The door, head for the door."

Struggling up on shaky legs, he was gratified to see Sue, Paige, and Case come alive, shake off the paralysis of fear, and dash for the exit from the room that lead into the hallway. He squared his shoulders in preparation for further combat with that being that had invaded his home. Crouching, he was ready for one more, perhaps final, lunging tackle, the smashing contact that had stopped so many collegians, when his knee buckled. The knee, the fucking knee! The impact with the wall had reinjured it. Helplessly, he watched through a red haze of pain as his adversary followed Sue, Paige, and Case with steps made menacing by their slow deliberateness.

Sam Dothan's Kawasaki whirred to a stop in front of the house in time for him to hear a crash. Jesus Christ, somebody really was tearing the place apart! He noticed the smell as he swung off the saddle, the sweet-sour stench tinted with a strong whiff of ammonia. The last time Sam had breathed something like that had been when neighbors' complaints had lead him to search an abandoned shack. He had found a dead wino, a body partially eaten by rats, and bloated in the heat of summer. He had puked then, and he felt like he might now. The taco taste that rose in his throat was flavored with bile. But this wasn't the housing projects, this was Ansley Park. Surely not here. Two women and a child tumbled from the front door, the larger of the two screaming something about leaving her husband, clearly panicked. Her husband. Sam imagined the scenario: the woman had come home to find . . .

The smaller of the women was very pretty, Sam noticed right off despite the unflattering orange glow of the streetlight. He hitched up his gun belt purposefully and marched up the driveway.

The big woman, he noted, wasn't really big, just well padded with ample body straining against a dress too small. But she could move, the way she was running toward him. "My husband," she panted, "my husband's inside with, with something!"

Sam sighed and assumed his best policeman-doing-his-job voice. "Take it easy, lady. I'll . . ."

He never finished. The woman in front of him grabbed him in a hug that nearly squeezed his breath away, alternately moaning and screaming in his ear.

"Thank God you're here," the pretty lady said through trembling lips. She looked like she wasn't far from hysteria, either. But she was holding on somehow. Probably for the child who was grasping her hand with one of his and a crutch with the other. They stood on the middle of the front porch, half of which was screened in from the days before air-conditioning when screens kept bugs out but allowed the breeze in.

Managing to free himself of Sue, Sam stepped onto the porch. If he'd ever seen people terrified, and he had, these folks qualified. "Now, exactly what's . . ."

Again, he didn't finish. The front door flew from its hinges. It didn't open, it just fell outward as though the house was sticking out its tongue. Instinctively, Sam jumped sideways, his hand reaching for his service revolver. He motioned for the woman and the kid to get out of his way, a warning hardly necessary since both had put him between them and the dark opening where the door had been. Nerves prickled under his skin as though his shirt were full of straw as he slowly moved to peer inside.

Holy shit! He'd never seen anything like that. A staggering corpse was what it looked like. He made himself think before he said, "All right, very funny." Ansley Park, my ass! Weirdos dressed up in freaky outfits, that's what it was. Happened every time there was another showing of one of those cult movies. But Sam had never witnessed a getup like this. That jawless, gaping hole of a mouth, how the hell had he managed that? And the dead stink? And who in the hell wanted to smell like a rotting corpse?

"All right," he repeated in a voice that wasn't quite as authoritarian as he would have liked, "this is THE PO-LICE. You're disturbing the peace. I'm telling you . . ."

For the third time events prevented a finish to his remarks. The guy in the scary costume picked up a chair from the hallway, picked it up in a hand that looked like a skeleton's, a chair that Sam would have had a hard time lifting, a big upholstered number. Fuck police regulations. Sam drew his .38 just as the chair came flying at him. Goddamn!

If he hadn't jumped out of the way, that friggin' chair would have broken some bones. Sam fired a shot into the roof of the porch. "I told you, this is THE POLICE!"

His assailant was unimpressed. Instead of submitting, he was reaching for the mate to the chair he had already tossed as lightly as a baseball. But he wasn't really paying attention to Sam. That one eye, the one that looked like a kid's aggie marble, was staring at the woman with the child. Sam crouched into the classic shooter's position. "Halt! Halt or I'll shoot!" The moment he spoke, Sam almost snickered with the nervous laughter of fright. He sounded like Sergeant Preston of the goddamn Mounted Police! The man/thing in from of him was drawing back to let go with that chair. "Okay, asshole." The front sight of the pistol was squarely on the man's knee. A disabling shot, knock the mother down. That was what he had been taught as a rookie, although he doubted his instructors had seen anything like this. Sam squeezed the trigger. It was the first time he had shot at something besides a paper target. As the gun bucked, he was irrationally surprised that the sound and feel were the same as on the police range. For a moment he smelled burned cordite, a sweet odor compared with the stench from the house. The round had gone where he wanted it. He could see the tear in the knee of the ragged trousers that had not been there seconds before.

That was the only difference. Shit. Must have missed the leg itself. The man—the whatever it was—began to swing the chair, preparing a blow at the woman that could well knock her head off. So much for disabling fire. Sam leveled the front sight squarely on the man's breast bone and pumped a shot where he figured it would have maximum effect. Besides the crash of the gunshot, there was no further result other than the bullet kicking up spurts of the dirt that caked the body of the thing. Body armor. The fucking politicians wouldn't allow good, hard-hitting, soft point ammo. Even if dumdums didn't penetrate a vest, the impact would tell the guy he meant business. Now the man, the suspect, the perpetrator, the *thing* had that chair above its head. Sam retreated toward the edge of the porch, his gun level again. The politicians decreed no head shots unless the officer was in more than immediate jeopardy (whatever that gibberish meant). Okay, fine. Sam could explain this away while he was on suspension for an illegal shooting. Better to talk from behind a desk than a hospital bed. Besides, if he didn't stop this thing those civilians might get hurt. He raised his sight and fired. No doubt the slugs had gone where he wanted them. The top of the skull/head splintered. And the *thing* came on, oozing gray slime that might have once been a brain from its shattered forehead.

Sam gaped in horror. This was no fruitcake in a fright suit—a guess that had slithered around behind the dark curtains of Sam's mind was now center stage. Why wasn't he surprised? Any *thing* that kept coming with half a head, that bullets wouldn't stop was something he had no business trying to subdue. Backup, call for backup, the SWAT team with enough firepower to stop a tank, anything normal. And what was slowly plodding out of the house *wasn't* normal. He glanced over his shoulder. The Kawasaki and its radio were too far away. By the time he got on the air, he, or the woman, would be beyond help. Sam was going to have to resolve this himself. He took a step back, lifting the revolver. Try for the eye. If he couldn't kill, maybe he could blind. Just a little farther back and . . . He fell off the edge of the porch.

Sam hit the ground with a jarring thud that knocked the gun from his grasp. Frantically, he groped in the dark, unable to tear his eyes from the slow but certain progress of that dead body

as it plodded, chair raised, toward the woman and child, both
of whom had backed themselves into the screened portion of
the porch. Sam had no time to curse the stupidity of people
who cut off their own retreat. Even if he found the gun, the
angle now was such that he dared not use it for fear of hitting
the civilians. He scrambled to his feet just as the hulking figure
was closing in on the woman and child. It meant to crush the
trapped pair with that chair and there wasn't a fucking thing
Sam could do. Her face trembling in fear, the woman acted
almost calmly as she stepped in front of her child in a frail
effort to protect him.

With infuriating slowness, Joe Stubb's vision began to
return. Though blurred, he could see the artificial horizon,
tilted against the stops. Jesus! The plane must be nearly
standing on its wingtip! Resisting the impulse to react
swiftly, he slowly pressed the right rudder pedal as he eased
the control yoke to the right. Despite the smoothness of his
movements, the Tri-Islander gave a shudder that ran
throughout its frame. A fierce buffet from the storm almost
pushed the aircraft back into the steep bank.

"Shee-it!" Joe muttered, glimpsing the altimeter. The
height above sea level read in tens of feet rather than thousands and the needle was still unwinding. As though han-
dling fragile glass, Joe applied gentle back pressure to the
yoke, gratified to see the ominous hand of the altimeter stop
and begin a slow climb.

For the first time since being blinded, he was aware of
the worried voice in his earphones. "TCNA Six, can you
read Miami Center?"

"Five by Five," Joe answered in what he intended to be
a calm, professional tone.

"We've lost you off the scope." The voice became peevish. "You descended below your assigned altitude of six thousand."

With a weary grin, Joe nodded. "Yeah, guess we did. Hit a thunderstorm out here."

"You haven't answered any of my transmissions in the last four minutes."

Joe had to laugh although he still had his hands full with an airplane that was bucking like a wild horse. That was the trouble with flying at night, he had to file an international instrument flight plan, giving a large share of control of the flight to some guy sitting in a nice dry room in Miami, the control for this area of the Caribbean. "Yeah," he agreed amiably, "I couldn't hear in the first place, and in the second, I've been kinda busy."

The reply was even more annoyed. "Regulations require response to communications."

Joe glanced reproachfully over at Ernest who was slumped in his seat, heaving with frightened sobs. Lot of help that boy was going to be. The copilot was the one who was supposed to handle the radio, particularly when Center was dishing out biddy-shit like this. He depressed his mike button to speak. "Tell you what: you fly your radar set, I'll fly this plane."

He grinned at the frustration the controller would suffer. Although the United States' FAA provided radar coverage and, therefore, separation in this sector, there wasn't a lot they could do about the pilot of a foreign aircraft who chose to be somewhat independent. Fuck 'em. He reached over to prod Ernest. "C'mon boy! We gonna be jus' fine!" If he heard, Ernest didn't respond.

They were out of the storm as quickly as they had entered it. No decreasing turbulence, no slackening of rain and hail. Phillip was buffeted against his seat belt and then he wasn't, a transition as sudden and complete as walking from a dark room into one well lit. The shining coin of the moon above illuminated the edges of the clouds that floated serenely by, ships on a smooth black sea. Phillip sighed loudly enough to disturb the reverie of his seatmate. The Haitian's eyes fluttered open.

"Guess we made it," Phillip said as he smiled.

A friendly grin broke out on Devoux's black face. "Yes, we make it now," he agreed. "Quite an exciting ride. More thrilling than Six Flags, eh?"

Was Pete putting him on? Phillip searched Devoux's expression. No, the guy didn't seem at all scared. Jesus, the guy was either acting, was a fool, or was very brave. "Yeah, a real thrill," he said as calmly as he could.

Marie deSault shrieked with delight at her vision. The woman, and probably the boy, would die as she watched. The woman was foolishly trying to protect the child, although neither would survive the crushing blow that was coming. The sight of the woman became fuzzy again, started to fade. Not now, no, don't let it happen now, the *hounan*'s mind wailed. What was happening, what was weakening the power? Could it be that the woman's concern for her son was overriding the fear upon which the power rested? Was it possible that the thought of the boy's safety was stronger than her belief in voodoo? Something moved in front of the woman, a small figure, quick and darting. Then Marie deSault could see nothing.

The big stinky man was going to hurt Momma, all right. There wasn't any doubt. He'd busted into Uncle Reid and Aunt Sue's house. He was a bad man. Now Momma couldn't get away. Well, the last thing that Daddy had said before he left was that Case was the man of the house and he had to take care of Momma. Man of the house, just like a grownup.

Case's small chest had swelled with pride that his father would trust him to take care of things. And here he was, hiding behind his mother like some dumb old girl. And the policeman wasn't going to be any help. Case had figured that out when the bullets didn't stop the man. Of course bullets weren't any good, Case had reasoned with a logic tempered by his avid reading of comic books. Anybody that could toss Uncle Reid around like that had to be as strong as Superman, anyway. Aunt Sue was just standing out there in the driveway, screaming. That wasn't going to stop the man, either. Case would have to take matters into his own hands to deserve the trust his father had given him.

He wrenched free of his mother's protective grasp, wobbling on his crutch toward the stinky man. (*Stinky Man:* he lifts large chairs with a single hand, bullets don't bother him. He must be a first cousin to the Hulk.)

"Case!" His mother's agonized scream almost made him forget what he had to do. Even encumbered with his crutch, Case easily dodged a swipe of a bony hand that could have taken his head off. The man might be big and very, very strong, but he was also very, very slow and clumsy. Now Case was behind him, apparently forgotten.

"Kid, wait!" the policeman called, scrambling back onto the porch. Case was going to have to make his move before the policeman could restrain him. The man who was going to hurt Momma, Stinky Man, took another shuffling step forward, dragging his back leg just like Case had noticed him doing before. Lunging, Case fell to his knees as he jammed his crutch between those legs and threw his full sixty-five pounds forward. At first, he thought he'd failed, blown the only chance he was going to get. Then, like a cut tree about to fall, the man began to sway, the weight of the chair helping him lose his balance. It seemed like hours until, chair and all, he toppled forward with a crash that sent splinters flying from the wooden porch.

Sam couldn't believe what he saw: the kid had tripped that *thing* up with his crutch. Just stuck it in there and heaved as neat as you please. "Here, Lady," he yelled. "Get out of there before he can get up."

Paige needed no suggestions. She was around the prostrate form and out onto the open part of the porch in long, running strides. The police officer, his gun relocated, stood warily, pointing it, waiting for the thing to move. "Do me a favor," he said without moving his gaze from the figure sprawled facedown, "go inside, call the station house. Tell 'em Sam Dothan needs backup, lots of it."

Sam was gratified to see how quickly the woman moved to do as he asked. But it was beginning to look like there wasn't any hurry. That thing wasn't moving. Maybe the fall had knocked him out, though Sam doubted it. If it showed any signs of getting back up, he wanted to be as far away as he could get, taking these people with him, but years of training wouldn't let him run, not until he had to, at least.

"Reid!" the big woman wailed from the driveway.

"I'm okay, Sue, really I am."

Sam whirled to look into the hallway. A man nearly as big as the one on the porch was staggering toward the open doorway, holding onto the wall for support. "I guess I was unconscious or something."

With his hand over his nose in a futile effort to diminish the smell, Reid stooped over the figure sprawled on his front porch. "Dead," he commented. "I'd guess he's been dead for months, maybe a year."

Paige's eyes met Reid's as she returned from making the call. Even in the shadows, he could see her apprehension. "You don't think . . ."

He nodded. "That's exactly what I think. What else?"

She gasped, clutching Case to her. "If she could do this and Phillip's going to march right into her, her place . . ."

Sam had been following the conversation, his head swivelling as though observing a verbal tennis match. "Who's 'she,' and how do you figure a stiff that has been dead for months came alive?" His mind was already forming a mental scab over the terror he had just experienced, like the laughs he'd had about the junkie that had pulled a gun on him a few years ago. The brain was protecting itself, discarding the impossible, eager to deal with real, understandable problems. His principal problem now that the action was over was how the hell was he going to write up a report that didn't send him straight to the department shrink? If he'd thought it through, he wouldn't have asked for backup, he would've suggested everybody forget the whole thing.

Sue had also been listening. Wiping the river of mascara running from one of her tear-filled eyes, she asked, "Reid, do you and Paige know something I don't? I demand an explanation."

"So do I," Sam said, although he was certain the explanation was going to be nuttier than what had already happened.

Reid shrugged his resignation. "Go ahead, Paige. Might as well tell them."

For the first time, Case spoke up. "Can you tell 'em some place that doesn't stink?"

When Paige finished, the group was standing at the curb, giving occasional nervous glances toward the dark form on the porch. Toys that moved, weird snakes, and monsters in swimming pools—enough for Sam to feel justified in having the whole bunch sent to the top floor of Grady Hospital, the mental ward. But the thing on the porch was real enough. Sam looked at it again to reassure himself it would still be there when the other cops arrived. If it disappeared in a puff of magic smoke or something, he'd have a top floor suite himself.

Sam could see the woman was fighting back tears. No wonder. If half of her loony story were true, even just the part about the thing on the porch, she wasn't ever going to see Phillip Owens again.

Marie deSault's ability to see was different from her power to know. Even if she had not witnessed the events of the last few minutes, she was aware she had failed again, whether because of the distance, the state of the white woman's mind, or the unpredictability of small children. She snarled in frustration. Although she did not understand the mechanics of the powers the *loas* had bestowed on her, she knew now she had strained them to the limits by dividing her attentions. By keeping the *loas* here to greet the white man and the foolish little Haitian, she had used whatever reserve there was to resurrect a corpse from a nearby grave and will it to the faraway place to attack the woman. The messenger of death was down and once he had reassumed the position of the tomb, the life Samedi had given him was gone. She dared not expend more effort, not with her chief victim about to arrive. Once he was here, she would not have the distance to weaken the powers. And he would be here in an hour.

Chapter 18

Phillip was surprised at the activity at the Cap-Haïtien Airport. He'd thought, perhaps hoped, that there would be no taxis available at night, giving him an excuse to postpone the confrontation until daylight. But there they were, the now familiar assortment of vintage American cars, each of their drivers eager for a fare. Concentrating on the details at hand, he pushed his mounting fear aside as he presented his passport, paid an arrival fee somewhat smaller than he had been charged before, and submitted his suitbag for inspection. Devoux's command of Creole expedited their progress. Before leaving Atlanta, Phillip had considered the purchase of a handgun. Simply killing the *hounan* would have been easy, he supposed, until he had realized that a pistol presented no real threat to one who possessed the awesome powers he had witnessed. Besides, the chance that the weapon might have been detected in his bag by Customs was too great. Possession of a firearm was a crime harshly punished in most Caribbean countries and he couldn't risk being thrown in jail before he had accomplished what he had come to do. No, he would simply have to rely on the plan he had made.

"Going out to deal with that woman now is nuts!" logic

screamed as they cleared officialdom and approached the throng of cabs.

The mind's answer was calm, unruffled, "And what would you suggest? Sitting right here in her backyard? How well are you going to sleep, knowing she's not hundreds of miles away but almost next door?"

"Sleep, my ass. Sit up till sunrise, but don't go wandering off to God only knows where in the dark."

"And wait for another one of her cute little tricks? No thanks. Let's get this over. Then we can really get a good night's sleep."

The argument was still grumbling in Phillip's mind when he approached the first car, a late sixties' vintage Ford product. Peering into the dark interior, he saw the form of the driver, his head resting against the seat back as he snored lightly.

Phillip cleared his throat loudly and the cabbie came alive. "Monsieur? You want a ride to hotel?" He leaned over to open the passenger door. In the light from the terminal building Phillip saw a yawn cross the still sleepy face.

"No, not yet anyway." Phillip tossed his suitbag into the backseat. "I want to go to wherever I might find Marie deSault."

The effect was as if Phillip had tossed a grenade onto the seat. The cabbie, now fully awake, sat upright so suddenly he bumped his head on the door frame. "Monsieur?"

Devoux repeated the request in Creole.

Even in the shadows, there was no mistaking the look of unmitigated terror on the driver's face as he surveyed this insane American and his equally crazy Haitian companion. Phillip had anticipated the reaction. Reaching into a pocket, he unfolded a fifty-dollar bill, more than the average monthly wage in Haiti. "I want to go *now*."

The taxi driver was in an obvious quandary. He started

to reach for the money, then hesitated. "We cannot drive there," he said finally in a mixture of relief and disappointment. "The car will not travel the road."

"How close can you get us?" Phillip let the bill flap gently in the breeze.

The black face screwed into a pensive expression. "Two miles, perhaps three. But you cannot make it up the path at night. Perhaps in the morning?"

"*Now,*" Phillip repeated. "If you can't get any closer than two or three miles, you can let us out and the money's yours."

Greed overcame caution. "Get in."

The car lurched its way through dark streets. Phillip was surprised how foreboding the town looked, even more so than when he and Paige had fled back to the hotel. The moonlight painted the dome of the church with a silver brush, its walls a ghostly white. Each house was shuttered tightly as though to keep the night at bay. Once, turning a corner, a scabrous dog watched their passage with eyes bloodred in the taxi's headlights. It was the only living creature Phillip saw. Gradually, the houses were no longer elbowing each other for room on rough paved streets. The road was hard-packed, rutted dirt, and climbed at an angle that required a protesting first gear. Instead of gaily painted stucco, dwellings were now wattle and daub with shaggy thatched roofs. The huts became farther spaced until he could no longer see more than one at a time spotlighted in the car's lights that wavered with each bump. Towering trees were outlined against the night sky, their reaching branches forbidding giant arms that seemed to reach out to scrape the top of the cab with menacing whispers. The end of the road came abruptly. No signs, no widened turnaround, just the end as though the surface of the earth itself had terminated.

Phillip climbed out, reaching for his suitbag in the backseat. "You'll wait?"

The driver, his eyes wide, shook his head. "No. I bring you where you want. Can't wait."

Devoux argued in animated Creole before shrugging defeat. "It is no use. Even if he were to agree to wait, he would only sneak away like a beaten dog. I apologize for the cowardly conduct of one of my people." The anthropologist hung his head in mortification.

Lightly placing a reassuring hand on his companion's shoulder, Phillip forced a grin. "No sweat, Pete. You've got balls enough for the whole country."

Pete smiled. "Thanks."

Opening his bag, Phillip withdrew two large hiking boots and a pair of flashlights, one of which he secured to his belt. While he laced up the boots, he could sense the driver's eagerness to be gone. Placing his shoes and the bag back in the cab, he asked, "Can you deliver these to the hotel, then? I'll pick them up on our way back."

"Okay." It was clear from the man's expression, visible in the moonlight, that he was skeptical Phillip and Devoux were going to be coming back.

For the first time he noticed Devoux was making no such preparations. "Pete, you're going up that hill in street shoes?"

Devoux was startled by the question. "Perhaps I should go barefoot. I travelled the mountains without shoes for much of my life. No, these will suffice."

"Now," Phillip said in a voice he hoped concealed his own doubts, "where is that path you mentioned and how far do we go?"

The driver pointed and Phillip played the beam of his flashlight in the general direction. There was a gap in the dense vegetation, more of a gully washed by water runoff than a path. "Follow that," the cabbie instructed. "There's a, er, the road bends away from the place you want. When you come to a fork, you go straight."

Phillip forced a jocular tone. "We can't miss it, right?"

The cabbie gave him a long, searching look, the kind of look one might bestow on a terminal cancer patient. "You be lucky, you miss it."

Phillip was about to ask for more specific directions, but the cab's door slammed shut and the car jerked backward with a grinding of gears. Phillip watched the old Ford retreat in reverse. The glow of the moon was bright enough to make out its driver as he made the sign of the cross in four directions.

"Well, now we go get her, right?" Devoux asked in a tone more appropriate to commencing a holiday.

"Uh, yeah." Phillip was determined to show no apprehension to his companion. God, the little guy was gutsy.

Phillip's light became a beacon for every mosquito within sight, he was sure as he slapped at his face. They did not seem to bother Devoux. The climb was even steeper than it had seemed and Phillip was sweating heavily in the cool night air. Roots hidden in the shadows took on a life of their own as they snatched at his boots. Devoux moved without difficulty, his swaying gait carrying him effortlessly uphill. Frequently, he stopped to let Phillip catch up. Once or twice there was a sound of something in the brush beside the road. A lizard disturbed by the light, Phillip told himself not very convincingly. Once, as he paused to wipe his face with a handkerchief, he heard a howl that came from no particular direction, a mournful, animal cry that reminded him of the wolf pack he'd heard while camping on Michigan's Upper Peninsula years ago. But there were no wolves in Haiti.

The sound undoubtedly was the wailing of the souls of

deSault's victims, Devoux decided with detached, academic interest. Knowing its origin made it no less terrifying, though. If he could restrain his mind to matters of anthropological significance, he might be able to mask his fear from Phillip. Nonetheless, he touched his neck to make sure the rosary was in place.

They had passed two rude huts when they saw a glimmer. Not the warm glow of a lantern, but the cold, pale shine of a firefly. They stopped to watch from the shadows of an overhanging tree as the illumination moved toward them. Something caught in Phillip's throat as he saw a luminescent form tread down the hill—a young girl, nude, shining with some inner light that made her iridescent. Only when she was a few feet away did he see the coated crust that lined the slash from the pubis to chin. Involuntarily he recoiled. He was looking at the girl he and Paige had seen slaughtered in the graveyard! He reached for the object in his pocket, but hesitated as she passed by. Through her, like smoke, he could see the twisted roots and knotted growth on the other side of the path. She turned, giving them a grin that was anything but friendly, cold dead eyes staring, and disappeared just as though someone had turned off a slide projector. She was there and then she wasn't. Phillip stood still for several moments before he was certain the vision was gone. His sweat was becoming icy cold.

"Very interesting," Devoux said from behind him. "I gather that to be a projection of the image of a sacrificial virgin. I suspect deSault is trying to frighten us." And she's being *very* successful, he thought, at least with me.

Phillip gulped back the panic that was blocking his voice. "You, you mean she *knows* we're coming?"

Devoux nodded calmly. "I would think so, yes. If she could find you in the States, she could hardly miss you here."

Logical, but hardly comforting. Phillip suppressed the urge to wait until tomorrow and abandon the whole thing and go home. The memory of Case being dragged into the pool stoked anger like coal in a furnace, an anger that demanded satisfaction. Now.

They continued to follow the path's course upward, glancing over their shoulders every few seconds. God, but was Phillip thirsty! He had been stupid not to bring a canteen. Just ahead, out of the flashlight's beam, he heard the tinkle of water. A spring or a pond, perhaps, unpolluted because of the sparse population this far up the mountain. Quickening his step, he saw a stream sluicing its way down hill. Above the stream was its source, a small pond so clear Phillip's light reflected off the sandy bottom, revealing a bubbling spring.

"Do you suppose we can drink here?" he asked.

"Yes, I could use a bit of cool water."

They knelt in the marshy clay, cupping their hands to dip into the cool water. A flicker of a shadow darted across the column of light, a shape far too big to live in this small stream. With a choking scream, Phillip threw himself backward just as something splashed, showering him with warm droplets.

The sweat was running down his skin like cold rain down a windowpane as he groped tentatively for his light, now dark. Unfastening the second one from his belt, he played its shaft of illumination across the water, where ripples were spreading, evidence that the placid surface had been disturbed. The flash was gone. Shit! The same thing that had been in the pool at home? Phillip forced his mind to think rather than react. "What was the name you had called it? Simbi, *loa* of fresh water, ponds, and springs?"

"Yes, Simbi," Devoux said slowly. "I think if she really had intended to drag us into the water, she could have done it. The *hounan* and her *loa* are again attempting to frighten us. Make our minds easier to work with.'' The thought made him feel slightly more secure.

''The old Haitian mind-fuck,'' Phillip commented in a weak attempt at humor.

Still thirsty, they resumed the hike up the rutted path. The moon, a welcome addition to the flash's light, had disappeared, either behind the mountain or a cloud, and the night's blackness had become almost tangible, not the absence of light but a force of its own. Phillip estimated they had travelled about a half mile beyond the spring when a group of lights bobbed down the path toward them. This time they saw three, four young women, each mutilated like the first, each with the same grisly smile. Like an evil shepherd, the form of Samedi walked behind. He stopped, doffing his tall hat in mimicry of a courtly gesture before his mouth opened in a soundless laugh.

At his heels, a dog bared it fangs and snapped silently at Phillip. The animal's long fur was matted with . . . mud? No, blood that oozed from an incision along its stomach, a cut from which entrails dragged in the dust. With a start, Phillip realized he was seeing the specter of Rhett. Post autopsy.

Phillip stopped and shut his eyes, conjuring up the memory picture of Case's last birthday. His face smeared with cake icing, the little boy mugged for the camera, complaining after each shot, ''Can I go outside now?'' Paige turned a pleading glance at her husband. ''Come on, Phillip. You've got enough pictures to fill an album already.'' Without relinquishing his recollection, Phillip slowly opened his eyes to see the figures dim and fade in much the same manner as a flashlight bulb does as the battery loses power. They vanished, leaving only the night. Phillip grinned. Maybe, just maybe, Devoux had been right.

Ahead of him he could hear his companion muttering. It sounded like prayers again.

The fork in the road was easily seen. Straight ahead, the water-worn path; to the right, one made by usage. They went straight. There was another glow ahead, this one reddish as though from a fire. Yet it came from no source Phillip could ascertain nor did it cast shadows. Fifty yards farther was another hut, indistinguishable from the others he had passed except its door and single window were open. Inside, he could see more light, brighter than that outside. They had arrived.

As if to confirm his conclusion, there was a sigh beside him. "We are here," Devoux said.

They paused long enough for Phillip to take the tape recorder from his breast pocket and plug in a set of small headphones. Then they went in. At first, the brightness nearly blinded them, a brightness that flickered like flame but gave no heat. Against the far wall was a sort of altar set with the equipment Phillip would have expected. But there was other stuff, too: strange effigies, a brass bell, a mirror, and a pitcher. His inventory of the objects came to a stop when he saw her, an ancient crone, eyes filmy white with cataracts. She leered at him with empty gums, a grin that could not have been more malevolent had she bared tiger's fangs. "Marie deSault?" he asked, somehow knowing she would not answer.

But she did, with a high-pitched, evil-sounding laugh that galloped down his spine with icy fingers. So this was the *hounan*, the witch, who had nearly drowned Case, who had killed Rhett, and tried to kill him. She didn't look like a powerful sorceress of voodoo. For the first time since he left Atlanta, Phillip was encouraged. Hell, this old bitch was blind and probably didn't weigh eighty pounds. Just kill her with his bare hands. He and Devoux would be long out of Haiti before anyone found her. One good wrench of that fragile neck, one twist, and he could forget the whole bad dream. He took a step forward, his boots crunching in the dry dirt of the floor.

As though someone had turned up a rheostat, the glare in the hut flared brighter and a long, thrashing form hung down from the ceiling. A snake, the biggest Phillip had ever seen, with a broad, flat head as wide as both of Phillip's hands. The serpent flashed bloodred eyes that seemed lit from within. Its hiss became a low silibant voice, and Phillip recoiled at the sound of his own name.

"Your mind, Phillip, close it to her *now*," Devoux said softly. In his peripheral vision, Phillip saw that the Haitian was fingering a string of beads—the rosary.

Another peal of foul laughter bent the old woman nearly double. The snake dropped across Phillip's shoulders with enough weight to knock him to his knees. He struggled vainly while the reptile's coils grew tight. He reached for his breast pocket only to touch another scaly coil wrapped so firmly around his chest he could not force a hand beneath it. As though sparked by his touch, the snake's grip began tightening as one would secure a knot, a tightening that was forcing the breath from Phillip's lungs.

"Phillip!" He heard Devoux's warning cry but was able to respond only with a choking croak.

With every bit of strength he could summon, Phillip tried to expand his muscles, break the deadly grasp while he fought to keep his brain from short-circuiting with terror. No use. Already his vision was beginning to darken at the edges like a TV picture tube in its terminal stages. With the detachment of the hopeless, he realized he could never divert his mind while the very essence of life was being crushed from him. His mind. Now it was playing tricks, flashing his life before him, he supposed, as he saw himself

attempting to elude tacklers against the blurred background
of University Stadium. No, wait. Memory was trying to tell
him something his fear had made him forget: the limp leg,
going limp to wiggle from a linebacker's grasp.

He could no longer see and there was an ominous buzzing
in his ears when he let himself go lax. For a second, an
instant, the smallest sub-division of time, he could move
within the deadly grasp. It seemed an eternity. His hand felt
as though it moved with the slowness of a clock's hour as
he searched for his shirt pocket.

The relentless crush resumed as though its relaxation had
been a mere flinch but Phillip's fingers touched the recorder
and pushed the ''on'' button. What happened now was beyond his control.

''Daddy?'' the little girl's voice asked shyly through the
headset.

Phillip's memory saw her. He forced himself to concentrate. Becky in her pink dress. Not yet two, but beautiful.
He had dressed her up and spent a Sunday afternoon driving
around to friends' homes to show her off. Until she had
discovered a friendly, very muddy cocker spaniel. The dress
had been ruined; Margaret had wailed. Phillip had laughed.
Becky wouldn't be able to get into it in another month anyway.

Becky . . .

The child's mud-streaked face faded and Phillip was in
the hut again. But the snake was gone, evaporated like rain
on hot pavement.

''Thank God,'' Devoux's relief whispered from somewhere behind him. That was when he noticed that the hateful, insane laughter had stopped also.

With rage ignited by fear, Phillip fixed the woman in his
eyes with the deadly intent of a gun sight. The fucking
snake! No doubt a manifestation related to the one that had

killed Rhett. The one that could have killed Case. He felt a
hatred hotter than he had ever experienced. Killing the old
woman would not only be necessary, it would be an orgasm
of delight. He anticipated the feel of her neck in his hands
with overwhelming pleasure. He moved toward her only
vaguely aware of the animal's growl that rattled in his throat.

"Your mind, Phillip." Devoux saw the clear intent.
"Your mind. You'll never . . ."

Phillip stood, his chest throbbing with hurt. The possibility of crushed ribs only flickered across his conscious
mind as he stepped toward the intended victim. A step, then
a second.

He was close now, close enough to see her move spittle
flecked lips, close enough to hear low muttering in a language made more menacing by its incomprehensibility. At
the moment she finished her chant, her incantation, a flash
of heat sucked the air from Phillip's already bruised lungs,
lungs that were still laboring from the embrace of the serpent. Fire! Phillip was surrounded by a wavering, dancing
wall of flame. He smelled the bitter stench of his beard on
fire before he felt the searing of his chin. Beating his face,
he turned to see Devoux, eyes closed, muttering in a cocoon
of flickering orange. There was no retreat. He, also, was
surrounded by flames that were reaching for him with burning fingers but consumed nothing in the hut.

A stab of pain ran up his leg as his pant leg caught fire
and ignited as though soaked in gasoline. He tried to ignore
the burning agony, to listen to the tape. "This is Becky
[giggle]. I hope you won't get mad . . ." Becky, smiling
with delight as Phillip completed a daisy chain and looped
it around her tiny neck that afternoon in the park. She was,
what, five? Yes, five. Margaret was at home, sleeping off
another night of scotch. He felt hot tears on his cheeks,
tears of bittersweet memories of a child who would never

be the lovely woman Phillip had known would emerge from the chrysalis of the little girl's body. She had accepted his gift that afternoon like a queen receiving tribute until her solemnity collapsed and she had thrown her arms around him, reaching up to pull his face into range of her kisses.

The hut was silent for a moment as he let the vision of Becky slip back into the recesses of the past. The old woman wasn't laughing now. Phillip made the transition from recall to the present and heard a moaning whistling sound that came from all around him. He felt a cold wind on his face, a wind that was growing in intensity. But not a hair on the *hounan's* head was affected by the howling storm, a blast of wind that slammed him against the side of the hut. God, he thought absently, this is more powerful than that typhoon in the Philippines two years ago. The force of the storm kept him pinned to the wall, an insect impaled on a pin. His vision was beginning to blur from the tears lashed from his eyes by the wind, and he gasped as he tried to keep the breath the sheer power of the gale was snatching from him.

The air was filled with forms that moved freely despite the power of the wind. Birds, ugly and without feathers, with cruel, hooked beaks that snapped at him, and insects with evil red eyes and long stingers that drew blood at each touch. Something flapped by his face and he raised an arm to shield his eyes only to feel a strip of flesh torn from his hand.

The first gust tore the glasses from Devoux's face and he stared myopically at the things swirling before him. The wind shrieked, blending into the laugh of the *hounan*, tugging at him. Phillip was just standing there—there was no chance of being heard over the scream of the hurricanelike wind. Have to touch him, get his attention, remind him to close his mind, Devoux thought. Holding onto a wall to remain erect, Devoux stretched out his other arm, the one holding the rosary. It was snatched from his hand and dashed against the mud wall like so many seeds carelessly sown. Turning to retrieve them, he heard a sound distinct from the howl of the storm and was fixed in his steps by the horror of his doom. Buzzing with concerted fury, thousands of bees covered his body, their stings fiery pricks in his skin. Frantically, he continued his litany. ". . . Full of grace, fruit of thy womb . . ."

He instantly realized the futility of his effort; it was no use. He could not tear his thoughts from the fear he had of bees, a fear that was a terror beating against the inside of his chest wall with jackhammer strokes. Another part of his brain, still the academic, wondered if his vulnerability to stings was known to the *hounan* or if they had simply been included randomly. He was certain he would never know, for his throat was already constricting, each gulp of breath labored and painful. He opened his mouth to gasp, drawing in . . . not sweet, life-giving air, but more bees! He spit, gagging, but still his mouth, his throat was filled with the things. He could feel them walking on his swelling tongue, probing into the cavern of his throat, crawling into his sinus cavity, stinging, burning. He grasped his neck, squeezing as though to dislodge the creeping mass whose buzzing from inside his head filled his ears.

His arms and legs were becoming heavy, difficult to move so that he was unaware he was sliding down the wall, crumpling to the dirt floor. What attention he could focus was concentrated on the thousands of tiny feet that were parading across eyes he could no longer close. The stings were becoming mere pricks now, hardly noticeable, and his vision, already blurred without his glasses, was rapidly darkening.

Phillip saw his companion collapse in a cloud of insects,

saw the loose, and now useless beads and guessed what had happened. Those things were killing him! Ignoring the creatures that were biting, tearing, stinging his own flesh, Phillip lunged toward his friend. Somehow, he could help swat the loathsome things away, crush them. But even with his full weight against the squall, he was transfixed as though his feet were in cement.

Devoux must have seen him, for his effort was to slowly point to his own ear—the headset. Listen to your tape, he seemed to indicate. Then he was still. Phillip reached a bee-encrusted hand to his shirt pocket and thumbed the button.

". . . 'cause I know I'm not 'sposed to be . . ."

Becky, with adultlike manners as she appeared from her mother's dressing room, her child's face smeared with lipstick in a grotesque exaggeration of a mouth. "Well, how do I look?" she asked in a perfect parody of Margaret about to go out for the evening. Phillip had been unable to restrain a ringing laugh then, and he smiled at the memory now. He had not had the heart to administer punishment. Instead, he had done the best he could to remove the makeup before Margaret came up from downstairs. He had, though, extracted a promise of no encores.

He chuckled aloud at the memory before he realized the wind was gone, leaving only the musty smell of the hut. "Well, old woman," he said aloud, "take your best shot."

Devoux, prone on the floor, was still. Phillip felt a surge of an apprehension unrelated to the horrors he had just witnessed. Devoux. Pete. Perhaps unconscious, certainly not . . . Surely the fates that had allowed the little Haitian to escape this country, then return to face the *hounan* could not, *would* not be so cruelly indifferent as to allow Pete to perish now. Somewhere in that part of our minds that accepts bitter truths even though we are still denying them, Phillip began to fear that Pete was gone. Before he could acknowledge his sorrows, before he even was certain of his loss, he started to go to the crumpled figure only feet away.

His better judgment stopped him. To turn his back on that hateful old bitch, that sorceress, might be a fatal mistake. Perhaps she had spent her powers, he thought. She was no longer grinning that hideous, death's head grimace. Now might be the time to finish it. He could anticipate the feel of the fragile bones of the scrawny neck, hear the final snap.

A chill ran from his feet to his knees and he glanced down. Water. Water was filling the hut, or that part of it where he stood as though he were in a bathtub when somebody turned on the spigot. A wall of water was building up around him although the door and window were open and the area of the altar and the old woman were as dry as before. It was as if he were standing inside a large, invisible aquarium. The water had no source. It was simply rising in the area immediately around him, rising quickly.

He felt a nudge at his boot and looked down through the water already at his waist. Crabs. Large, misshapen crabs had come from nowhere, crabs with huge, jagged claws and black pinhead eyes that stared up at him malevolently. One scooted upward and dug a pincher twice the size of its body into the flesh of his leg. Phillip swatted at it with his hand only to have his palm impaled on the spikes that covered its shell. Instinctively, Phillip smashed the crustacean against his hip and watched it dissolve in green slime that bubbled like acid.

He felt a slash of pain in his calf that made him look down again. Fish—small, but with mouths of needlelike teeth had joined the crabs. Fish that were already jumping from the rising surface to tear at his shirt. One leapt for his face, barely missing his eyes. There was no doubt what those things were going to do when the water reached the level of his throat. And the water was still rising.

Rising. God! The moisture would kill the batteries that ran the recorder! He reached again for the pocket, but his hand wouldn't budge. Two of the larger fish had it by the fingers, ripping the flesh as they pulled his hand down. The water level was inches from his shirt pocket.

Phillip tugged, gritting his teeth against the tearing of the skin, but another fish added its weight and he could not lift his arm. The bottom of the pocket was now wet.

Standing on tiptoe, Phillip lunged forward, slapping at one hand with the other. He could stretch his body no higher and still the water covered almost half the pocket.

He lunged sideways, back and forth, shaking like a wet dog. The teeth only sank in deeper. His pocket was underwater.

"Daddee . . ." For a millisecond, he thought, somehow, the recorder had started itself. But the familiar voice wasn't coming from his headset, it was coming . . . He stared in horrified fascination. On the surface of the water, now almost to his chin, a shape was taking form, a blob that was growing arms and legs and . . . and long blond hair. He sucked in his breath as Becky's dead face supplicated him, "Daddee . . ."

Her lips were blue with chill, her lifeless eyes glazed over in death, and her hair, that beautiful hair that floated around the pale, dead face like a living halo . . . . "Daddee," she beseeched in a near whisper, "where are you? Why didn't you get me out of the pool? I needed you, Daddy, I needed you so much."

And she had. The guilt that had hibernated so long now awoke and crept from its lair to gnaw on his perceptions, his conscience. The syllogism was frightful in its simplicity: Phillip had knowingly left his child with an alcoholic, an irresponsible person. The results could have been predicted. The blame was his.

The acknowledgment was more painful than the fire, the wind, the crushing embrace of the snake. *"Nooo . . ."* Phillip neither knew nor cared whether the shriek of denial was something he was screaming or if it existed only in his head. It was all clear now, understandable with a ruthless logic. His insensitivity to his daughter's safety was a crime for which his own life should be forfeited. And he was willing to pay the penalty, a penalty that seemed not only fair, but desirable.

The recorder, the *hounan*, voodoo. None seemed important now, not now that Becky was here. If he could join her, why struggle? Shortly, the water would be over his head, his lips would also turn blue and his eyes, like hers, would dull. "I'm coming, sweetheart," he muttered, "I'm coming to be with you."

He reached out to touch the cold flesh, his flesh. He was tired, so damn tired of the struggle of the last few . . . minutes? Hours? Whatever, he could relax, rest, and in a short while he would be with Becky. Rest, relax. He sighed wearily, his breath creating ripples on the water below his chin.

As though to enforce his decision, Becky motioned him closer. "I want a kiss, Daddy, give me a kiss."

A kiss. When had he last heard that? Becky? No, since then. That part of him that had not succumbed, that spark of will that refuses to die, began to turn the pages of his memory with frantic fingers . . . A kiss, a kiss.

Case.

A few years ago, before he had become too old for affection between father and son, Case had reached up from his bed just before Phillip had turned off the lights. "A kiss, Daddy, give me a kiss."

Case. The small boy at home. The son who nearly died when that thing in the swimming pool grabbed him, who could have died by snakebite, who would die if Phillip did not rid the world of that leering creature by the altar. This Becky he saw was her creation, not his daughter . . . A trick, an apparition, so evil, so cunning he had almost given in.

''No!'' either he or his mind roared. To go with this, this Becky *thing*, was unthinkable, obscene. Better to use the real Becky's voice to send this thing away.

But the tape.

The tape. It would be useless now. The tape. Its pitiful message was etched into his memory with the acid of bereavement. Maybe, perhaps . . . He shut his eyes for what might be the last time and remembered where Becky's message had left off, the part that cut deepest into the nerve of his soul.

''. . . I wanted to tell you I love you, Daddy.'' The memory elicited more agony than the teeth and claws that were tearing at him. A pitifully small coffin in an over-furnished room. Sunlight from a window spun gold in the long hair that he would never brush free of tangles again. The tiny face had a ghost of a smile as though she knew he was there at last.

Phillip thought the groan he heard was his own. Instead, he heard it again as the thought-picture faded and he saw the crone slowly collapsing to the floor, vainly holding onto the altar for support. She was chanting, mumbling something in a voice too weak to be understood. And the water was gone, vanished with its evil minions. In two steps, he was beside her, his hands reaching for her throat. Inches away from homicide, he stopped. There would be no need. Crumpled on the dirt like a bag of soiled clothes, she gave that choking, rattling sound he recognized from the men he had seen die in faraway battles. With a final sigh, she was still, her emaciated body lying against the altar like a rag doll discarded by a child. Flinching at the touch of her already cool skin, he felt for a pulse, listened at the bony chest for a heartbeat. There was neither. Taking the mirror from the altar, he held it in front of her face for an ancient postmortem. No breath fogged the glass. He felt no elation of victory, no satisfaction of seeing a foe vanquished. The weariness of his receding adrenalin high was temporarily insulating him from emotion: joy, hate. He only felt tired, like a runner who must catch his breath before savoring a close win. He took one last look at the open eyes that now stared into eternity and turned to Devoux.

The Haitian's face was swollen like an overstuffed sausage, his eyes squeezed nearly shut by puffy cheeks. Kneeling, Phillip lifted Devoux to a sitting position against him. There was breath, faint and ragged, but breath.

"Pete," Phillip asked, "what can I do?"

Between lips shut from the swelling came a whisper, inaudible words. Lowering his head to Devoux's mouth, Phillip could barely hear, "Allergy to bee stings."

"I can get you into town," Phillip encouraged.

"No good," he gasped, "be dead in another few minutes."

Phillip tugged the limp form erect. "Like shit! I'm going to carry you." He managed a weak grin. "After all, it's downhill."

"No." The whisper was getting fainter. "No time. Leave me, please."

Phillip started for the door, dragging Devoux. "You showed me the way to destroy her. I'm not going to leave you."

The Haitian managed a weak gesture. "I'm dying." There was an ominous pause as he struggled to continue speaking. "Let the natives find me here with her. They, they . . . they will think I killed her. Help . . . them believe they can do same with . . . other *hounans*." The ghost of a smile twitched those swollen lips. "I'll be a hero. Always wanted . . . wanted . . ."

Devoux was still, his eyes fixed pleadingly on Phillip's face. He was dead.

Phillip eased him to the floor. "You're a hero, all right. Bravest man I ever knew. And I never got the chance to say 'thanks.'"

At the door, he paused, the interior of the hut swimming through tears. He raised his hand to his forehead in a salute, repeating, "Bravest man I ever knew." He knew Peter Devoux would be proud to be called a hero.

Slowly, cautiously, his emotions returned and he savored each as he might sample dishes of an unfamiliar cuisine. Relief had the strongest flavor, relief that his and his family's ordeal was over. But that taste was almost obscured by the pungent sting of grief—sorrow that a noble and brave man had died. Behind the other two, on the tongue of his soul, there was a mellowness: anticipation, expectation of a life without fear. It had been so long since he had tasted this last, he barely recognized it, although it was the best of all.

Outside, the sky was gray with a cheerless but promising preview of dawn. The chatter of birds beginning to stir filled Phillip's ears with a joyful sound and he breathed deeply, savoring the freshness of the air. Even the weariness that follows terror and sorrow could not weigh him down nor could the thought of the long walk ahead. One thing at a time: hike to the hotel, call Paige. He would call as soon as he got to the hotel. If there was phone service, a shaky assumption in this part of the world. He started down the hill with the light step of a man pleased to find himself alive. Were Devoux with him, he would have whistled with joy, a joy now denied him by his loss.

Pausing at the spring, he drank thirstily, enjoying the feeling of the sweet water as it rolled down his parched throat. The coolness of the water soothed the ragged, torn flesh of his hand as he dipped it below the surface. Removing his shoes, he trailed his burned leg in a semicircle across the spring. The glass of the lost flashlight winked merrily up at him from the bottom. A sound, a rustling footstep behind him, caused him to jerk erect. A group of women were kneeling along the stream, rubbing clothes with sand before pounding them on rocks. And Paige bitched about doing wash! He smiled. He didn't feel like smiling, but he did it anyway. The women returned his smile with wide grins. One pointed to the direction from which he had come and asked something in Creole. Phillip shrugged, conveying his ignorance of the language. She pointed again, this time opening her mouth with lips over her teeth to simulate bare gums, her eyes closed. The *hounan*—she was telling him he had passed a much feared person. He nodded and snapped his finger. "Poof!"

She did not understand, so Phillip stretched out on the ground, folding his arms across his chest like a corpse and closing his eyes. The women jabbered excitedly among themselves before one managed a single English word. "Dead?" she asked.

Nodding vigorously, Phillip repeated, "Poof!" He paused, adding, "Devoux. Dr. Peter Devoux killed her." He hoped at least one of the women understood and would spread the name.

The mountainside echoed the relieved laughter of the women.

His thirst slaked, Phillip stood, watching the women at their chore. Black magic, curses, death. All that was behind him now, a renewal of his existence. If he was to have another try at life, he owed it to himself to improve the quality of the years left, years he owed to Devoux. He had a wife and a son, healthy and alive, and, now, safe. He would always remember his daughter, but that tape, the sound of her voice that reduced him to sobs . . . Reaching into his pocket, he opened the recorder and removed the cassette. It twinkled in the light of the rising sun as he sent it spinning into the air.

Phillip paused a moment longer, watching the ripples subside. "So long, Becky," he said aloud, "I'll always love you. But now I'm letting you go, getting on with the rest of my life. Good-bye." He had shed two burdens this morning. If only Devoux were here to share his relief.

Epilogue

꽃

The jolt of the 10-11's landing woke Phillip from the nap
that had only been interrupted when he changed planes in
Miami. Rubbing sleepy eyes, he watched the lights of Atlanta's mid-field terminal flash by the window like a small
city as the big Delta jet trembled with reverse thrust, came
to a stop, and sedately taxied off the active runway like a
dowager leaving the dance floor. For a split second, he
thought he was returning home after another ordinary job.
Then he noticed the stark emptiness of the assigned seat
next to him and the reality of the last twenty-four hours was
a weight on his shoulders. He felt a weary sadness throbbing like the pain from his hastily bandaged hand. There
was an emptiness, also, a missing longing for a man he had
known only a few days, a man who made the world a better
place for being in it. Haiti, deSault, Devoux. They all
seemed as ephemeral as a dream, a nightmare. As soon as
the plane came to a stop, the usual crowd of passengers
stood as though that would speed disembarcation. Phillip
watched through eyes that felt as though sand had been
thrown in them. God, was he looking forward to a hot bath
and sleep. Sleep that would, he hoped, temporarily relieve
him of reality.

As the line in the aisle shuffled forward, he stood, stretched, and removed his suitbag from the overhead rack. He supposed Paige would be waiting for him in the terminal, although when he had called that morning, he had told her it was unnecessary. He'd take a cab home. Predictably, the connection from the hotel had been a bad one and she was so glad to hear he was safe, she had not noticed the sadness in his voice.

"Daddy!" The happy cry came from somewhere in the terminal. Phillip's eyes had to adjust to the brilliance before he spotted Case waving his crutch as though it were a victorious banner.

Paige's arms were around Phillip as her lips pressed against his almost before he saw her. "Hello, handsome. Welcome home," she said in her sexiest voice. Stepping back, she glanced around. "Where's Dr. Devoux? I not only want to thank him for keeping you safe, but . . ." She searched Phillip's haggard face. "He's not here, is he?"

Phillip felt the guilt of a survivor, the feeling of being alive when another has died in a seemingly random process. An artillery shell obliviates one bunker while the men in the next are unscathed. Luck, fate, joss. Guilt. He studied the beige carpet. "No, he won't be coming back." The memory of that small black body on the dirt floor of the hut cast a gloomy shadow over the reunion. "He was probably the bravest man I ever knew."

The pain of sorrow on Paige's face almost matched his own. "Oh, God! That man went there to help you and he's . . ." She could not bring herself to say it.

Case, poling himself along on his crutch, reached the couple and almost fell as he tried to hug his father. Phillip caught him under the arms and hugged him, smiling with the joy children often bring when it is most needed. "Don't even ask, Case," Phillip growled with good nature, "I remembered to bring you something."

"A surprise!" Case whooped. "A surprise! What's . . ."

"Now don't get yourself excited," Phillip said, turning toward the exit. "Besides, it's past your bed time." He gave Paige a look of mock disapproval.

She smiled. "Fat chance I had of getting him to bed! You know how he is when you're coming home."

An hour later, Case had reluctantly allowed himself to be tucked in, falling asleep before Phillip turned off the lights in his bedroom. Paige was downstairs, a pitcher of martinis in the freezer. She released the sob she had been suppressing and threw her arms around her husband. "Phillip, I'm so sad about Dr. Devoux. We owe him so much and I never even met him."

Kissing her gently, he led her to a chair. "Yes, we do. I know it's not much in the way of thanks, but I'm going to write the story of what happened."

"But . . ."

"I know, a lot of people will think I've gone nuts. But there's enough corroboration: three adults and a cop witnessed what happened next door—that incident you told me about on the way home. God, I can't believe Case doing what he did!"

"He's your son." She smiled wanly.

He opened the freezer and poured a stem glass full of liquid oily with the cold. "I guess he is at that. Then there's what happened at the pool, and the vet and herpetologist who saw that mamba. I guess a few folks will be open-minded enough to believe, all right."

"No matter what they think, you owe it to Peter Devoux to tell what happened. He died trying to save you . . . and us."

Phillip sighed and nodded slowly. "Jesus, but that tastes

good! Yeah, I don't know if that rosary would have done him any good, but he did lose it reaching for me.''

Paige lifted her glass. ''To Dr. Devoux.''

''To Pete,'' Phillip said. ''Now I'm about ready for some sleep.''

Becky did not come to Phillip that night and he enjoyed a dreamless slumber. As the sun pried its way between the curtains the next morning, it bathed Phillip's face in a halo of gold. Yawning, he sat up in bed, immediately aware of Paige's absence. His unasked question was answered by the clatter of cookware from the kitchen. He grinned, astonished that she had gotten up before he had and had managed to slip away without waking him. And cooking breakfast before going to work! That was a first. Today, his first day without fear in many, was going to be a good one, as would all the fear-free days to follow.

High up a mountain, not far from Cap-Haïtien, a man stirred, sat up on his straw mattress, and glanced around the dark interior of his hut. His internal clock, that mechanism that governs the lives of those who live close to the land, told him he had slept later than usual. Daylight was already leaking around the edges of his single window. He should have been outside, tending to his banana trees an hour ago. Then he remembered and he understood. Sometime in the ghost of dawn, he had awakened to discover he was standing in front of the small altar, the altar he had tended since his initiation rites years ago, the altar he had used to perform ceremonies for the practitioners nearby. He had been, and was, a *hounan* with such limited powers as the *loas* chose to bestow upon him, a small fish in a very black pond.

But that had miraculously changed. As he had stood in

front of the altar, curious as to why he was there, a dim, cheerless light had illuminated the interior of the hut. On the edge of a shadowed corner, something had moved, slithering forward with its scales making a whispering sound on the dirt floor. Whether the huge snake had actually spoken or had communicated by some sort of mind contact made no difference, the message was unmistakable: there was a large, bearded white man. That man, and his woman, must die. The *hounan* would be given the means to accomplish this task, although the white man and his woman lived in a faraway land. Do this, the snake had told him, do this and you will be the most powerful *hounan* in Cap-Haïtien. The Haitian had felt the powers, tangible as clothes on his body, and he would use them. The task would be easy.

Easy with his new powers, easy with what was already happening not far away in a hut much like his. There were two corpses lying on the dirt floor. One, that of an old woman, was already decomposing in the tropical heat. That one was of no interest to the *hounan*. The other, that of a small Haitian man, looked as though he was merely sleeping, an appearance enhanced by the fact that he now stirred and slowly sat erect and then stiffly climbed to his feet. Unlike most people awaking, he did not yawn, nor did he rub his eyes, eyes that no longer were a kindly brown. Instead, the eyes had a dull glow, the color of pebbles polished by water.

There was another figure in the hut, a spectral figure that wavered like heat rising from asphalt, the figure of a tall black man with a stovepipe hat and a pipe in his mouth. It was toward this figure—apparition—that the recently arisen man turned. Though no words were spoken, some sort of communication was taking place, for the small Haitian nodded slowly, obediently. His face was without expression, although he was thinking. Or trying to. Trying hard, although the dull senses that he possessed could not recall his name or how he had come to be here, nor did he care. He could understand what he was being told, though. Very clearly. He was going someplace far to the north to meet a large white man, a person whose image was familiar, yet lost somewhere in the fog of a long-ago dream. He was to do something, although he did not yet know what. Those instructions would be given later. All he knew was that he would obey. How he was to get there, or why, didn't matter. What was important was that he would do exactly as commanded. As minutes passed, the past and the dream disappeared as though these were the first moments of his life. No, not life, existence . . . an existence of which the sole purpose was to do as the tall man with the hat ordered. He was ready and he would obey.